EIGHT MEN

EIGHT MEN

STORIES BY

Richard
Wright

**With an Introduction by
Paul Gilroy**

HarperPerennial
A Division of HarperCollinsPublishers

HarperCollins books may be purchased for educational, business, or sales promotional use. For information please write: Special Markets Department, HarperCollins Publishers, Inc., 10 East 53rd Street, New York, NY 10022.

First HarperPerennial edition published 1996.

Library of Congress Cataloging-in-Publication Data

Wright, Richard, 1908–1960.
    Eight Men / by Richard Wright. — 1st ed.
      p. cm.
    ISBN 0-06-097681-0
    1. Afro-American men—Fiction.   I. Title.
  [PS3545.R815E4   1996]
  813'.52—dc20   96-21614

04 05 06 07 08 ❖/RRD 20 19 18 17 16 15 14 13 12 11

Contents

Introduction to the HarperPerennial Edition

Eight Men was conceived and assembled during Richard Wright's European exile. It was initially published in 1961, being the first of three volumes to emerge after their author had met his premature and tragic death. These circumstances and Wright's failure to complete an introduction to the book have made it controversial in assessments of his work. Some critics have viewed the collection as a low point in Wright's supposedly dwindling creative output and suggested that his plan for its publication was a short-term strategy designed to resolve an acute financial crisis. These assertions have sounded more plausible in the context of another, bigger, and extremely contentious argument about the waning of Wright's creativity. This views his immersion in Parisian intellectual and political life as regrettable because it led the world's preeminent Negro writer far away from the vital roots of his creativity in the Southern

Black Belt. This kind of commentary on Wright regards his exposure to "alien" political and philosophical influences as disastrous rather than enriching. It argues that France somehow contaminated the version of literary authenticity that he had established by articulating African-American experiences in a way that was universally resonant.

It is possible that the publication of *Eight Men* was partly a response to the harsh critical judgments on Wright's European-produced novels, *The Outsider* and *The Long Dream*. It may also be true that anxiety about the direction and saleability of his new books had been increased by the disinterest shown in his travel writing and other nonfiction by puzzled readers whose expectations about Wright and his future work had been generated in thrilling but unsettling encounters with *Black Boy* and *Native Son*. With these possibilities in mind, it is less surprising that *Eight Men* has sometimes been dismissed as little more than the unhappy product of Wright's tentative disenchantment with editors and agents who pressured him toward a formulaic repetition of his earlier successes. Would he, outside of prompting by poor artistic and economic fortunes, have produced anything like this particular combination of materials? Looking back on *Eight Men* more than thirty years after the book's initial appearance, this line of questioning does not seem a fruitful way to approach its contents. The difficulties surrounding the book's conception are certainly relevant in attempts to fathom Wright's artistic choices and the overall design behind *Eight Men*'s publication, but they need not undermine the coherence of the project. Contrary to some critical orthodoxies, there are thematic convergences connecting what might appear, at first sight, to be a diverse anthology formed from texts produced for radio broadcast, old and new short fiction, and slices of autobiography. Pending final verdicts on the trying period in which Wright developed his idea for the book and on the complex relationship between the fragments that comprise *Eight Men,* his earlier more successful work, and the revolutionary literary patterns it established, there are other ways in which the book can be appreciated and recognized as a fitting companion to his better-known writings.

Eight Men's central focus on masculinity provides one valuable key to this reassessment. It not only speaks directly to contemporary concerns but can also be used to illuminate aspects of Wright's thinking that have been overlooked and misunderstood, particularly where his own figure has been subsumed by the nihilistic power of his imaginative creations. A second, related, sign of *Eight Men*'s enduring worth lies in the way it has been marked by its author's sensitivity to the interplay of distinctive psychological factors with economic, cultural, and historical forces. This combination of interests and insights was unusual for its time. It bears the imprint of Wright's investigations into the psychological relations characteristic of colonial societies as well as his long-standing engagement with the political and social issues that arose from thinking about black mental health in the United States. These issues are addressed respectively in "Man, God Ain't Like That...," a humorous piece that parodies the psychological theories of Octave Mannoni and "The Man Who Killed a Shadow," a discomfiting tale that introduces the interrelation of racism and sexuality in a striking reversal of some stereotypical notions of predator and quarry. Wright demonstrates that some of the supposed beneficiaries of white supremacy are no less likely to be unhinged by its operations than its black victims. These chapters testify to Wright's prescience in identifying, at a very early point, problems that have only recently become widely recognized and only grudgingly been accorded a legitimate place in black political thought.

The treatment of sexuality is important because it disrupts crude analyses of Wright by revealing the full range and complexity of his insights into the workings of black masculinity and its complex relationship to racial oppression. *Eight Men* challenges the brute machismo and uncomplicated misogyny so often imputed to him on the simplistic basis that overidentifies his own attitudes and responses with those of his murderous and antisocial male characters. It draws attention to aspects of his development that many commentators have chosen to ignore, for the male protagonists found in *Eight Men* are as likely to be devoted and sensitive husbands and fathers as they are to be the asocial or brutal figures created in his best-known work. The analysis of black masculinity toward which *Eight Men* points can also contribute to contemporary discussions of race, politics, and gender, which have recently begun to develop their own urgent inquiries into the issues that preoccupied Wright. Statistics on homicide and other forms of black-on-black violence have lent a new topicality to his considerations of the kind of masculinity that seeks a firearm as the measure of its confirmation. The centrality of violent fantasies to contemporary black popular cultures also suggests that something insightful might still be waiting to be released from Wright's speculations about the instances of projection, inversion, and sublimation found in the compensatory, fratricidal subcultures of young black people. The fragile threads that tie the collection together are composed of Wright's meditations on the character and dynamism of black masculinity—enacted, feared, celebrated, worried over, lived, and beheld both by outsiders and initiates. *Eight Men* contains a sustained attempt to address the linkages between what are now too blithely called race and gender relations. Though it encompasses many other elements, the anthology can be most profitably read as a study of the relationship between the social pathologies of white supremacy and the formation of black male subjectivity. We can suppose that Wright's opening story, "The Man Who Was Almost a Man," was placed first in the collection for more than merely chronological reasons. It had been predated into print by "The Man Who Saw a Flood," which is the earliest piece. As an introduction, it sensitizes the reader toward a number of core issues that recur in what follows and should be familiar from Wright's other writings.

The first of these is his strong sense of the fundamental role of violence, both symbolic and actual in mediating racial domination and conditioning the exercise of racialized power. Time and again, the pieces in *Eight Men* draw out the central significance of violence, against the self, against the racial Other, and most important, against those who occupy the positions closest to the person who perpetrates the violence.

The idea of closeness, of proximity to others, is also fundamental to Wright's thinking in *Eight Men*. For, in a world that has been split along the color line, people can be physically close while remaining separated by "a vast psychological distance." Blacks and whites enjoy radically different forms of consciousness and are sundered from each other even when they occupy the same spaces. The stresses this creates are powerful enough to drive people on both sides of the color line out of their minds. Even if they are able to retain a tenuous grip on sanity, there are myriad tragedies to be discovered in the systematic inability of racialized groups to communicate, to recognize each other's humanity, and to act justly on the bases of shared human worth and common human status.

As Wright moved out of Marxism and toward a standpoint he felt was more faithful to the exacting demands of black experience in the modern world, the obligation to specify the limits of an alternative, less triumphal, humanism loomed large.

Alienation from self, from other people and from the problematic, creative, essence of a racially indivisible humanity acquired a different significance. The problem of estrangement was no longer to be confined to the vehicles that racism based in economic exploitation readily provided for it. This change of emphasis was pronounced where Wright turned his attention toward the hurt and wrong that blacks do to one another. Though they may operate together, this variety of injury is not the same phenomenon as the damage wrought upon black lives and hopes by white power. Here he spotlights the ambivalent role of the black family. That beleaguered space of intimacy affords protection and support to its occupants, but the emotional and psychological price of nurturance is a high one. Family life can easily become restricting, disabling, and destructive. The racial consciousness of family members must be channeled, orchestrated so that their lives fit the lowly expectations of an unjust world that is premised upon the denial of their humanity. This may be motivated by love, but its consequences can be catastrophic. There are significant parallels here with feminist evaluations of the family as a site of oppression for the women whose unpaid and unrecognized labor makes it habitable, but *Eight Men* explores the problems of family life in a distinctive way by highlighting how black households train their boys into manhood while simultaneously habituating them to a social and economic system that is incapable of recognizing it. To be men, these boys will have to act consciously and decisively against the machinations of power in the private, domestic world as well as in the destructive public potency of the Jim Crow system that configures black households to the specifications of its own dismal desires. The desperate, therapeutic gunplay with which Dave Saunders follows his pathetic attack on the mule in "The Man Who Was Almost a Man," means that he has wasted the precious bullets that could have been saved for a more liberatory assault on ol man Hawkins' big white house. "Lawd, ef Ah had just one mo bullet Ah'd taka shot at tha house. Ah'd like t scare ol man Hawkins jusa little . . . Jusa enough t let im know Dave Saunders is a man." The story that follows, "The Man Who Lived Underground," a dazzling fragment from a longer work that had been rejected by Wright's original publisher, also addresses the existential relationship between "race," masculinity, and power. Here, too, a black man playfully points a weapon in the direction of an "imaginary foe."

Wright's interest in the ambivalent role of the black family is connected to his attempts to quantify the difficulties involved in founding and maintaining a racial community characterized by mutuality and solidarity. He implies that this becomes almost impossible in modern urban conditions where capitalism and the power of white supremacy combine and promote an intense individualism that Wright identifies as a "wild and restless loneliness." The effects of this isolation are neatly encapsulated in the sad tale of black workers slaving away unseen, ignorant, and unappreciated in the citadels of scientific knowledge with which Wright closes the book. A full participant now in the dramas of subaltern masculinity, he notes speaking of one fellow worker, "We had nothing in common except that we were . . . black and lost." Wright is prepared to probe the significance of the petty, perverse hatreds that his abject colleagues employ to make their dehumanized lives bearable: "Perhaps Brand and Cooke, lacking interests that could absorb them, fuming like children over trifles, simply invented their hatred of each other in order to have something to feel deeply about." This alienated interaction between blacks is foreclosed by poverty, misery, and hunger. It offers its participants an empty simulation of authentic human coexistence, but it is made to bear an additional burden. It operates as a valve, a functional element that is essential to the harmony and stability of the white powers it serves. In this segregated world, the full destructive impact of that fateful link between the private, nurturing activity that takes place in the family and public systems of racialized governance is registered in the consciousness of black men. In seeking recognition for their humanity, they can generate a powerful oppositional movement, capable of transforming American society as a whole. Here, the black male demonstrators of the 1960s marching silently in pursuit of civil rights while carrying placards that bore the affirmative legend "I am a man" come to mind as something like the fulfillment of Wright's aspirations. However, *Eight Men*'s focus on masculinity does not become triumphantly masculinist. Though he makes the anatomization of masculinity a priority, the male psyche is not the only place where the wounds made by white supremacy refuse to heal. Women—black and white—are recognized as actors in the theater of "race." Their moral and political agency is neither peripheral nor supplementary to the principal action. Wright's commentary upon the dream world of mass culture, which draws women into its net of empty hopes and his related conviction that the appeal of religion is much stronger to black women than it is to men, confirm that he recognizes other possibilities apart from the ones that he has chosen to explore. Prospects for healthy and mutually satisfying relationships between black men and women look bleak if examined through Wright's confessional account of the cruel and immoral business of selling insurance on Chicago's South Side. They improve dramatically when considered through the frames provided by "The Man Who Saw a Flood" and "Man of All Work".

It is not possible to make facile generalizations about the representative characteristics of the black men in this book. They are not all isolated or indifferent figures, disconnected from family and community. Indeed, Dave Saunders, the father who fails to discipline him, and Tom, the long-suffering father in "The Man Who Saw a Flood" are all tightly bound in networks of kinship and responsibility for others. In "The Man Who Went to Chicago," Wright presents himself in a similar role, defined by the filial piety demonstrated in caring for his relatives. Carl in "Man of All Work" is similarly embedded in circuits of responsibility that derive from the roles of provider, father, and husband. They are connected only by the way that their alienation is registered in their consciousness of themselves as men.

"Man of All Work," which was written as a radio play, is the centerpiece of Wright's exploration of gender. It is a difficult piece for anyone who sees Wright's work exclusively through the lens that *Native Son* provides, not least for its explicitly humorous character. In what might almost be a parody of the machismo that Wright supposedly celebrated, the story begins with the eponymous Carl, rising in the night without complaint to feed his baby daughter. The same tender act gets taught to his son well before the main strands of the narrative come together.

Carl is unable to find employment. Desperate for money, dressed in drag, renamed Lucy, and fortified with the belief that whites look at blacks without really seeing them, he sets out to find work as a domestic servant in a well-to-do white family. Their child is too young to be blind to the founding absurdity of racial classification and sees immediately that something is not quite right about this bristly and overly muscular presentation of black femininity. However, the performance is all too convincing for the father of the house who tries to make Lucy/Carl submit to the sexual advances that have driven away her/his predecessor. The outraged white wife, sickened by her husband's venality, shoots the object of his transgressive desire. In manifesting the violence that is always latent within contact between blacks and whites, she precipitates the circumstances in which Carl's cross-dressing is revealed. Through her, as with the librarian in "The Man Who Killed a Shadow," Wright identifies the articulation of race and gender and enumerates some of the gender-specific forms that racism can assume.

Several of the stories in *Eight Men* are not set in the United States. By being located elsewhere, they express the changing scale of Wright's political imagination. Though it is far from the special terrors of the Jim Crow South and its Northern surrogates, the misunderstanding between Olaf Jenson, the Danish night porter, and the nameless black superman who scares him is a systematic one. It, too, pivots on the incapacity to confer that inter-subjective, masculine recognition that remains for Wright the premise of authentic, modern freedoms.

Eight Men is being republished now in the middle of one of those lengthy periods in African-American political culture when the integrity of the race as a whole is being defined exclusively as the integrity of its menfolk. Their status has been felt to depend upon a race-specific mode of masculinity that was damaged by the operations of white supremacy through slavery and since. Black masculinity has once again become the focus of restorative and compensatory activities that bear upon the race's capacity to act in pursuit of its own interests. This involves a political project that is understood along nationalistic lines and which therefore depends all the more crucially on the nation's power to reproduce itself in appropriately manly forms. Masculinity is both the necessary catalyst and the prized outcome of that reproductive process. The manhood of African-Americans must be renewed and repaired if their political fortunes are to be improved. An elaborate literature of self-help, self-analysis, and self-worth has grown up around the idea that black masculinity can, in redeeming itself, transform the plight of those who have undergone procedures of symbolic castration that deny them access to the personal and political benefits of authentic maleness. Without this intervention, long after slavery and Jim Crowism have been dismantled, black men are doomed to remain mere boys in a world dominated and manipulated by real men whose superior status is conveyed in their common whiteness. These are complex issues that connect, as Richard Wright did long ago, the social and economic with the psychological and cultural. Trapped among the tragic shadows cast by larger-than-life heroes drawn from the worlds of sports and entertainment as well as the arena of official politics, the crisis of black life is plausibly and persistently but mistakenly apprehended as a crisis of black masculinity.

On one side stand the wretched but peculiarly heroic figures of men like O. J. Simpson, Tupac Shakur, and Mayor Marion Barry; on the other, the well-intentioned demand for positive role models is being raised. Calls for gender-segregated education and the reinstitutionalization of father-centered parenting can be heard amidst a new discourse on the multiple pathologies of matrifocal social life. These controversies provide an appropriate setting for the rediscovery of Richard Wright's *Eight Men*. It seems as though the implosion of racial identity that marks our time has opened up another way of thinking about Wright's work and exploring the bequest he has made to the future.

—Paul Gilroy

EIGHT MEN

THE MAN WHO WAS

ALMOST A MAN

DAVE STRUCK OUT across the fields, looking homeward through paling light. Whut's the use talkin wid em niggers in the field? Anyhow, his mother was putting supper on the table. Them niggers can't understan nothing. One of these days he was going to get a gun and practice shooting, then they couldn't talk to him as though he were a little boy. He slowed, looking at the ground. Shucks, Ah ain scareda them even ef they are biggern me! Aw, Ah know whut Ahma do. Ahm going by ol Joe's sto n git that Sears Roebuck catlog n look at them guns. Mebbe Ma will lemme buy one when she gits mah pay from ol man Hawkins. Ahma beg her t gimme some money. Ahm ol ernough to hava gun. Ahm seventeen. Almost a man. He strode, feeling his long loose-jointed limbs. Shucks, a man oughta hava little gun aftah he done worked hard all day.

He came in sight of Joe's store. A yellow lantern glowed on the front porch. He mounted steps and went through the screen door, hearing it bang behind him. There was a strong smell of coal oil and mackerel fish. He felt very confident until he saw fat Joe walk in through the rear door, then his courage began to ooze.

"Howdy, Dave! Whutcha want?"

"How yuh, Mistah Joe? Aw, Ah don wanna buy nothing. Ah jus wanted t see ef yuhd lemme look at tha catlog erwhile."

"Sure! You wanna see it here?"

"Nawsuh. Ah wans t take it home wid me. Ah'll bring it back termorrow when Ah come in from the fiels."

"You plannin on buying something?"

"Yessuh."

"Your ma lettin you have your own money now?"

"Shucks. Mistah Joe, Ahm gittin t be a man like anybody else!"

Joe laughed and wiped his greasy white face with a red bandanna.

"Whut you plannin on buyin?"

Dave looked at the floor, scratched his head, scratched his thigh, and smiled. Then he looked up shyly.

"Ah'll tell yuh, Mistah Joe, ef yuh promise yuh won't tell."

"I promise."

"Waal, Ahma buy a gun."

"A gun? Whut you want with a gun?"

"Ah wanna keep it."

"You ain't nothing but a boy. You don't need a gun."

"Aw, lemme have the catlog, Mistah Joe. Ah'll bring it back."

Joe walked through the rear door. Dave was elated. He

looked around at barrels of sugar and flour. He heard Joe coming back. He craned his neck to see if he were bringing the book. Yeah, he's got it. Gawddog, he's got it!

"Here, but be sure you bring it back. It's the only one I got."

"Sho, Mistah Joe."

"Say, if you wanna buy a gun, why don't you buy one from me? I gotta gun to sell."

"Will it shoot?"

"Sure it'll shoot."

"Whut kind is it?"

"Oh, it's kinda old . . . a left-hand Wheeler. A pistol. A big one."

"Is it got bullets in it?"

"It's loaded."

"Kin Ah see it?"

"Where's your money?"

"Whut yuh wan fer it?"

"I'll let you have it for two dollars."

"Just two dollahs? Shucks, Ah could buy tha when Ah git mah pay."

"I'll have it here when you want it."

"Awright, suh. Ah be in fer it."

He went through the door, hearing it slam again behind him. Ahma git some money from Ma n buy me a gun! Only two dollahs! He tucked the thick catalogue under his arm and hurried.

"Where yuh been, boy?" His mother held a steaming dish of black-eyed peas.

"Aw, Ma, Ah jus stopped down the road t talk wid the boys."

"Yuh know bettah t keep suppah waitin."

He sat down, resting the catalogue on the edge of the table.

"Yuh git up from there and git to the well n wash yosef! Ah ain feedin no hogs in mah house!"

She grabbed his shoulder and pushed him. He stumbled out of the room, then came back to get the catalogue.

"Whut this?"

"Aw, Ma, it's jusa catlog."

"Who yuh git it from?"

"From Joe, down at the sto."

"Waal, thas good. We kin use it in the outhouse."

"Naw, Ma." He grabbed for it. "Gimme ma catlog, Ma."

She held onto it and glared at him.

"Quit hollerin at me! Whut's wrong wid yuh? Yuh crazy?"

"But Ma, please. It ain mine! It's Joe's! He tol me t bring it back t im termorrow."

She gave up the book. He stumbled down the back steps, hugging the thick book under his arm. When he had splashed water on his face and hands, he groped back to the kitchen and fumbled in a corner for the towel. He bumped into a chair; it clattered to the floor. The catalogue sprawled at his feet. When he had dried his eyes he snatched up the book and held it again under his arm. His mother stood watching him.

"Now, ef yuh gonna act a fool over that ol book, Ah'll take it n burn it up."

"Naw, Ma, please."

"Waal, set down n be still!"

He sat down and drew the oil lamp close. He thumbed page after page, unaware of the food his mother set on the table. His father came in. Then his small brother.

"Whutcha got there, Dave?" his father asked.

"Jusa catlog," he answered, not looking up.

"Yeah, here they is!" His eyes glowed at blue-and-black revolvers. He glanced up, feeling sudden guilt. His father was watching him. He eased the book under the table and rested it on his knees. After the blessing was asked, he ate. He scooped up peas and swallowed fat meat without chewing. Buttermilk helped to wash it down. He did not want to mention money before his father. He would do much better by cornering his mother when she was alone. He looked at his father uneasily out of the edge of his eye.

"Boy, how come yuh don quit foolin wid tha book n eat yo suppah?"

"Yessuh."

"How you n ol man Hawkins gitten erlong?"

"Suh?"

"Can't yuh hear? Why don yuh lissen? Ah ast yu how wuz yuh n ol man Hawkins gittin erlong?"

"Oh, swell, Pa. Ah plows mo lan than anybody over there."

"Waal, yuh oughta keep yo mind on whut yuh doin."

"Yessuh."

He poured his plate full of molasses and sopped it up slowly with a chunk of cornbread. When his father and brother had left the kitchen, he still sat and looked again at the guns in the catalogue, longing to muster courage enough to present his case to his mother. Lawd, ef Ah only had tha pretty one! He could almost feel the slickness of the weapon with his fingers. If he had a gun like that he would polish it and keep it shining so it would never rust. N Ah'd keep it loaded, by Gawd!

"Ma?" His voice was hesitant.

"Hunh?"

"Ol man Hawkins give yuh mah money yit?"

"Yeah, but ain no usa yuh thinking bout throwin nona it

erway. Ahm keepin tha money sos yuh kin have cloes t go to school this winter."

He rose and went to her side with the open catalogue in his palms. She was washing dishes, her head bent low over a pan. Shyly he raised the book. When he spoke, his voice was husky, faint.

"Ma, Gawd knows Ah wans one of these."

"One of whut?" she asked, not raising her eyes.

"One of these," he said again, not daring even to point. She glanced up at the page, then at him with wide eyes.

"Nigger, is yuh gone plumb crazy?"

"Aw, Ma—"

"Git outta here! Don yuh talk t me bout no gun! Yuh a fool!"

"Ma, Ah kin buy one fer two dollahs."

"Not ef Ah knows it, yuh ain!"

"But yuh promised me one—"

"Ah don care whut Ah promised! Yuh ain nothing but a boy yit!"

"Ma, ef yuh lemme buy one Ah'll *never* ast yuh fer nothing no mo."

"Ah tol yuh t git outta here! Yuh ain gonna toucha penny of tha money fer no gun! Thas how come Ah has Mistah Hawkins t pay yo wages t me, cause Ah knows yuh ain got no sense."

"But, Ma, we needa gun. Pa ain got no gun. We needa gun in the house. Yuh kin never tell whut might happen."

"Now don yuh try to maka fool outta me, boy! Ef we did hava gun, yuh wouldn't have it!"

He laid the catalogue down and slipped his arm around her waist.

"Aw, Ma, Ah done worked hard alla summer n ain ast yuh fer nothin, is Ah, now?"

"Thas whut yuh spose t do!"

"But Ma, Ah wans a gun. Yuh kin lemme have two dollahs outta mah money. Please, Ma. I kin give it to Pa . . . Please, Ma! Ah loves yuh, Ma."

When she spoke her voice came soft and low.

"Whut yu wan wida gun, Dave? Yuh don need no gun. Yuh'll git in trouble. N ef yo pa jus thought Ah let yuh have money t buy a gun he'd hava fit."

"Ah'll hide it, Ma. It ain but two dollahs."

"Lawd, chil, whut's wrong wid yuh?"

"Ain nothin wrong, Ma. Ahm almos a man now. Ah wans a gun."

"Who gonna sell yuh a gun?"

"Ol Joe at the sto."

"N it don cos but two dollahs?"

"Thas all, Ma. Jus two dollahs. Please, Ma."

She was stacking the plates away; her hands moved slowly, reflectively. Dave kept an anxious silence. Finally, she turned to him.

"Ah'll let yuh git tha gun ef yuh promise me one thing."

"Whut's tha, Ma?"

"Yuh bring it straight back t me, yuh hear? It be fer Pa."

"Yessum! Lemme go now, Ma."

She stooped, turned slightly to one side, raised the hem of her dress, rolled down the top of her stocking, and came up with a slender wad of bills.

"Here," she said. "Lawd knows yuh don need no gun. But yer pa does. Yuh bring it right back t me, yuh hear? Ahma put it up. Now ef yuh don, Ahma have yuh pa lick yuh so hard yuh won fergit it."

"Yessum."

He took the money, ran down the steps, and across the yard.

"Dave! Yuuuuuh Daaaaave!"

He heard, but he was not going to stop now. "Naw, Lawd!"

The first movement he made the following morning was to reach under his pillow for the gun. In the gray light of dawn he held it loosely, feeling a sense of power. Could kill a man with a gun like this. Kill anybody, black or white. And if he were holding his gun in his hand, nobody could run over him; they would have to respect him. It was a big gun, with a long barrel and a heavy handle. He raised and lowered it in his hand, marveling at its weight.

He had not come straight home with it as his mother had asked; instead he had stayed out in the fields, holding the weapon in his hand, aiming it now and then at some imaginary foe. But he had not fired it; he had been afraid that his father might hear. Also he was not sure he knew how to fire it.

To avoid surrendering the pistol he had not come into the house until he knew that they were all asleep. When his mother had tiptoed to his bedside late that night and demanded the gun, he had first played possum; then he had told her that the gun was hidden outdoors, that he would bring it to her in the morning. Now he lay turning it slowly in his hands. He broke it, took out the cartridges, felt them, and then put them back.

He slid out of bed, got a long strip of old flannel from a trunk, wrapped the gun in it, and tied it to his naked thigh while it was still loaded. He did not go in to breakfast. Even though it was not yet daylight, he started for Jim Hawkins' plantation. Just as the sun was rising he reached the barns where the mules and plows were kept.

"Hey! That you, Dave?"

He turned. Jim Hawkins stood eying him suspiciously.

"What're yuh doing here so early?"

"Ah didn't know Ah wuz gittin up so early, Mistah Hawkins. Ah wuz fixin t hitch up ol Jenny n take her t the fiels."

"Good. Since you're so early, how about plowing that stretch down by the woods?"

"Suits me, Mistah Hawkins."

"O.K. Go to it!"

He hitched Jenny to a plow and started across the fields. Hot dog! This was just what he wanted. If he could get down by the woods, he could shoot his gun and nobody would hear. He walked behind the plow, hearing the traces creaking, feeling the gun tied tight to his thigh.

When he reached the woods, he plowed two whole rows before he decided to take out the gun. Finally, he stopped, looked in all directions, then untied the gun and held it in his hand. He turned to the mule and smiled.

"Know whut this is, Jenny? Naw, yuh wouldn know! Yuhs jusa ol mule! Anyhow, this is a gun, n it kin shoot, by Gawd!"

He held the gun at arm's length. Whut t hell, Ahma shoot this thing! He looked at Jenny again.

"Lissen here, Jenny! When Ah pull this ol trigger, Ah don wan yuh t run n acka fool now!"

Jenny stood with head down, her short ears pricked straight. Dave walked off about twenty feet, held the gun far out from him at arm's length, and turned his head. Hell, he told himself, Ah ain afraid. The gun felt loose in his fingers; he waved it wildly for a moment. Then he shut his eyes and tightened his forefinger. Bloom! A report half deafened him and he thought his right hand was torn from his arm. He heard Jenny whinnying and galloping over the field, and he found himself on his knees, squeezing his fingers hard between his legs. His hand was numb; he jammed it into his mouth, trying to warm it, trying to stop the pain. The gun lay at his feet. He did not quite know what had happened. He stood up and stared at the gun as though it were a living thing. He gritted his teeth and kicked the gun. Yuh almos broke mah arm! He turned to look for Jenny; she was far over the fields, tossing her head and kicking wildly.

"Hol on there, ol mule!"

When he caught up with her she stood trembling, walling her big white eyes at him. The plow was far away; the traces had broken. Then Dave stopped short, looking, not believing. Jenny was bleeding. Her left side was red and wet with blood. He went closer. Lawd, have mercy! Wondah did Ah shoot this mule? He grabbed for Jenny's mane. She flinched, snorted, whirled, tossing her head.

"Hol on now! Hol on."

Then he saw the hole in Jenny's side, right between the ribs. It was round, wet, red. A crimson stream streaked down the front leg, flowing fast. Good Gawd! Ah wuzn't shootin at tha mule. He felt panic. He knew he had to stop that blood, or Jenny would bleed to death. He had never seen so much blood in all his life. He chased the mule for half a mile, trying to catch her. Finally she stopped, breathing hard, stumpy tail half arched. He caught her mane and led her back to where the plow and gun lay. Then he stooped and grabbed handfuls of damp black earth and tried to plug the bullet hole. Jenny shuddered, whinnied, and broke from him.

"Hol on! Hol on now!"

He tried to plug it again, but blood came anyhow. His fingers were hot and sticky. He rubbed dirt into his palms, trying to dry them. Then again he attempted to plug the bullet hole, but Jenny shied away, kicking her heels high. He stood helpless. He had to do something. He ran at Jenny; she dodged him. He watched a red stream of blood flow down Jenny's leg and form a bright pool at her feet.

"Jenny . . . Jenny," he called weakly.

His lips trembled. She's bleeding t death! He looked in the direction of home, wanting to go back, wanting to get help. But he saw the pistol lying in the damp black clay. He had a queer feeling that if he only did something, this would not be; Jenny would not be there bleeding to death.

When he went to her this time, she did not move. She stood with sleepy, dreamy eyes; and when he touched her she gave a low-pitched whinny and knelt to the ground, her front knees slopping in blood.

"Jenny . . . Jenny . . ." he whispered.

For a long time she held her neck erect; then her head sank, slowly. Her ribs swelled with a mighty heave and she went over.

Dave's stomach felt empty, very empty. He picked up the gun and held it gingerly between his thumb and forefinger. He buried it at the foot of a tree. He took a stick and tried to cover the pool of blood with dirt—but what was the use? There was Jenny lying with her mouth open and her eyes walled and glassy. He could not tell Jim Hawkins he had shot his mule. But he had to tell something. Yeah, Ah'll tell em Jenny started gittin wil n fell on the joint of the plow. . . . But that would hardly happen to a mule. He walked across the field slowly, head down.

It was sunset. Two of Jim Hawkins' men were over near the edge of the woods digging a hole in which to bury Jenny. Dave was surrounded by a knot of people, all of whom were looking down at the dead mule.

"I don't see how in the world it happened," said Jim Hawkins for the tenth time.

The crowd parted and Dave's mother, father, and small brother pushed into the center.

"Where Dave?" his mother called.

"There he is," said Jim Hawkins.

His mother grabbed him.

"Whut happened, Dave? Whut yuh done?"

"Nothin."

"C mon, boy, talk," his father said.

Dave took a deep breath and told the story he knew nobody believed.

"Waal," he drawled. "Ah brung ol Jenny down here sos Ah could do mah plowin. Ah plowed bout two rows, just like yuh see." He stopped and pointed at the long rows of upturned earth. "Then somethin musta been wrong wid ol Jenny. She wouldn ack right a-tall. She started snortin n kickin her heels. Ah tried t hol her, but she pulled erway, rearin n goin in. Then when the point of the plow was stickin up in the air, she swung erroun n twisted herself back on it . . . She stuck herself n started t bleed. N fo Ah could do anything, she wuz dead."

"Did you ever hear of anything like that in all your life?" asked Jim Hawkins.

There were white and black standing in the crowd. They murmured. Dave's mother came close to him and looked hard into his face. "Tell the truth, Dave," she said.

"Looks like a bullet hole to me," said one man.

"Dave, whut yuh do wid the gun?" his mother asked.

The crowd surged in, looking at him. He jammed his hands into his pockets, shook his head slowly from left to right, and backed away. His eyes were wide and painful.

"Did he hava gun?" asked Jim Hawkins.

"By Gawd, Ah tol yuh tha wuz a gun wound," said a man, slapping his thigh.

His father caught his shoulders and shook him till his teeth rattled.

"Tell whut happened, yuh rascal! Tell whut . . ."

Dave looked at Jenny's stiff legs and began to cry.

"Whut yuh do wid tha gun?" his mother asked.

"Whut wuz he doin wida gun?" his father asked.

"Come on and tell the truth," said Hawkins. "Ain't nobody going to hurt you . . ."

His mother crowded close to him.

"Did yuh shoot tha mule, Dave?"

Dave cried, seeing blurred white and black faces.

"Ahh ddinn gggo tt sshooot hher . . . Ah ssswear ffo Gawd Ahh ddin. . . . Ah wuz a-tryin t sssee ef the old gggun would sshoot—"

"Where yuh git the gun from?" his father asked.

"Ah got it from Joe, at the sto."

"Where yuh git the money?"

"Ma give it t me."

"He kept worryin me, Bob. Ah had t. Ah tol im t bring the gun right back t me . . . It was fer yuh, the gun."

"But how yuh happen to shoot that mule?" asked Jim Hawkins.

"Ah wuzn shootin at the mule, Mistah Hawkins. The gun jumped when Ah pulled the trigger . . . N fo Ah knowed anythin Jenny was there a-bleedin."

Somebody in the crowd laughed. Jim Hawkins walked close to Dave and looked into his face.

"Well, looks like you have bought you a mule, Dave."

"Ah swear fo Gawd, Ah didn go t kill the mule, Mistah Hawkins!"

"But you killed her!"

All the crowd was laughing now. They stood on tiptoe and poked heads over one another's shoulders.

"Well, boy, looks like yuh done bought a dead mule! Hahaha!"

"Ain tha ershame."

"Hohohohoho."

Dave stood, head down, twisting his feet in the dirt.

"Well, you needn't worry about it, Bob," said Jim Hawkins to Dave's father. "Just let the boy keep on working and pay me two dollars a month."

"Whut yuh wan fer yo mule, Mistah Hawkins?"

Jim Hawkins screwed up his eyes.

"Fifty dollars."

"Whut yuh do wid tha gun?" Dave's father demanded.

Dave said nothing.

"Yuh wan me t take a tree n beat yuh till yuh talk!"

"Nawsuh!"

"Whut yuh do wid it?"

"Ah throwed it erway."

"Where?"

"Ah . . . Ah throwed it in the creek."

"Waal, c mon home. N firs thing in the mawnin git to tha creek n fin tha gun."

"Yessuh."

"Whut yuh pay fer it?"

"Two dollahs."

"Take tha gun n git yo money back n carry it t Mistah Hawkins, yuh hear? N don fergit Ahma lam you black bottom good fer this! Now march yosef on home, suh!"

Dave turned and walked slowly. He heard people laughing. Dave glared, his eyes welling with tears. Hot anger bubbled in him. Then he swallowed and stumbled on.

That night Dave did not sleep. He was glad that he had gotten out of killing the mule so easily, but he was hurt. Something hot seemed to turn over inside him each time he remembered how they had laughed. He tossed on his bed, feeling his hard pillow. N Pa says he's gonna beat me . . . He remembered other beatings, and his back quivered. Naw, naw, Ah sho don wan im t beat me tha way no mo. Dam em all! Nobody ever gave him anything. All he did was work. They treat me like a mule, n then they beat me. He gritted his teeth. N Ma had t tell on me.

Well, if he had to, he would take old man Hawkins that two dollars. But that meant selling the gun. And he wanted to keep that gun. Fifty dollars for a dead mule.

He turned over, thinking how he had fired the gun. He had an itch to fire it again. Ef other men kin shoota gun, by Gawd, Ah kin! He was still, listening. Mebbe they all sleepin now. The house was still. He heard the soft breathing of his brother. Yes, now! He would go down and get that gun and see if he could fire it! He eased out of bed and slipped into overalls.

The moon was bright. He ran almost all the way to the edge of the woods. He stumbled over the ground, looking for the spot where he had buried the gun. Yeah, here it is. Like a hungry dog scratching for a bone, he pawed it up. He puffed his black cheeks and blew dirt from the trigger and barrel. He broke it and found four cartridges unshot. He looked around; the fields were filled with silence and moonlight. He clutched the gun stiff and hard in his fingers. But, as soon as he wanted to pull the trigger, he shut his eyes and turned his head. Naw, Ah can't shoot wid mah eyes closed n mah head turned. With effort he held his eyes open; then he squeezed. *Blooooom!* He was stiff, not breathing. The gun was still in his hands. Dammit, he'd done it! He fired again. *Blooooom!* He smiled. *Blooooom!*

Blooooom! Click, click. There! It was empty. If anybody could shoot a gun, he could. He put the gun into his hip pocket and started across the fields.

When he reached the top of a ridge he stood straight and proud in the moonlight, looking at Jim Hawkins' big white house, feeling the gun sagging in his pocket. Lawd, ef Ah had just one mo bullet Ah'd taka shot at tha house. Ah'd like t scare ol man Hawkins jusa little . . . Jusa enough t let im know Dave Saunders is a man.

To his left the road curved, running to the tracks of the Illinois Central. He jerked his head, listening. From far off came a faint *hoooof-hoooof; hoooof-hoooof; hoooof-hoooof*. . . . He stood rigid. Two dollahs a mont. Les see now . . . Tha means it'll take bout two years. Shucks! Ah'll be dam!

He started down the road, toward the tracks. Yeah, here she comes! He stood beside the track and held himself stiffly. Here she comes, erroun the ben . . . C mon, yuh slow poke! C mon! He had his hand on his gun; something quivered in his stomach. Then the train thundered past, the gray and brown box cars rumbling and clinking. He gripped the gun tightly; then he jerked his hand out of his pocket. Ah betcha Bill wouldn't do it! Ah betcha . . . The cars slid past, steel grinding upon steel. Ahm ridin yuh ternight, so hep me Gawd! He was hot all over. He hesitated just a moment; then he grabbed, pulled atop of a car, and lay flat. He felt his pocket; the gun was still there. Ahead the long rails were glinting in the moonlight, stretching away, away to somewhere, somewhere where he could be a man . . .

THE MAN WHO LIVED

UNDERGROUND

I'VE GOT TO HIDE, he told himself. His chest heaved as he waited, crouching in a dark corner of the vestibule. He was tired of running and dodging. Either he had to find a place to hide, or he had to surrender. A police car swished by through the rain, its siren rising sharply. They're looking for me all over . . . He crept to the door and squinted through the fogged plate glass. He stiffened as the siren rose and died in the distance. Yes, he had to hide, but where? He gritted his teeth. Then a sudden movement in the street caught his attention. A throng of tiny columns of water snaked into the air from the perforations of a manhole cover. The columns stopped abruptly, as though the perforations had become clogged; a gray spout of sewer water jutted up from underground and lifted the circular metal cover, juggled it for a moment, then let it fall with a clang.

He hatched a tentative plan: he would wait until the siren sounded far off, then he would go out. He smoked and waited, tense. At last the siren gave him his signal; it wailed, dying, going away from him. He stepped to the sidewalk, then paused and looked curiously at the open manhole, half expecting the cover to leap up again. He went to the center of the street and stooped and peered into the hole, but could see nothing. Water rustled in the black depths.

He started with terror; the siren sounded so near that he had the idea that he had been dreaming and had awakened to find the car upon him. He dropped instinctively to his knees and his hands grasped the rim of the manhole. The siren seemed to hoot directly above him and with a wild gasp of exertion he snatched the cover far enough off to admit his body. He swung his legs over the opening and lowered himself into watery darkness. He hung for an eternal moment to the rim by his finger tips, then he felt rough metal prongs and at once he knew that sewer workmen used these ridges to lower themselves into manholes. Fist over fist, he let his body sink until he could feel no more prongs. He swayed in dank space; the siren seemed to howl at the very rim of the manhole. He dropped and was washed violently into an ocean of warm, leaping water. His head was battered against a wall and he wondered if this were death. Frenziedly his fingers clawed and sank into a crevice. He steadied himself and measured the strength of the current with his own muscular tension. He stood slowly in water that dashed past his knees with fearful velocity.

He heard a prolonged scream of brakes and the siren broke off. Oh, God! They had found him! Looming above his head in the rain a white face hovered over the hole. "How did this damn thing get off?" he heard a policeman ask. He saw the steel cover move slowly until the hole looked like a quarter moon turned black. "Give me a hand here," someone called. The cover clanged into place, muffling the sights and sounds of the upper world. Knee-deep in the pulsing current, he breathed with aching chest, filling his lungs with the hot stench of yeasty rot.

From the perforations of the manhole cover, delicate lances of hazy violet sifted down and wove a mottled pattern upon the surface of the streaking current. His lips parted as a car swept past along the wet pavement overhead, its heavy rumble soon dying out, like the hum of a plane speeding through a dense cloud. He had never thought that cars could sound like that; everything seemed strange and unreal under here. He stood in darkness for a long time, knee-deep in rustling water, musing.

The odor of rot had become so general that he no longer smelled it. He got his cigarettes, but discovered that his matches were wet. He searched and found a dry folder in the pocket of his shirt and managed to strike one; it flared weirdly in the wet gloom, glowing greenishly, turning red, orange, then yellow. He lit a crumpled cigarette; then, by the flickering light of the match, he looked for support so that he would not have to keep his muscles flexed against the pouring water. His pupils narrowed and he saw to either side of him two steaming walls that rose and curved inward some six feet above his head to form a dripping, mouse-colored dome. The bottom of the sewer was a sloping V-trough. To the left, the sewer vanished in ashen fog. To the right was a steep down-curve into which water plunged.

He saw now that had he not regained his feet in time, he would have been swept to death, or had he entered any other manhole he would have probably drowned. Above the rush of the current he heard sharper juttings of water; tiny streams were spewing into the sewer from smaller conduits. The match died; he struck another and saw a mass of debris sweep past him and clog the throat of the down-curve. At once the water began rising rapidly. Could he climb out before he drowned? A long hiss sounded and the debris was sucked from sight; the current lowered. He understood now what had made the water toss the manhole cover; the down-curve had become temporarily obstructed and the perforations had become clogged.

He was in danger; he might slide into a down-curve; he might wander with a lighted match into a pocket of gas and blow himself up; or he might contract some horrible disease . . . Though he wanted to leave, an irrational impulse held him rooted. To the left, the convex ceiling swooped to a height of less than five feet. With cigarette slanting from pursed lips, he waded with taut muscles, his feet sloshing over the slimy bottom, his shoes sinking into spongy slop, the slate-colored water cracking in creamy foam against his knees. Pressing his flat left palm against the lowered ceiling, he struck another match and saw a metal pole nestling in a niche of the wall. Yes, some sewer workman had left it. He reached for it, then jerked his head away as a whisper of scurrying life whisked past and was still. He held the match close and saw a huge rat, wet with slime, blinking beady eyes and baring tiny fangs. The light blinded the rat and the frizzled head moved aimlessly. He grabbed the pole and let it fly against the rat's soft body; there was shrill piping and the grizzly body splashed into the dun-colored water and was snatched out of sight, spinning in the scuttling stream.

He swallowed and pushed on, following the curve of the misty cavern, sounding the water with the pole. By the faint light of another manhole cover he saw, amid loose wet brick, a hole with walls of damp earth leading into blackness. Gingerly he poked the pole into it; it was hollow and went beyond the length of the pole. He shoved the pole before him, hoisted himself upward, got to his hands and knees, and crawled. After a few yards he paused, struck to wonderment by the silence; it seemed that he had traveled a million miles away from the world. As he inched forward again he could sense the bottom of the dirt tunnel becoming dry and lowering slightly. Slowly he rose and to his astonishment he stood erect. He could not hear the rustling of the water now and he felt confoundingly alone, yet lured by the darkness and silence.

He crept a long way, then stopped, curious, afraid. He put his right foot forward and it dangled in space; he drew back in fear. He thrust the pole outward and it swung in emptiness. He trembled, imagining the earth crumbling and burying him alive. He scratched a match and saw that the dirt floor sheered away steeply and widened into a sort of cave some five feet below him. An old sewer, he muttered. He cocked his head, hearing a feathery cadence which he could not identify. The match ceased to burn.

Using the pole as a kind of ladder, he slid down and stood in darkness. The air was a little fresher and he could still hear vague noises. Where was he? He felt suddenly that someone was standing near him and he turned sharply, but there was only darkness. He poked cautiously and felt a brick wall; he followed it and the strange sounds grew louder. He ought to get out of here. This was crazy. He could not remain here for any length of time; there was no food and no place to sleep. But the faint sounds tantalized him; they were strange but familiar. Was it a motor? A baby crying? Music? A siren? He groped on, and the sounds came so clearly that he could feel the pitch and timbre of human voices. Yes, singing! That was it! He listened with open mouth. It was a church service. Enchanted, he groped toward the waves of melody.

> *Jesus, take me to your home above*
> *And fold me in the bosom of Thy love . . .*

The singing was on the other side of a brick wall. Excited, he wanted to watch the service without being seen. Whose church was it? He knew most of the churches in this area above ground, but the singing sounded too strange and detached for him to guess. He looked to the left, to the right, down to the black dirt, then upward and was startled to see a bright sliver of light slicing the darkness like the blade of a razor. He struck one of his two remaining matches and saw rusty pipes running along an old concrete ceiling. Photographically he located the exact position of the pipes in his mind. The match flame sank and he sprang upward; his hands clutched a pipe. He swung his legs and tossed his body onto the bed of pipes and they creaked, swaying up and down; he thought that the tier was about to crash, but nothing happened. He edged to the crevice and saw a segment of black men and women, dressed in white robes, singing, holding tattered songbooks in their black palms. His first impulse was to laugh, but he checked himself.

What was he doing? He was crushed with a sense of guilt. Would God strike him dead for that? The singing swept on and he shook his head, disagreeing in spite of himself. They oughtn't to do that, he thought. But he could think of no reason *why* they should not do it. Just singing with the air of the sewer blowing in on them . . . He felt that he was gazing upon something abysmally obscene, yet he could not bring himself to leave.

After a long time he grew numb and dropped to the dirt. Pain throbbed in his legs and a deeper pain, induced by the sight of those black people groveling and begging for something they could never get, churned in him. A vague conviction made him feel that those people should stand unrepentant and yield no quarter in singing and praying, yet *he* had run away from the police, had pleaded with them to believe in *his* innocence. He shook his head, bewildered.

How long had he been down here? He did not know. This was a new kind of living for him; the intensity of feelings he had experienced when looking at the church people sing made him certain that he had been down here a long time, but his mind told him that the time must have been short. In this darkness the only notion he had of time was when a match flared and measured time by its fleeting light. He groped back through the hole toward the sewer and the waves of song subsided and finally he could not hear them at all. He came to where the earth hole ended and he heard the noise of the current and time lived again for him, measuring the moments by the wash of water.

The rain must have slackened, for the flow of water had lessened and came only to his ankles. Ought he to go up into the streets and take his chances on hiding somewhere else? But they would surely catch him. The mere thought of dodging and running again from the police made him tense. No, he would stay and plot how to elude them. But what could he do down here? He walked forward into the sewer and came to another manhole cover; he stood beneath it, debating. Fine pencils of gold spilled suddenly from the little circles in the manhole cover and trembled on the surface of the current. Yes, street lamps . . . It must be night . . .

He went forward for about a quarter of an hour, wading

aimlessly, poking the pole carefully before him. Then he stopped, his eyes fixed and intent. What's that? A strangely familiar image attracted and repelled him. Lit by the yellow stems from another manhole cover was a tiny nude body of a baby snagged by debris and half-submerged in water. Thinking that the baby was alive, he moved impulsively to save it, but his roused feelings told him that it was dead, cold, nothing, the same nothingness he had felt while watching the men and women singing in the church. Water blossomed about the tiny legs, the tiny arms, the tiny head, and rushed onward. The eyes were closed, as though in sleep; the fists were clenched, as though in protest; and the mouth gaped black in a soundless cry.

He straightened and drew in his breath, feeling that he had been staring for all eternity at the ripples of veined water skimming impersonally over the shriveled limbs. He felt as condemned as when the policemen had accused him. Involuntarily he lifted his hand to brush the vision away, but his arm fell listlessly to his side. Then he acted; he closed his eyes and reached forward slowly with the soggy shoe of his right foot and shoved the dead baby from where it had been lodged. He kept his eyes closed, seeing the little body twisting in the current as it floated from sight. He opened his eyes, shivered, placed his knuckles in the sockets, hearing the water speed in the somber shadows.

He tramped on, sensing at times a sudden quickening in the current as he passed some conduit whose waters were swelling the stream that slid by his feet. A few minutes later he was standing under another manhole cover, listening to the faint rumble of noises above ground. Streetcars and trucks, he mused. He looked down and saw a stagnant pool of gray-green sludge; at intervals a balloon pocket rose from the scum, glistening a bluish-purple, and burst. Then another. He turned, shook his head, and tramped back to the dirt cave by the church, his lips quivering.

Back in the cave, he sat and leaned his back against a dirt wall. His body was trembling slightly. Finally his senses quieted and he slept. When he awakened he felt stiff and cold. He had to leave this foul place, but leaving meant facing those policemen who had wrongly accused him. No, he could not go back aboveground. He remembered the beating they had given him and how he had signed his name to a confession, a confession which he had not even read. He had been too tired when they had shouted at him, demanding that he sign his name; he had signed it to end his pain.

He stood and groped about in the darkness. The church singing had stopped. How long had he slept? He did not know. But he felt refreshed and hungry. He doubled his fist nervously, realizing that he could not make a decision. As he walked about he stumbled over an old rusty iron pipe. He picked it up and felt a jagged edge. Yes, there was a brick wall and he could dig into it. What would he find? Smiling, he groped to the brick wall, sat, and began digging idly into damp cement. I can't make any noise, he cautioned himself. As time passed he grew thirsty, but there was no water. He had to kill time or go aboveground. The cement came out of the wall easily; he extracted four bricks and felt a soft draft blowing into his face. He stopped, afraid. What was beyond? He waited a long time and nothing happened; then he began digging again, soundlessly, slowly; he enlarged the hole and crawled through into a dark room and collided with another wall. He felt his way to the right; the wall ended and his fingers toyed in space, like the antennae of an insect.

He fumbled on and his feet struck something hollow, like

wood. What's this? He felt with his fingers. Steps . . . He stooped and pulled off his shoes and mounted the stairs and saw a yellow chink of light shining and heard a low voice speaking. He placed his eye to a keyhole and saw the nude waxen figure of a man stretched out upon a white table. The voice, low-pitched and vibrant, mumbled indistinguishable words, neither rising nor falling. He craned his neck and squinted to see the man who was talking, but he could not locate him. Above the naked figure was suspended a huge glass container filled with a blood-red liquid from which a white rubber tube dangled. He crouched closer to the door and saw the tip end of a black object lined with pink satin. A coffin, he breathed. This is an undertaker's establishment . . . A fine-spun lace of ice covered his body and he shuddered. A throaty chuckle sounded in the depths of the yellow room.

He turned to leave. Three steps down it occurred to him that a light switch should be nearby; he felt along the wall, found an electric button, pressed it, and a blinding glare smote his pupils so hard that he was sightless, defenseless. His pupils contracted and he wrinkled his nostrils at a peculiar odor. At once he knew that he had been dimly aware of this odor in the darkness, but the light had brought it sharply to his attention. Some kind of stuff they use to embalm, he thought. He went down the steps and saw piles of lumber, coffins, and a long workbench. In one corner was a tool chest. Yes, he could use tools, could tunnel through walls with them. He lifted the lid of the chest and saw nails, a hammer, a crowbar, a screwdriver, a light bulb, and a long length of electric wire. Good! He would lug these back to his cave.

He was about to hoist the chest to his shoulders when he discovered a door behind the furnace. Where did it lead? He tried to open it and found it securely bolted. Using the crowbar so as to make no sound, he pried the door open; it swung on creaking hinges, outward. Fresh air came to his face and he caught the faint roar of faraway sound. Easy now, he told himself. He widened the door and a lump of coal rattled toward him. A coalbin . . . Evidently the door led into another basement. The roaring noise was louder now, but he could not identify it. Where was he? He groped slowly over the coal pile, then ranged in darkness over a gritty floor. The roaring noise seemed to come from above him, then below. His fingers followed a wall until he touched a wooden ridge. A door, he breathed.

The noise died to a low pitch; he felt his skin prickle. It seemed that he was playing a game with an unseen person whose intelligence outstripped his. He put his ear to the flat surface of the door. Yes, voices . . . Was this a prize fight stadium? The sound of the voices came near and sharp, but he could not tell if they were joyous or despairing. He twisted the knob until he heard a soft click and felt the springy weight of the door swinging toward him. He was afraid to open it, yet captured by curiosity and wonder. He jerked the door wide and saw on the far side of the basement a furnace glowing red. Ten feet away was still another door, half ajar. He crossed and peered through the door into an empty, high-ceilinged corridor that terminated in a dark complex of shadow. The belling voices rolled about him and his eagerness mounted. He stepped into the corridor and the voices swelled louder. He crept on and came to a narrow stairway leading circularly upward; there was no question but that he was going to ascend those stairs.

Mounting the spiraled staircase, he heard the voices roll in a steady wave, then leap to crescendo, only to die away, but always remaining audible. Ahead of him glowed red letters:

E—X—I—T. At the top of the steps he paused in front of a black curtain that fluttered uncertainly. He parted the folds and looked into a convex depth that gleamed with clusters of shimmering lights. Sprawling below him was a stretch of human faces, tilted upward, chanting, whistling, screaming, laughing. Dangling before the faces, high upon a screen of silver, were jerking shadows. A movie, he said with slow laughter breaking from his lips.

He stood in a box in the reserved section of a movie house and the impulse he had had to tell the people in the church to stop their singing seized him. These people were laughing at their lives, he thought with amazement. They were shouting and yelling at the animated shadows of themselves. His compassion fired his imagination and he stepped out of the box, walked out upon thin air, walked on down to the audience; and, hovering in the air just above them, he stretched out his hand to touch them . . . His tension snapped and he found himself back in the box, looking down into the sea of faces. No; it could not be done; he could not awaken them. He sighed. Yes, these people were children, sleeping in their living, awake in their dying.

He turned away, parted the black curtain, and looked out. He saw no one. He started down the white stone steps and when he reached the bottom he saw a man in trim blue uniform coming toward him. So used had he become to being underground that he thought that he could walk past the man, as though he were a ghost. But the man stopped. And he stopped.

"Looking for the men's room, sir?" the man asked, and, without waiting for an answer, he turned and pointed. "This way, sir. The first door to your right."

He watched the man turn and walk up the steps and go out

of sight. Then he laughed. What a funny fellow! He went back
to the basement and stood in the red darkness, watching the
glowing embers in the furnace. He went to the sink and turned
the faucet and the water flowed in a smooth silent stream that
looked like a spout of blood. He brushed the mad image from
his mind and began to wash his hands leisurely, looking about
for the usual bar of soap. He found one and rubbed it in his
palms until a rich lather bloomed in his cupped fingers, like
a scarlet sponge. He scrubbed and rinsed his hands meticu-
lously, then hunted for a towel; there was none. He shut off
the water, pulled off his shirt, dried his hands on it; when he
put it on again he was grateful for the cool dampness that
came to his skin.

Yes, he was thirsty; he turned on the faucet again, bowled
his fingers and when the water bubbled over the brim of his
cupped palms, he drank in long, slow swallows. His bladder
grew tight; he shut off the water, faced the wall, bent his head,
and watched a red stream strike the floor. His nostrils wrinkled
against acrid wisps of vapor; though he had tramped in
the waters of the sewer, he stepped back from the wall so
that his shoes, wet with sewer slime, would not touch his
urine.

He heard footsteps and crawled quickly into the coalbin.
Lumps rattled noisily. The footsteps came into the basement
and stopped. Who was it? Had someone heard him and come
down to investigate? He waited, crouching, sweating. For a
long time there was silence, then he heard the clang of metal
and a brighter glow lit the room. Somebody's tending the
furnace, he thought. Footsteps came closer and he stiffened.
Looming before him was a white face lined with coal dust, the
face of an old man with watery blue eyes. Highlights spotted
his gaunt cheekbones, and he held a huge shovel. There was a

screechy scrape of metal against stone, and the old man lifted a shovelful of coal and went from sight.

The room dimmed momentarily, then a yellow glare came as coal flared at the furnace door. Six times the old man came to the bin and went to the furnace with shovels of coal, but not once did he lift his eyes. Finally he dropped the shovel, mopped his face with a dirty handkerchief, and sighed: "Wheeew!" He turned slowly and trudged out of the basement, his footsteps dying away.

He stood, and lumps of coal clattered down the pile. He stepped from the bin and was startled to see the shadowy outline of an electric bulb hanging above his head. Why had not the old man turned it on? Oh, yes . . . He understood. The old man had worked here for so long that he had no need for light; he had learned a way of seeing in his dark world, like those sightless worms that inch along underground by a sense of touch.

His eyes fell upon a lunch pail and he was afraid to hope that it was full. He picked it up; it was heavy. He opened it. *Sandwiches!* He looked guiltily around; he was alone. He searched farther and found a folder of matches and a half-empty tin of tobacco; he put them eagerly into his pocket and clicked off the light. With the lunch pail under his arm, he went through the door, groped over the pile of coal, and stood again in the lighted basement of the undertaking establishment. I've got to get those tools, he told himself. And turn off that light. He tiptoed back up the steps and switched off the light; the invisible voice still droned on behind the door. He crept down and, seeing with his fingers, opened the lunch pail and tore off a piece of paper bag and brought out the tin and spilled grains of tobacco into the makeshift concave. He rolled it and wet it with spittle, then inserted one end into his

mouth and lit it: he sucked smoke that bit his lungs. The nico-
tine reached his brain, went out along his arms to his finger
tips, down to his stomach, and over all the tired nerves of his
body.

He carted the tools to the hole he had made in the wall.
Would the noise of the falling chest betray him? But he would
have to take a chance; he had to have those tools. He lifted
the chest and shoved it; it hit the dirt on the other side of the
wall with a loud clatter. He waited, listening; nothing happened. Head first, he slithered through and stood in the cave.
He grinned, filled with a cunning idea. Yes, he would now go
back into the basement of the undertaking establishment and
crouch behind the coal pile and dig another hole. Sure! Fumbling, he opened the tool chest and extracted a crowbar, a
screwdriver, and a hammer; he fastened them securely about
his person.

With another lumpish cigarette in his flexed lips, he crawled
back through the hole and over the coal pile and sat, facing
the brick wall. He jabbed with the crowbar and the cement
sheered away; quicker than he thought, a brick came loose. He
worked an hour; the other bricks did not come easily. He
sighed, weak from effort. I ought to rest a little, he thought.
I'm hungry. He felt his way back to the cave and stumbled
along the wall till he came to the tool chest. He sat upon it,
opened the lunch pail, and took out two thick sandwiches. He
smelled them. Pork chops . . . His mouth watered. He closed
his eyes and devoured a sandwich, savoring the smooth rye
bread and juicy meat. He ate rapidly, gulping down lumpy
mouthfuls that made him long for water. He ate the other
sandwich and found an apple and gobbled that up too, sucking
the core till the last trace of flavor was drained from it. Then,
like a dog, he ground the meat bones with his teeth, enjoying

the salty, tangy marrow. He finished and stretched out full length on the ground and went to sleep. . . .

. . . His body was washed by cold water that gradually turned warm and he was buoyed upon a stream and swept out to sea where waves rolled gently and suddenly he found himself walking upon the water how strange and delightful to walk upon the water and he came upon a nude woman holding a nude baby in her arms and the woman was sinking into the water holding the baby above her head and screaming *help* and he ran over the water to the woman and he reached her just before she went down and he took the baby from her hands and stood watching the breaking bubbles where the woman sank and he called *lady* and still no answer yes dive down there and rescue that woman but he could not take this baby with him and he stooped and laid the baby tenderly upon the surface of the water expecting it to sink but it floated and he leaped into the water and held his breath and strained his eyes to see through the gloomy volume of water but there was no woman and he opened his mouth and called *lady* and the water bubbled and his chest ached and his arms were tired but he could not see the woman and he called again *lady lady* and his feet touched sand at the bottom of the sea and his chest felt as though it would burst and he bent his knees and propelled himself upward and water rushed past him and his head bobbed out and he breathed deeply and looked around where was the baby the baby was gone and he rushed over the water looking for the baby calling *where is it* and the empty sky and sea threw back his voice *where is it* and he began to doubt that he could stand upon the water and then he was sinking and as he struggled the water rushed him downward spinning dizzily and he opened his mouth to call for help and water surged into his lungs and he choked . . .

He groaned and leaped erect in the dark, his eyes wide. The images of terror that thronged his brain would not let him sleep. He rose, made sure that the tools were hitched to his belt, and groped his way to the coal pile and found the rectangular gap from which he had taken the bricks. He took out the crowbar and hacked. Then dread paralyzed him. How long had he slept? Was it day or night now? He had to be careful. Someone might hear him if it were day. He hewed softly for hours at the cement, working silently. Faintly quivering in the air above him was the dim sound of yelling voices. Crazy people, he muttered. They're still there in that movie . . .

Having rested, he found the digging much easier. He soon had a dozen bricks out. His spirits rose. He took out another brick and his fingers fluttered in space. Good! What lay ahead of him? Another basement? He made the hole larger, climbed through, walked over an uneven floor and felt a metal surface. He lighted a match and saw that he was standing behind a furnace in a basement; before him, on the far side of the room, was a door. He crossed and opened it; it was full of odds and ends. Daylight spilled from a window above his head.

Then he was aware of a soft, continuous tapping. What was it? A clock? No, it was louder than a clock and more irregular. He placed an old empty box beneath the window, stood upon it, and looked into an areaway. He eased the window up and crawled through; the sound of the tapping came clearly now. He glanced about; he was alone. Then he looked upward at a series of window ledges. The tapping identified itself. That's a typewriter, he said to himself. It seemed to be coming from just above. He grasped the ridges of a rain pipe and lifted himself upward; through a half-inch opening of window he saw a doorknob about three feet away. No, it was not a doorknob; it was a small circular disk made of stainless steel with many fine markings upon it. He held his breath; an eerie white hand, seemingly detached from its arm, touched the metal knob and whirled it, first to the left, then to the right. It's a safe! . . . Suddenly he could see the dial no more; a huge metal door swung slowly toward him and he was looking into a safe filled with green wads of paper money, rows of coins wrapped in brown paper, and glass jars and boxes of various sizes. His heart quickened. Good Lord! The white hand went in and out of the safe, taking wads of bills and cylinders of coins. The hand vanished and he heard the muffled click of the big door as it closed. Only the steel dial was visible now. The typewriter still tapped in his ears, but he could not see it. He blinked, wondering if what he had seen was real. There was more money in that safe than he had seen in all his life.

As he clung to the rain pipe, a daring idea came to him and he pulled the screwdriver from his belt. If the white hand twirled that dial again, he would be able to see how far to left and right it spun and he would have the combination! His blood tingled. I can scratch the numbers right here, he thought. Holding the pipe with one hand, he made the sharp edge of the screwdriver bite into the brick wall. Yes, he could do it. Now, he was set. Now, he had a reason for staying here in the underground. He waited for a long time, but the white hand did not return. Goddamn! Had he been more alert, he could have counted the twirls and he would have had the combination. He got down and stood in the areaway, sunk in reflection.

How could he get into that room? He climbed back into the basement and saw wooden steps leading upward. Was that the room where the safe stood? Fearing that the dial was now being twirled, he clambered through the window, hoisted himself up the rain pipe, and peered; he saw only the naked gleam of the steel dial. He got down and doubled his fists. Well, he would explore the basement. He returned to the basement room and mounted the steps to the door and squinted through the keyhole; all was dark, but the tapping was still somewhere near, still faint and directionless. He pushed the door in; along one wall of a room was a table piled with radios and electrical equipment. A radio shop, he muttered.

Well, he could rig up a radio in his cave. He found a sack, slid the radio into it, and slung it across his back. Closing the door, he went down the steps and stood again in the basement, disappointed. He had not solved the problem of the steel dial and he was irked. He set the radio on the floor and again hoisted himself through the window and up the rain pipe and squinted; the metal door was swinging shut. Goddamn! He's worked the combination again. If I had been patient, I'd have had it! How could he get into that room? He *had* to get into it. He could jimmy the window, but it would be much better if he could get in without any traces. To the right of him, he calculated, should be the basement of the building that held the safe; therefore, if he dug a hole right *here*, he ought to reach his goal.

He began a quiet scraping; it was hard work, for the bricks were not damp. He eventually got one out and lowered it softly to the floor. He had to be careful; perhaps people were beyond this wall. He extracted a second layer of brick and found still another. He gritted his teeth, ready to quit. I'll dig one more, he resolved. When the next brick came out he felt air blowing into his face. He waited to be challenged, but nothing happened.

He enlarged the hole and pulled himself through and stood in quiet darkness. He scratched a match to flame and saw steps; he mounted and peered through a keyhole: Darkness . . . He strained to hear the typewriter, but there was only silence. Maybe the office had closed? He twisted the knob and swung the door in; a frigid blast made him shiver. In the shadows before him were halves and quarters of hogs and lambs and steers hanging from metal hooks on the low ceiling, red meat encased in folds of cold white fat. Fronting him was frost-coated glass from behind which came indistinguishable sounds. The odor of fresh raw meat sickened him and he backed away. A meat market, he whispered.

He ducked his head, suddenly blinded by light. He narrowed his eyes; the red-white rows of meat were drenched in yellow glare. A man wearing a crimson-spotted jacket came in and took down a bloody meat cleaver. He eased the door to, holding it ajar just enough to watch the man, hoping that the darkness in which he stood would keep him from being seen. The man took down a hunk of steer and placed it upon a bloody wooden block and bent forward and whacked with the cleaver. The man's face was hard, square, grim; a jet of mustache smudged his upper lip and a glistening cowlick of hair fell over his left eye. Each time he lifted the cleaver and brought it down upon the meat, he let out a short, deep-chested grunt. After he had cut the meat, he wiped blood off the wooden block with a sticky wad of gunny sack and hung the cleaver upon a hook. His face was proud as he placed the chunk of meat in the crook of his elbow and left.

The door slammed and the light went off; once more he stood in shadow. His tension ebbed. From behind the frosted glass he heard the man's voice: "Forty-eight cents a pound, ma'am." He shuddered, feeling that there was something he had to do. But what? He stared fixedly at the cleaver, then he sneezed and was terrified for fear that the man had heard him. But the door did not open. He took down the cleaver and examined the sharp edge smeared with cold blood. Behind the ice-coated glass a cash register rang with a vibrating, musical tinkle.

Absent-mindedly holding the meat cleaver, he rubbed the glass with his thumb and cleared a spot that enabled him to see into the front of the store. The shop was empty, save for the man who was now putting on his hat and coat. Beyond the front window a wan sun shone in the streets; people passed and now and then a fragment of laughter or the whir of a speeding auto came to him. He peered closer and saw on the right counter of the shop a mosquito netting covering pears, grapes, lemons, oranges, bananas, peaches, and plums. His stomach contracted.

The man clicked out the light and he gritted his teeth, muttering, Don't lock the icebox door . . . The man went through the door of the shop and locked it from the outside. Thank God! Now, he would eat some more! He waited, trembling. The sun died and its rays lingered on in the sky, turning the streets to dusk. He opened the door and stepped inside the shop. In reverse letters across the front window was: NICK'S FRUITS AND MEATS. He laughed, picked up a soft ripe yellow pear and bit into it; juice squirted; his mouth ached as his saliva glands reacted to the acid of the fruit. He ate three pears, gobbled six bananas, and made away with several oranges, taking a bite out of their tops and holding them to his lips and squeezing them as he hungrily sucked the juice.

He found a faucet, turned it on, laid the cleaver aside, pursed his lips under the stream until his stomach felt about to burst. He straightened and belched, feeling satisfied for the first time since he had been underground. He sat upon the floor, rolled and lit a cigarette, his bloodshot eyes squinting against the film of drifting smoke. He watched a patch of sky turn red, then purple; night fell and he lit another cigarette, brooding. Some part of him was trying to remember the world he had left, and another part of him did not want to remember it. Sprawling before him in his mind was his wife, Mrs. Wooten for whom he worked, the three policemen who had picked him up . . . He possessed them now more completely than he had ever possessed them when he had lived aboveground. How this had come about he could not say, but he had no desire to go back to them. He laughed, crushed the cigarette, and stood up.

He went to the front door and gazed out. Emotionally he hovered between the world aboveground and the world underground. He longed to go out, but sober judgment urged him to remain here. Then impulsively he pried the lock loose with one swift twist of the crowbar; the door swung outward. Through the twilight he saw a white man and a white woman coming toward him. He held himself tense, waiting for them to pass; but they came directly to the door and confronted him.

"I want to buy a pound of grapes," the woman said.

Terrified, he stepped back into the store. The white man stood to one side and the woman entered.

"Give me a pound of dark ones," the woman said.

The white man came slowly forward, blinking his eyes.

"Where's Nick?" the man asked.

"Were you just closing?" the woman asked.

"Yes, ma'am," he mumbled. For a second he did not breathe, then he mumbled again: "Yes, ma'am."

"I'm sorry," the woman said.

The street lamps came on, lighting the store somewhat. Ought he run? But that would raise an alarm. He moved slowly, dreamily, to a counter and lifted up a bunch of grapes and showed them to the woman.

"Fine," the woman said. "But isn't that more than a pound?"

He did not answer. The man was staring at him intently.

"Put them in a bag for me," the woman said, fumbling with her purse.

"Yes, ma'am."

He saw a pile of paper bags under a narrow ledge; he opened one and put the grapes in.

"Thanks," the woman said, taking the bag and placing a dime in his dark palm.

"Where's Nick?" the man asked again. "At supper?"

"Sir? Yes, sir," he breathed.

They left the store and he stood trembling in the doorway. When they were out of sight, he burst out laughing and crying. A trolley car rolled noisily past and he controlled himself quickly. He flung the dime to the pavement with a gesture of contempt and stepped into the warm night air. A few shy stars trembled above him. The look of things was beautiful, yet he felt a lurking threat. He went to an unattended newsstand and looked at a stack of papers. He saw a headline: HUNT NEGRO FOR MURDER.

He felt that someone had slipped up on him from behind and was stripping off his clothes; he looked about wildly, went quickly back into the store, picked up the meat cleaver where he had left it near the sink, then made his way through the icebox to the basement. He stood for a long time, breathing heavily. They know I didn't do anything, he muttered. But how could he prove it? He had signed a confession. Though innocent, he felt guilty, condemned. He struck a match and held it near the steel blade, fascinated and repelled by the dried blotches of blood. Then his fingers gripped the handle of the cleaver with all the strength of his body, he wanted to fling the cleaver from him, but he could not. The match flame wavered and fled; he struggled through the hole and put the cleaver in the sack with the radio. He was determined to keep it, for what purpose he did not know.

He was about to leave when he remembered the safe. Where was it? He wanted to give up, but felt that he ought to make one more try. Opposite the last hole he had dug, he tunneled again, plying the crowbar. Once he was so exhausted that he lay on the concrete floor and panted. Finally he made another hole. He wriggled through and his nostrils filled with the fresh smell of coal. He struck a match; yes, the usual steps led upward. He tiptoed to a door and eased it open. A fair-haired white girl stood in front of a steel cabinet, her blue eyes wide upon him. She turned chalky and gave a high-pitched scream. He bounded down the steps and raced to his hole and clambered through, replacing the bricks with nervous haste. He paused, hearing loud voices.

"What's the matter, Alice?"

"A man . . ."

"What man? Where?"

"A man was at that door . . ."

"Oh, nonsense!"

"He was looking at me through the door!"

"Aw, you're dreaming."

"I *did* see a man!"

The girl was crying now.

"There's nobody here."

Another man's voice sounded.

"What is it, Bob?"

"Alice says she saw a man in here, in that door!"

"Let's take a look."

He waited, poised for flight. Footsteps descended the stairs.

"There's nobody down here."

"The window's locked."

"And there's no door."

"You ought to fire that dame."

"Oh, I don't know. Women are that way."

"She's too hysterical."

The men laughed. Footsteps sounded again on the stairs. A door slammed. He sighed, relieved that he had escaped. But he had not done what he had set out to do; his glimpse of the room had been too brief to determine if the safe was there. He had to know. Boldly he groped through the hole once more; he reached the steps and pulled off his shoes and tiptoed up and peered through the keyhole. His head accidentally touched the door and it swung silently in a fraction of an inch; he saw the girl bent over the cabinet, her back to him. Beyond her was the safe. He crept back down the steps, thinking exultingly: I found it!

Now he had to get the combination. Even if the window in the areaway was locked and bolted, he could gain entrance when the office closed. He scoured through the holes he had dug and stood again in the basement where he had left the radio and the cleaver. Again he crawled out of the window and lifted himself up the rain pipe and peered. The steel dial showed lonely and bright, reflecting the yellow glow of an unseen light. Resigned to a long wait, he sat and leaned against a wall. From far off came the faint sounds of life aboveground; once he looked with a baffled expression at the dark sky. Frequently he rose and climbed the pipe to see the white hand spin the dial, but nothing happened. He bit his lip with impatience. It was not the money that was luring him, but the mere fact that he could get it with impunity. Was the hand now twirling the dial? He rose and looked, but the white hand was not in sight.

Perhaps it would be better to watch continuously? Yes; he clung to the pipe and watched the dial until his eyes thickened with tears. Exhausted, he stood again in the areaway. He heard a door being shut and he clawed up the pipe and looked. He jerked tense as a vague figure passed in front of him. He stared unblinkingly, hugging the pipe with one hand and holding the screwdriver with the other, ready to etch the combination upon the wall. His ears caught: *Dong . . . Dong . . . Dong . . . Dong . . . Dong . . . Dong . . . Dong . . .* Seven o'clock, he whispered. Maybe they were closing now? What kind of a store would be open as late as this? he wondered. Did anyone live in the rear? Was there a night watchman? Perhaps the safe was *already* locked for the night! Goddamn! While he had been eating in that shop, they had locked up everything . . . Then, just as he was about to give up, the white hand touched the dial and turned it once to the right and stopped at six. With quivering fingers, he etched 1—R—6 upon the brick wall with the tip of the screwdriver. The hand twirled the dial twice to the left and stopped at two, and he engraved 2—L—2 upon the wall. The dial was spun four times to the right and stopped at six again; he wrote 4—R—6. The dial rotated three times to the left and was centered straight up and down; he wrote 3—L—0. The door swung open and again he saw the piles of green money and the rows of wrapped coins. I got it, he said grimly.

Then he was stone still, astonished. There were two hands now. A right hand lifted a wad of green bills and deftly slipped it up the sleeve of a left arm. The hands trembled; again the right hand slipped a packet of bills up the left sleeve. He's stealing, he said to himself. He grew indignant, as if the money belonged to him. Though *he* had planned to steal the money, he despised and pitied the man. He felt that his stealing the money and the man's stealing were two entirely different things. He wanted to steal the money merely for the sensation involved in getting it, and he had no intention whatever of spending a penny of it; but he knew that the man who was now stealing it was going to spend it, perhaps for pleasure. The huge steel door closed with a soft click.

Though angry, he was somewhat satisfied. The office would close soon. I'll clean the place out, he mused. He imagined the entire office staff cringing with fear; the police would question everyone for a crime they had not committed, just as they had questioned him. And they would have no idea of how the money had been stolen until they discovered the holes he had tunneled in the walls of the basements. He lowered himself and laughed mischievously, with the abandoned glee of an adolescent.

He flattened himself against the wall as the window above him closed with rasping sound. He looked; somebody was bolting the window securely with a metal screen. That won't help you, he snickered to himself. He clung to the rain pipe until the yellow light in the office went out. He went back into the basement, picked up the sack containing the radio and cleaver, and crawled through the two holes he had dug and groped his way into the basement of the building that held the safe. He moved in slow motion, breathing softly. Be careful now, he told himself. There might be a night watchman . . . In his memory was the combination written in bold white characters as upon a blackboard. Eel-like he squeezed through the last hole and crept up the steps and put his hand on the knob and pushed the door in about three inches. Then his courage ebbed; his imagination wove dangers for him.

Perhaps the night watchman was waiting in there, ready to shoot. He dangled his cap on a forefinger and poked it past the jamb of the door. If anyone fired, they would hit his cap; but nothing happened. He widened the door, holding the crowbar high above his head, ready to beat off an assailant. He stood like that for five minutes; the rumble of a streetcar brought him to himself. He entered the room. Moonlight floated in from a side window. He confronted the safe, then checked himself. Better take a look around first . . . He stepped about and found a closed door. Was the night watchman in there? He opened it and saw a washbowl, a faucet, and a commode. To the left was still another door that opened into a huge dark room that seemed empty; on the far side of that room he made out the shadow of still another door. Nobody's here, he told himself.

He turned back to the safe and fingered the dial; it spun with ease. He laughed and twirled it just for fun. Get to work, he told himself. He turned the dial to the figures he saw on the blackboard of his memory; it was so easy that he felt that the safe had not been locked at all. The heavy door eased loose and he caught hold of the handle and pulled hard, but the door swung open with a slow momentum of its own. Breath-less, he gaped at wads of green bills, rows of wrapped coins, curious glass jars full of white pellets, and many oblong green metal boxes. He glanced guiltily over his shoulder; it seemed impossible that someone should not call to him to stop.

They'll be surprised in the morning, he thought. He opened the top of the sack and lifted a wad of compactly tied bills; the money was crisp and new. He admired the smooth, clean-cut edges. The fellows in Washington sure know how to make this stuff, he mused. He rubbed the money with his fingers, as though expecting it to reveal hidden qualities. He lifted the wad to his nose and smelled the fresh odor of ink. Just like any other paper, he mumbled. He dropped the wad into the sack and picked up another. Holding the bag, he thought and laughed.

There was in him no sense of possessiveness; he was intrigued with the form and color of the money, with the manifold reactions which he knew that men aboveground held toward it. The sack was one-third full when it occurred to him to examine the denominations of the bills; without realizing it, he had put many wads of one-dollar bills into the sack. Aw, nuts, he said in disgust. Take the big ones . . . He dumped the one-dollar bills onto the floor and swept all the hundred-dollars bills he could find into the sack, then he raked in rolls of coins with crooked fingers.

He walked to a desk upon which sat a typewriter, the same machine which the blond girl had used. He was fascinated by it; never in his life had he used one of them. It was a queer instrument of business, something beyond the rim of his life. Whenever he had been in an office where a girl was typing, he had almost always spoken in whispers. Remembering vaguely what he had seen others do, he inserted a sheet of paper into the machine; it went in lopsided and he did not know how to straighten it. Spelling in a soft diffident voice, he pecked out his name on the keys: *freddaniels*. He looked at it and laughed. He would learn to type correctly one of these days.

Yes, he would take the typewriter too. He lifted the machine and placed it atop the bulk of money in the sack. He did not feel that he was stealing, for the cleaver, the radio, the money, and the typewriter were all on the same level of value, all meant the same thing to him. They were the serious toys of the men who lived in the dead world of sunshine and rain he had left, the world that had condemned him, branded him guilty.

But what kind of a place is this? He wondered. What was in that dark room to his rear? He felt for his matches and found that he had only one left. He leaned the sack against the safe and groped forward into the room, encountering smooth, metallic objects that felt like machines. Baffled, he touched a wall and tried vainly to locate an electric switch. Well, he *had* to strike his last match. He knelt and struck it, cupping the flame near the floor with his palms. The place seemed to be a factory, with benches and tables. There were bulbs with green shades spaced about the tables; he turned on a light and twisted it low so that the glare was limited. He saw a half-filled packet of cigarettes and appropriated it. There were stools at the benches and he concluded that men worked here at some trade. He wandered and found a few half-used folders of matches. If only he could find more cigarettes! But there were none.

But what kind of a place was this? On a bench he saw a pad of paper captioned: PEER'S—MANUFACTURING JEWEL-ERS. His lips formed an "O," then he snapped off the light and ran back to the safe and lifted one of the glass jars and stared at the tiny white pellets. Gingerly he picked up one and found that it was wrapped in tissue paper. He peeled the paper and saw a glittering stone that looked like glass, glinting white and blue sparks. Diamonds, he breathed.

Roughly he tore the paper from the pellets and soon his palm quivered with precious fire. Trembling, he took all four glass jars from the safe and put them into the sack. He grabbed one of the metal boxes, shook it, and heard a tinny rattle. He pried off the lid with the screwdriver. Rings! Hundreds of them ... Were they worth anything? He scooped up a handful and jets of fire shot fitfully from the stones. These are dia-monds too, he said. He pried open another box. Watches! A chorus of soft, metallic ticking filled his ears. For a moment he could not move, then he dumped all the boxes into the sack.

He shut the safe door, then stood looking around, anxious not to overlook anything. Oh! He had seen a door in the room where the machines were. What was in there? More valuables? He re-entered the room, crossed the floor, and stood undecided before the door. He finally caught hold of the knob and pushed the door in; the room beyond was dark. He advanced cautiously inside and ran his fingers along the wall for the usual switch, then he was stark still. *Something had moved in the room!* What was it? Ought he to creep out, taking the rings and diamonds and money? Why risk what he already had? He waited and the ensuing silence gave him confidence to explore further. Dare he strike a match? Would not a match flame make him a good target? He tensed again as he heard a faint sigh; he was now convinced that there was something alive near him, something that lived and breathed. On tiptoe he felt slowly along the wall, hoping that he would not collide with anything. Luck was with him; he found the light switch.

No; don't turn the light on . . . Then suddenly he realized that he did not know in what direction the door was. Goddamn! He had to turn the light on or strike a match. He fingered the switch for a long time, then thought of an idea. He knelt upon the floor, reached his arm up to the switch and flicked the button, hoping that if anyone shot, the bullet would go above his head. The moment the light came on he narrowed his eyes to see quickly. He sucked in his breath and his body gave a violent twitch and was still. In front of him, so close that it made him want to bound up and scream, was a human face.

He was afraid to move lest he touch the man. If the man had opened his eyes at that moment, there was no telling what he might have done. The man—long and rawboned—was stretched out on his back upon a little cot, sleeping in his clothes, his head cushioned by a dirty pillow; his face, clouded by a dark stubble of beard, looked straight up to the ceiling. The man sighed, and he grew tense to defend himself; the man mumbled and turned his face away from the light. I've got to turn off that light, he thought. Just as he was about to rise, he saw a gun and cartridge belt on the floor at the man's side. Yes, he would take the gun and cartridge belt, not to use them, but just to keep them, as one takes a memento from a country fair. He picked them up and was about to click off the light when his eyes fell upon a photograph perched upon a chair near the man's head; it was the picture of a woman, smiling, shown against a background of open fields; at the woman's side were two young children, a boy and a girl. He smiled indulgently; he could send a bullet into that man's brain and time would be over for him . . .

He clicked off the light and crept silently back into the room where the safe stood; he fastened the cartridge belt about him and adjusted the holster at his right hip. He strutted about the room on tiptoe, lolling his head nonchalantly, then paused abruptly pulled the gun, and pointed it with grim face toward an imaginary foe. "Boom!" he whispered fiercely. Then he bent forward with silent laughter. That's just like they do it in the movies, he said.

He contemplated his loot for a long time, then got a towel from the washroom and tied the sack securely. When he looked up he was momentarily frightened by his shadow looming on the wall before him. He lifted the sack, dragged it down the basement steps, lugged it across the basement, gasping for breath. After he had struggled through the hole, he clumsily replaced the bricks, then tussled with the sack until he got it to the cave. He stood in the dark, wet with sweat, brooding about the diamonds, the rings, the watches, the money; he remembered the singing in the church, the people yelling in the movie, the dead baby, the nude man stretched out upon the white table . . . He saw these items hovering before his eyes and felt that some dim meaning linked them together, that some magical relationship made them kin. He stared with vacant eyes, convinced that all of these images, with their tongueless reality, were striving to tell him something . . .

Later, seeing with his fingers, he untied the sack and set each item neatly upon the dirt floor. Exploring, he took the bulb, the socket, and the wire out of the tool chest; he was elated to find a double socket at one end of the wire. He crammed the stuff into his pockets and hoisted himself upon the rusty pipes and squinted into the church; it was dim and empty. Somewhere in this wall were live electric wires; but where? He lowered himself, groped and tapped the wall with the butt of the screwdriver, listening vainly for hollow sounds. I'll just take a chance and dig, he said.

For an hour he tried to dislodge a brick, and when he struck a match, he found that he had dug a depth of only an inch! No use in digging here, he sighed. By the flickering light of a match, he looked upward, then lowered his eyes, only to glance up again, startled. Directly above his head, beyond the pipes, was a wealth of electric wiring. I'll be damned, he snickered.

He got an old dull knife from the chest and, seeing again with his fingers, separated the two strands of wire and cut away the insulation. Twice he received a slight shock. He scraped the wiring clean and managed to join the two twin ends, then screwed in the bulb. The sudden illumination blinded him and he shut his lids to kill the pain in his eyeballs. I've got that much done, he thought jubilantly.

He placed the bulb on the dirt floor and the light cast a blatant glare on the bleak clay walls. Next he plugged one end of the wire that dangled from the radio into the light socket and bent down and switched on the button; almost at once there was the harsh sound of static, but no words or music. Why won't it work? he wondered. Had he damaged the mechanism in any way? Maybe it needed grounding? Yes . . . He rummaged in the tool chest and found another length of wire, fastened it to the ground of the radio, and then tied the opposite end to a pipe. Rising and growing distinct, a slow strain of music entranced him with its measured sound. He sat upon the chest, deliriously happy.

Later he searched again in the chest and found a half-gallon can of glue; he opened it and smelled a sharp odor. Then he recalled that he had not even looked at the money. He took a wad of green bills and weighed it in his palm, then broke the seal and held one of the bills up to the light and studied it closely. *The United States of America will pay to the bearer on demand one hundred dollars,* he read in slow speech; then: *This note is legal tender for all debts, public and private. . . .* He broke into a musing laugh, feeling that he was reading of the doings of people who lived on some far-off planet. He turned the bill over and saw on the other side of it a delicately beautiful building gleaming with paint and set amidst green grass. He had no desire whatever to count the money; it was what it stood for—the various currents of life swirling aboveground—that captivated him. Next he opened the rolls of coins and let them slide from their paper wrappings to the ground; the bright, new gleaming pennies and nickles and dimes piled high at his feet, a glowing mound of shimmering copper and silver. He sifted them through his fingers, listening to their tinkle as they struck the conical heap.

Oh, yes! He had forgotten. He would now write his name on the typewriter. He inserted a piece of paper and poised his fingers to write. But what was his name? He stared, trying to remember. He stood and glared about the dirt cave, his name on the tip of his lips. But it would not come to him. Why was he here? Yes, he had been running away from the police. But why? His mind was blank. He bit his lips and sat again, feeling a vague terror. But why worry? He laughed, then pecked slowly: *itwasalonghotday*. He was determined to type the sentence without making any mistakes. How did one make capital letters? He experimented and luckily discovered how to lock the machine for capital letters and then shift it back to lower case. Next he discovered how to make spaces, then he wrote neatly and correctly: *It was a long hot day*. Just why he selected that sentence he did not know; it was merely the ritual of performing the thing that appealed to him. He took the sheet out of the machine and looked around with stiff neck and hard eyes and spoke to an imaginary person:

"Yes, I'll have the contracts ready tomorrow."

He laughed. That's just the way they talk, he said. He grew weary of the game and pushed the machine aside. His eyes fell upon the can of glue, and a mischievous idea bloomed in him, filling him with nervous eagerness. He leaped up and opened the can of glue, then broke the seals on all the wads of money. I'm going to have some wallpaper, he said with a luxurious, physical laugh that made him bend at the knees. He took the towel with which he had tied the sack and balled it into a swab and dipped it into the can of glue and dabbed glue onto the wall; then he pasted one green bill by the side of another. He stepped back and cocked his head. Jesus! That's funny . . . He slapped his thighs and guffawed. He had triumphed over the world aboveground! He was free! If only people could see this! He wanted to run from this cave and yell his discovery to the world.

He swabbed all the dirt walls of the cave and pasted them with green bills; when he had finished the walls blazed with a yellow-green fire. Yes, this room would be his hide-out; between him and the world that had branded him guilty would stand this mocking symbol. He had not stolen the money; he had simply picked it up, just as a man would pick up firewood in a forest. And that was how the world aboveground now seemed to him, a wild forest filled with death.

The walls of money finally palled on him and he looked about for new interests to feed his emotions. The cleaver! He drove a nail into the wall and hung the bloody cleaver upon it. Still another idea welled up. He pried open the metal boxes and lined them side by side on the dirt floor. He grinned at the gold and fire. From one box he lifted up a fistful of ticking gold watches and dangled them by their gleaming chains. He stared with an idle smile, then began to wind them up; he did not attempt to set them at any given hour, for there was no time for him now. He took a fistful of nails and drove them into the papered walls and hung the watches upon them, letting them swing down by their glittering chains, trembling and ticking busily against the backdrop of green with the lemon sheen of the electric light shining upon the metal watch casings, converting the golden disks into blobs of liquid yellow. Hardly had he hung up the last watch than the idea extended itself; he took more nails from the chest and drove them into the green paper and took the boxes of rings and went from nail to nail and hung up the golden bands. The blue and white sparks from the stones filled the cave with brittle laughter, as though enjoying his hilarious secret. People certainly can do some funny things, he said to himself.

He sat upon the tool chest, alternately laughing and shaking his head soberly. Hours later he became conscious of the gun sagging at his hip and he pulled it from the holster. He had seen men fire guns in movies, but somehow his life had never led him into contact with firearms. A desire to feel the sensation others felt in firing came over him. But someone might hear . . . Well, what if they did? They would not know where the shot had come from. Not in their wildest notions would they think that it had come from under the streets! He tightened his fingers on the trigger; there was a deafening report and it seemed that the entire underground had caved in upon his eardrums; and in the same instant there flashed an orange-blue spurt of flame that died quickly but lingered on as a vivid after-image. He smelled the acrid stench of burnt powder filling his lungs and he dropped the gun abruptly.

The intensity of his feelings died and he hung the gun and cartridge belt upon the wall. Next he lifted the jars of diamonds and turned them bottom upward, dumping the white pellets upon the ground. One by one he picked them up and peeled the tissue paper from them and piled them in a neat heap. He wiped his sweaty hands on his trousers, lit a cigarette, and commenced playing another game. He imagined that he was a rich man who lived aboveground in the obscene sunshine and he was strolling through a park of a summer morning, smiling, nodding to his neighbors, sucking an after-breakfast cigar. Many times he crossed the floor of the cave, avoiding the diamonds with his feet, yet subtly gauging his footsteps so that his shoes, wet with sewer slime, would strike the diamonds at some undetermined moment. After twenty minutes of sauntering, his right foot smashed into the heap and diamonds lay scattered in all directions, glinting with a million tiny chuckles of icy laughter. Oh, shucks, he mumbled in mock regret, intrigued by the damage he had wrought. He continued walking, ignoring the brittle fire. He felt that he had a glorious victory locked in his heart.

He stooped and flung the diamonds more evenly over the floor and they showered rich sparks, collaborating with him. He went over the floor and trampled the stones just deep enough for them to be faintly visible, as though they were set delicately in the prongs of a thousand rings. A ghostly light bathed the cave. He sat on the chest and frowned. Maybe *any*thing's right, he mumbled. Yes, if the world as men had made it was right, then anything else was right, any act a man took to satisfy himself, murder, theft, torture.

He straightened with a start. What was happening to him? He was drawn to these crazy thoughts, yet they made him feel vaguely guilty. He would stretch out upon the ground, then get up; he would want to crawl again through the holes he had dug, but would restrain himself; he would think of going again up into the streets, but fear would hold him still. He stood in the middle of the cave, surrounded by green walls and a laughing floor, trembling. He was going to do something, but what? Yes, he was afraid of himself, afraid of doing some nameless thing.

To control himself, he turned on the radio. A melancholy piece of music rose. Brooding over the diamonds on the floor was like looking up into a sky full of restless stars; then the illusion turned into its opposite: he was high up in the air

looking down at the twinkling lights of a sprawling city. The
music ended and a man recited news events. In the same
attitude in which he had contemplated the city, so now,
as he heard the cultivated tone, he looked down upon
land and sea as men fought, as cities were razed, as planes
scattered death upon open towns, as long lines of trenches
wavered and broke. He heard the names of generals and the
names of mountains and the names of countries and the names
and numbers of divisions that were in action on different
battle fronts. He saw black smoke billowing from the stacks
of warships as they neared each other over wastes of water
and he heard their huge guns thunder as red-hot shells
screamed across the surface of night seas. He saw hundreds
of planes wheeling and droning in the sky and heard the clatter
of machine guns as they fought each other and he saw planes
falling in plumes of smoke and blaze of fire. He saw steel
tanks rumbling across fields of ripe wheat to meet other tanks
and there was a loud clang of steel as numberless tanks collided. He saw troops with fixed bayonets charging in waves
against other troops who held fixed bayonets and men groaned
as steel ripped into their bodies and they went down to die
. . . The voice of the radio faded and he was staring at the
diamonds on the floor at his feet.

He shut off the radio, fighting an irrational compulsion to
act. He walked aimlessly about the cave, touching the walls
with his finger tips. Suddenly he stood still. *What was the
matter with him?* Yes, he knew . . . It was these walls; these
crazy walls were filling him with a wild urge to climb out
into the dark sunshine aboveground. Quickly he doused the
light to banish the shouting walls, then sat again upon the
tool chest. Yes, he was trapped. His muscles were flexed taut
and sweat ran down his face. He knew now that he could not

stay here and he could not go out. He lit a cigarette with shaking fingers; the match flame revealed the green-papered walls with militant distinctness; the purple on the gun barrel glinted like a threat; the meat cleaver brooded with its eloquent splotches of blood; the mound of silver and copper smoldered angrily; the diamonds winked at him from the floor; and the gold watches ticked and trembled, crowning time the king of consciousness, defining the limits of living . . . The match blaze died and he bolted from where he stood and collided brutally with the nails upon the walls. The spell was broken. He shuddered, feeling that, in spite of his fear, sooner or later he would go up into that dead sunshine and somehow say something to somebody about all this.

He sat again upon the tool chest. Fatigue weighed upon his forehead and eyes. Minutes passed and he relaxed. He dozed, but his imagination was alert. He saw himself rising, wading again in the sweeping water of the sewer; he came to a manhole and climbed out and was amazed to discover that he had hoisted himself into a room filled with armed policemen who were watching him intently. He jumped awake in the dark; he had not moved. He sighed, closed his eyes, and slept again; this time his imagination designed a scheme of protection for him. His dreaming made him feel that he was standing in a room watching over his own nude body lying stiff and cold upon a white table. At the far end of the room he saw a crowd of people huddled in a corner, afraid of his body. Though lying dead upon the table, he was standing in some mysterious way at his side, warding off the people, guarding his body, and laughing to himself as he observed the situation. They're scared of me, he thought.

He awakened with a start, leaped to his feet, and stood in the center of the black cave. It was a full minute before he

moved again. He hovered between sleeping and waking, un-
protected, a prey of wild fears. He could neither see nor hear.
One part of him was asleep; his blood coursed slowly and his
flesh was numb. On the other hand he was roused to a strange,
high pitch of tension. He lifted his fingers to his face, as though
about to weep. Gradually his hands lowered and he struck a
match, looking about, expecting to see a door through which
he could walk to safety; but there was no door, only the green
walls and the moving floor. The match flame died and it was
dark again.

Five minutes later he was still standing when the thought
came to him that he had been asleep. Yes . . . But he was not
yet fully awake; he was still queerly blind and deaf. How
long had he slept? Where was he? Then suddenly he recalled
the green-papered walls of the cave and in the same instant
he heard loud singing coming from the church beyond the
wall. Yes, they woke me up, he muttered. He hoisted himself
and lay atop the bed of pipes and brought his face to the narrow slit. Men and women stood here and there between pews.
A song ended and a young black girl tossed back her head and
closed her eyes and broke plaintively into another hymn:

> *Glad, glad, glad, oh, so glad*
> *I got Jesus in my soul . . .*

Those few words were all she sang, but what her words
did not say, her emotions said as she repeated the lines, vary-
ing the mood and tempo, making her tone express meanings
which her conscious mind did not know. Another woman
melted her voice with the girl's, and then an old man's voice
merged with that of the two women. Soon the entire con-
gregation was singing:

> *Glad, glad, glad, oh, so glad*
> *I got Jesus in my soul . . .*

They're wrong, he whispered in the lyric darkness. He felt that their search for a happiness they could never find made them feel that they had committed some dreadful offense which they could not remember or understand. He was now in possession of the feeling that had gripped him when he had first come into the underground. It came to him in a series of questions: Why was this sense of guilt so seemingly innate, so easy to come by, to think, to feel, so verily physical? It seemed that when one felt this guilt one was retracing in one's feelings a faint pattern designed long before; it seemed that one was always trying to remember a gigantic shock that had left a haunting impression upon one's body which one could not forget or shake off, but which had been forgotten by the conscious mind, creating in one's life a state of eternal anxiety.

He had to tear himself away from this; he got down from the pipes. His nerves were so taut that he seemed to feel his brain pushing through his skull. He felt that he had to do something, but he could not figure out what it was. Yet he knew that if he stood here until he made up his mind, he would never move. He crawled through the hole he had made in the brick wall and the exertion afforded him respite from tension. When he entered the basement of the radio store, he stopped in fear, hearing loud voices.

"Come on, boy! Tell us what you did with the radio!"

"Mister, I didn't steal the radio! I swear!"

He heard a dull thumping sound and he imagined a boy being struck violently.

"Please, mister!"

"Did you take it to a pawn shop?"

"No, sir! I didn't steal the radio! I got a radio at home," the boy's voice pleaded hysterically. "Go to my home and look!"

There came to his ears the sound of another blow. It was so funny that he had to clap his hand over his mouth to keep from laughing out loud. They're beating some poor boy, he whispered to himself, shaking his head. He felt a sort of distant pity for the boy and wondered if he ought to bring back the radio and leave it in the basement. No. Perhaps it was a good thing that they were beating the boy; perhaps the beating would bring to the boy's attention, for the first time in his life, the secret of his existence, the guilt that he could never get rid of.

Smiling, he scampered over a coal pile and stood again in the basement of the building where he had stolen the money and jewelry. He lifted himself into the areaway, climbed the rain pipe, and squinted through a two-inch opening of window. The guilty familiarity of what he saw made his muscles tighten. Framed before him in a bright tableau of daylight was the night watchman sitting upon the edge of a chair, stripped to the waist, his head sagging forward, his eyes red and puffy. The watchman's face and shoulders were stippled with red and black welts. Back of the watchman stood the safe, the steel door wide open showing the empty vault. Yes, they think he did it, he mused.

Footsteps sounded in the room and a man in a blue suit passed in front of him, then another, then still another. Policemen, he breathed. Yes, they were trying to make the watchman confess, just as they had once made him confess to a crime he had not done. He stared into the room, trying to recall something. Oh . . . Those were the same policemen who had beaten him, had made him sign that paper when he had been too tired and sick to care. Now, they were doing the same thing to the watchman. His heart pounded as he saw one of the policemen shake a finger into the watchman's face.

"Why don't you admit it's an inside job, Thompson?" the policeman said.

"I've told you all I know," the watchman mumbled through swollen lips.

"But nobody was here but you!" the policeman shouted.

"I was sleeping," the watchman said. "It was wrong, but I was sleeping all that night!"

"Stop telling us that lie!"

"It's the truth!"

"When did you get the combination?"

"I don't know how to open the safe," the watchman said.

He clung to the rain pipe, tense; he wanted to laugh, but he controlled himself. He felt a great sense of power; yes, he could go back to the cave, rip the money off the walls, pick up the diamonds and rings, and bring them here and write a note, telling them where to look for their foolish toys. No . . . What good would that do? It was not worth the effort. The watchman was guilty; although he was not guilty of the crime of which he had been accused, he was guilty, had always been guilty. The only thing that worried him was that the man who had been really stealing was not being accused. But he consoled himself: they'll catch him sometime during his life.

He saw one of the policemen slap the watchman across the mouth.

"Come clean, you bastard!"

"I've told you all I know," the watchman mumbled like a child.

One of the police went to the rear of the watchman's chair and jerked it from under him; the watchman pitched forward upon his face.

"Get up!" a policeman said.

Trembling, the watchman pulled himself up and sat limply again in the chair.

"Now, are you going to talk?"

"I've told you all I know," the watchman gasped.

"Where did you hide the stuff?"

"I didn't take it!"

"Thompson, your brains are in your feet," one of the policemen said. "We're going to string you up and get them back into your skull."

He watched the policemen clamp handcuffs on the watchman's wrists and ankles; then they lifted the watchman and swung him upside-down and hoisted his feet to the edge of a door. The watchman hung, head down, his eyes bulging. They're crazy, he whispered to himself as he clung to the ridges of the pipe.

"You going to talk?" a policeman shouted into the watchman's ear.

He heard the watchman groan.

"We'll let you hang there till you talk, see?"

He saw the watchman close his eyes.

"Let's take 'im down. He passed out," a policeman said.

He grinned as he watched them take the body down and dump it carelessly upon the floor. The policeman took off the handcuffs.

"Let 'im come to. Let's get a smoke," a policeman said.

The three policemen left the scope of his vision. A door slammed. He had an impulse to yell to the watchman that he could escape through the hole in the basement and live with him in the cave. But he wouldn't understand, he told himself. After a moment he saw the watchman rise and stand, swaying from weakness. He stumbled across the room to a desk, opened a drawer, and took out a gun. He's going to kill him-

self, he thought, intent, eager, detached, yearning to see the
end of the man's actions. As the watchman stared vaguely
about he lifted the gun to his temple; he stood like that for
some minutes, biting his lips until a line of blood etched its
way down a corner of his chin. No, he oughtn't do that, he
said to himself in a mood of pity.

"Don't!" he half whispered and half yelled.

The watchman looked wildly about; he had heard him. But
it did not help; there was a loud report and the watchman's
head jerked violently and he fell like a log and lay prone,
the gun clattering over the floor.

The three policemen came running into the room with drawn
guns. One of the policemen knelt and rolled the watchman's
body over and stared at a ragged, scarlet hole in the temple.

"Our hunch was right," the kneeling policeman said. "He was
guilty, all right."

"Well, this ends the case," another policeman said.

"He knew he was licked," the third one said with grim
satisfaction.

He eased down the rain pipe, crawled back through the
holes he had made, and went back into his cave. A fever
burned in his bones. He had to act, yet he was afraid. His
eyes stared in the darkness as though propped open by invisible hands, as though they had become lidless. His muscles
were rigid and he stood for what seemed to him a thousand
years.

When he moved again his actions were informed with pre-
cision, his muscular system reinforced from a reservoir of
energy. He crawled through the hole of earth, dropped into
the gray sewer current, and sloshed ahead. When his right
foot went forward at a street intersection, he fell backward

and shot down into water. In a spasm of terror his right hand grabbed the concrete ledge of a down-curve and he felt the streaking water tugging violently at his body. The current reached his neck and for a moment he was still. He knew that if he moved clumsily he would be sucked under. He held onto the ledge with both hands and slowly pulled himself up. He sighed, standing once more in the sweeping water, thankful that he had missed death.

He waded on through sludge, moving with care, until he came to a web of light sifting down from a manhole cover. He saw steel hooks running up the side of the sewer wall; he caught hold and lifted himself and put his shoulder to the cover and moved it an inch. A crash of sound came to him as he looked into a hot glare of sunshine through which blurred shapes moved. Fear scalded him and he dropped back into the pallid current and stood paralyzed in the shadows. A heavy car rumbled past overhead, jarring the pavement, warning him to stay in his world of dark light, knocking the cover back into place with an imperious clang.

He did not know how much fear he felt, for fear claimed him completely; yet it was not a fear of the police or of people, but a cold dread at the thought of the actions he knew he would perform if he went out into that cruel sunshine. His mind said no; his body said yes; and his mind could not understand his feelings. A low whine broke from him and he was in the act of uncoiling. He climbed upward and heard the faint honking of auto horns. Like a frantic cat clutching a rag, he clung to the steel prongs and heaved his shoulder against the cover and pushed it off halfway. For a split second his eyes were drowned in the terror of yellow light and he was in a deeper darkness than he had ever known in the underground.

Partly out of the hole, he blinked, regaining enough sight

to make out meaningful forms. An odd thing was happening: No one was rushing forward to challenge him. He had imagined the moment of his emergence as a desperate tussle with men who wanted to cart him off to be killed; instead, life froze about him as the traffic stopped. He pushed the cover aside, stood, swaying in a world so fragile that he expected it to collapse and drop him into some deep void. But nobody seemed to pay him heed. The cars were now swerving to shun him and the gaping hole.

"Why in hell don't you put up a red light, dummy?" a raucous voice yelled.

He understood; they thought that he was a sewer workman. He walked toward the sidewalk, weaving unsteadily through the moving traffic.

"Look where you're going, nigger!"

"That's right! Stay there and get killed!"

"You blind, you bastard?"

"Go home and sleep your drunk off!"

A policeman stood at the curb, looking in the opposite direction. When he passed the policeman, he feared that he would be grabbed, but nothing happened. Where was he? Was this real? He wanted to look about to get his bearings, but felt that something awful would happen to him if he did. He wandered into a spacious doorway of a store that sold men's clothing and saw his reflection in a long mirror: his cheekbones protruded from a hairy black face; his greasy cap was perched askew upon his head and his eyes were red and glassy. His shirt and trousers were caked with mud and hung loosely. His hands were gummed with a black stickiness. He threw back his head and laughed so loudly that passers-by stopped and stared.

He ambled on down the sidewalk, not having the merest

notion of where he was going. Yet, sleeping within him, was
the drive to go somewhere and say something to somebody.
Half an hour later his ears caught the sound of spirited singing.

> *The Lamb, the Lamb, the Lamb*
> *I hear thy voice a-calling*
> *The Lamb, the Lamb, the Lamb*
> *I feel thy grace a-falling*

A church! He exclaimed. He broke into a run and came to
brick steps leading downward to a subbasement. This is it!
The church into which he had peered. Yes, he was going in
and tell them. What? He did not know; but, once face to face
with them, he would think of what to say. Must be Sunday, he
mused. He ran down the steps and jerked the door open; the
church was crowded and a deluge of song swept over him.

> *The Lamb, the Lamb, the Lamb*
> *Tell me again your story*
> *The Lamb, the Lamb, the Lamb*
> *Flood my soul with your glory*

He stared at the singing faces with a trembling smile.
"Say!" he shouted.
Many turned to look at him, but the song rolled on. His arm
was jerked violently.
"I'm sorry, Brother, but you can't do that in here," a man
said.
"But, mister!"
"You can't act rowdy in God's house," the man said.
"He's filthy," another man said.
"But I want to tell 'em," he said loudly.
"He stinks," someone muttered.
The song had stopped, but at once another one began.

> *Oh, wondrous sight upon the cross*
> *Vision sweet and divine*
> *Oh, wondrous sight upon the cross*
> *Full of such love sublime*

He attempted to twist away, but other hands grabbed him and rushed him into the doorway.

"Let me alone!" he screamed, struggling.

"Get out!"

"He's drunk," somebody said. "He ought to be ashamed!"

"He acts crazy!"

He felt that he was failing and he grew frantic.

"But, mister, let me tell—"

"Get away from this door, or I'll call the police!"

He stared, his trembling smile fading in a sense of wonderment.

"The police," he repeated vacantly.

"Now, get!"

He was pushed toward the brick steps and the door banged shut. The waves of song came.

> *Oh, wondrous sight, wondrous sight*
> *Lift my heavy heart above*
> *Oh, wondrous sight, wondrous sight*
> *Fill my weary soul with love*

He was smiling again now. Yes, the police . . . That was it! Why had he not thought of it before? The idea had been deep down in him, and only now did it assume supreme importance. He looked up and saw a street sign: COURT STREET— HARTSDALE AVENUE. He turned and walked northward, his mind filled with the image of the police station. Yes, that was where they had beaten him, accused him, and had made him sign a confession of his guilt. He would go there and clear up everything, make a statement. What statement? He did not know. He was the statement, and since it was all so clear to him, surely he would be able to make it clear to others.

He came to the corner of Hartsdale Avenue and turned westward. Yeah, there's the station . . . A policeman came down the steps and walked past him without a glance. He mounted the stone steps and went through the door, paused; he was in a hallway where several policemen were standing, talking, smoking. One turned to him.

"What do you want, boy?"

He looked at the policeman and laughed.

"What in hell are you laughing about?" the policeman asked.

He stopped laughing and stared. His whole being was full of what he wanted to say to them, but he could not say it.

"Are you looking for the Desk Sergeant?"

"Yes, sir," he said quickly; then: "Oh, no, sir."

"Well, make up your mind, now."

Four policemen grouped themselves around him.

"I'm looking for the men," he said.

"What men?"

Peculiarly, at that moment he could not remember the names of the policemen; he recalled their beating him, the confession he had signed, and how he had run away from them. He saw the cave next to the church, the money on the walls, the guns, the rings, the cleaver, the watches, and the diamonds on the floor.

"They brought me here," he began.

"When?"

His mind flew back over the blur of the time lived in the underground blackness. He had no idea of how much time had elapsed, but the intensity of what had happened to him told him that it could not have transpired in a short space of time, yet his mind told him that time must have been brief.

"It was a long time ago." He spoke like a child relating a dimly remembered dream. "It was a long time," he repeated, following the promptings of his emotions. "They beat me . . . I was scared . . . I ran away."

A policeman raised a finger to his temple and made a derisive circle.

"Nuts," the policeman said.

"Do you know what place this is, boy?"

"Yes, sir. The police station," he answered sturdily, almost proudly.

"Well, who do you want to see?"

"The men," he said again, feeling that surely they knew the men. "You know the men," he said in a hurt tone.

"What's your name?"

He opened his lips to answer and no words came. He had forgotten. But what did it matter if he had? It was not important.

"Where do you live?"

Where did he live? It had been so long ago since he had lived up here in this strange world that he felt it was foolish even to try to remember. Then for a moment the old mood that had dominated him in the underground surged back. He leaned forward and spoke eagerly.

"They said I killed the woman."

"What woman?" a policeman asked.

"And I signed a paper that said I was guilty," he went on, ignoring their questions. "Then I ran off . . ."

"Did you run off from an institution?"

"No, sir," he said, blinking and shaking his head. "I came from under the ground. I pushed off the manhole cover and climbed out . . ."

"All right, now," a policeman said, placing an arm about

his shoulder. "We'll send you to the psycho and you'll be taken care of."

"Maybe he's a Fifth Columnist!" a policeman shouted.

There was laughter and, despite his anxiety, he joined in. But the laughter lasted so long that it irked him.

"I got to find those men," he protested mildly.

"Say, boy, what have you been drinking?"

"Water," he said. "I got some water in a basement."

"Were the men you ran away from dressed in white, boy?"

"No, sir," he said brightly. "They were men like you."

An elderly policeman caught hold of his arm.

"Try and think hard. Where did they pick you up?"

He knitted his brows in an effort to remember, but he was blank inside. The policeman stood before him demanding logical answers and he could no longer think with his mind; he thought with his feelings and no words came.

"I was guilty," he said. "Oh, no, sir. I wasn't then, I mean, mister!"

"Aw, talk sense. Now, where did they pick you up?"

He felt challenged and his mind began reconstructing events in reverse; his feelings ranged back over the long hours and he saw the cave, the sewer, the bloody room where it was said that a woman had been killed.

"Oh, yes, sir," he said, smiling. "I was coming from Mrs. Wooten's."

"Who is she?"

"I work for her."

"Where does she live?"

"Next door to Mrs. Peabody, the woman who was killed."

The policemen were very quiet now, looking at him intently.

"What do you know about Mrs. Peabody's death, boy?"

"Nothing, sir. But they said I killed her. But it doesn't make any difference. I'm guilty!"

"What are you talking about, boy?"

His smile faded and he was possessed with memories of the underground; he saw the cave next to the church and his lips moved to speak. But how could he say it? The distance between what he felt and what these men meant was vast. Something told him, as he stood there looking into their faces, that he would never be able to tell them, that they would never believe him even if he told them.

"All the people I saw was guilty," he began slowly.

"Aw, nuts," a policeman muttered.

"Say," another policeman said, "that Peabody woman was killed over on Winewood. That's Number Ten's beat."

"Where's Number Ten?" a policeman asked.

"Upstairs in the swing room," someone answered.

"Take this boy up, Sam," a policeman ordered.

"O.K. Come along, boy."

An elderly policeman caught hold of his arm and led him up a flight of wooden stairs, down a long hall, and to a door.

"Squad Ten!" the policeman called through the door.

"What?" a gruff voice answered.

"Someone to see you!"

"About what?"

The old policeman pushed the door in and then shoved him into the room.

He stared, his lips open, his heart barely beating. Before him were the three policemen who had picked him up and had beaten him to extract the confession. They were seated about a small table, playing cards. The air was blue with smoke and sunshine poured through a high window, lighting up fantastic smoke shapes. He saw one of the policemen look up; the policeman's face was tired and a cigarette dropped limply from one corner of his mouth and both of his fat, puffy eyes were squinting and his hands gripped his cards.

"Lawson!" the man exclaimed.

The moment the man's name sounded he remembered the names of all of them: Lawson, Murphy, and Johnson. How simple it was. He waited, smiling, wondering how they would react when they knew that he had come back.

"Looking for me?" the man who had been called Lawson mumbled, sorting his cards. "For what?"

So far only Murphy, the red-headed one, had recognized him.

"Don't you-all remember me?" he blurted, running to the table.

All three of the policemen were looking at him now. Lawson, who seemed the leader, jumped to his feet.

"Where in hell have you been?"

"Do you know 'im, Lawson?" the old policeman asked.

"Huh?" Lawson frowned. "Oh, yes. I'll handle 'im." The old policeman left the room and Lawson crossed to the door and turned the key in the lock. "Come here, boy," he ordered in a cold tone.

He did not move; he looked from face to face. Yes, he would tell them about his cave.

"He looks batty to me," Johnson said, the one who had not spoken before.

"Why in hell did you come back here?" Lawson said.

"I—I just didn't want to run away no more," he said. "I'm all right, now." He paused; the men's attitude puzzled him.

"You've been hiding, huh?" Lawson asked in a tone that denoted that he had not heard his previous words. "You told us you were sick, and when we left you in the room, you jumped out of the window and ran away."

Panic filled him. Yes, they were indifferent to what he would say! They were waiting for him to speak and they would laugh at him. He had to rescue himself from this bog; he had to force the reality of himself upon them.

"Mister, I took a sackful of money and pasted it on the walls . . ." he began.

"I'll be damned," Lawson said.

"Listen," said Murphy, "let me tell you something for your own good. We don't want you, see? You're free, free as air. Now go home and forget it. It was all a mistake. We caught the guy who did the Peabody job. He wasn't colored at all. He was an Eyetalian."

"Shut up!" Lawson yelled. "Have you no sense!"

"But I want to tell 'im," Murphy said.

"We can't let this crazy fool go," Lawson exploded. "He acts nuts, but this may be a stunt . . ."

"I was down in the basement," he began in a childlike tone, as though repeating a lesson learned by heart; "and I went into a movie . . ." His voice failed. He was getting ahead of his story. First, he ought to tell them about the singing in the church, but what words could he use? He looked at them appealingly. "I went into a shop and took a sackful of money and diamonds and watches and rings . . . I didn't steal 'em; I'll give 'em all back. I just took 'em to play with . . ." He paused, stunned by their disbelieving eyes.

Lawson lit a cigarette and looked at him coldly.

"What did you do with the money?" he asked in a quiet, waiting voice.

"I pasted the hundred-dollar bills on the walls."

"What walls?" Lawson asked.

"The walls of the dirt room," he said, smiling, "the room next to the church. I hung up the rings and the watches and I stamped the diamonds into the dirt . . ." He saw that they were not understanding what he was saying. He grew frantic to make them believe, his voice tumbled on eagerly. "I saw a dead baby and a dead man . . ."

"Aw, you're nuts," Lawson snarled, shoving him into a chair.

"But, mister . . ."

"Johnson, where's the paper he signed?" Lawson asked.

"What paper?"

"The confession, fool!"

Johnson pulled out his billfold and extracted a crumpled piece of paper.

"Yes, sir, mister," he said, stretching forth his hand. "That's the paper I signed . . ."

Lawson slapped him and he would have toppled had his chair not struck a wall behind him. Lawson scratched a match and held the paper over the flame; the confession burned down to Lawson's fingertips.

He stared, thunderstruck; the sun of the underground was fleeing and the terrible darkness of the day stood before him. They did not believe him, but he *had* to make them believe him!

"But, mister . . ."

"It's going to be all right, boy," Lawson said with a quiet, soothing laugh. "I've burned your confession, see? You didn't sign anything." Lawson came close to him with the black ashes cupped in his palm. "You don't remember a thing about this, do you?"

"Don't you-all be scared of me," he pleaded, sensing their uneasiness. "I'll sign another paper, if you want me to. I'll show you the cave."

"What's your game, boy?" Lawson asked suddenly.

"What are you trying to find out?" Johnson asked.

"Who sent you here?" Murphy demanded.

"Nobody sent me, mister," he said. "I just want to show you the room . . ."

"Aw, he's plumb bats," Murphy said. "Let's ship 'im to the psycho."

"No," Lawson said. "He's playing a game and I wish to God I knew what it was."

There flashed through his mind a definite way to make them believe him; he rose from the chair with nervous excitement.

"Mister, I saw the night watchman blow his brains out because you accused him of stealing," he told them. "But he didn't steal the money and diamonds. I took 'em."

Tigerishly Lawson grabbed his collar and lifted him bodily. *"Who told you about that?"*

"Don't get excited, Lawson," Johnson said. "He read about it in the papers."

Lawson flung him away.

"He couldn't have," Lawson said, pulling papers from his pocket. "I haven't turned in the reports yet."

"Then how *did* he find out?" Murphy asked.

"Let's get out of here," Lawson said with quick resolution. "Listen, boy, we're going to take you to a nice, quiet place, see?"

"Yes, sir," he said. "And I'll show you the underground."

"Goddamn," Lawson muttered, fastening the gun at his hip. He narrowed his eyes at Johnson and Murphy. "Listen," he spoke just above a whisper, "say nothing about this, you hear?"

"O.K.," Johnson said.

"Sure," Murphy said.

Lawson unlocked the door and Johnson and Murphy led him down the stairs. The hallway was crowded with policemen.

"What have you got there, Lawson?"

"What did he do, Lawson?"

"He's psycho, ain't he, Lawson?"

Lawson did not answer; Johnson and Murphy led him to the car parked at the curb, pushed him into the back seat. Lawson got behind the steering wheel and the car rolled forward.

"What's up, Lawson?" Murphy asked.

"Listen," Lawson began slowly, "we tell the papers that he spilled about the Peabody job, then he escapes. The Wop is caught and we tell the papers that we steered them wrong to trap the real guy, see? Now this dope shows up and acts nuts. If we let him go, he'll squeal that we framed him, see?"

"I'm all right, mister," he said, feeling Murphy's and Johnson's arm locked rigidly into his. "I'm guilty . . . I'll show you everything in the underground. I laughed and laughed . . ."

"Shut that fool up!" Lawson ordered.

Johnson tapped him across the head with a blackjack and he fell back against the seat cushion, dazed.

"Yes, sir," he mumbled. "I'm all right."

The car sped along Hartsdale Avenue, then swung onto Pine Street and rolled to State Street, then turned south. It slowed to a stop, turned in the middle of a block, and headed north again.

"You're going around in circles, Lawson," Murphy said.

Lawson did not answer; he was hunched over the steering wheel. Finally he pulled the car to a stop at a curb.

"Say, boy, tell us the truth," Lawson asked quietly. "Where did you hide?"

"I didn't hide, mister."

The three policemen were staring at him now; he felt that for the first time they were willing to understand him.

"Then what happened?"

"Mister, when I looked through all of those holes and saw how people were living, I loved 'em . . ."

"Cut out that crazy talk!" Lawson snapped. "Who sent you back here?"

"Nobody, mister."

"Maybe he's talking straight," Johnson ventured.

"All right," Lawson said. "Nobody hid you. Now, tell us *where* you hid."

"I went underground . . ."

"What goddamn underground do you keep talking about?"

"I just went . . ." He paused and looked into the street, then pointed to a manhole cover. "I went down in there and stayed."

"In the *sewer?*"

"Yes, sir."

The policemen burst into a sudden laugh and ended quickly. Lawson swung the car around and drive to Woodside Avenue; he brought the car to a stop in front of a tall apartment building.

"What're we going to do, Lawson?" Murphy asked.

"I'm taking him up to my place," Lawson said. "We've got to wait until night. There's nothing we can do now."

They took him out of the car and led him into a vestibule.

"Take the steps," Lawson muttered.

They led him up four flights of stairs and into the living room of a small apartment. Johnson and Murphy let go of his arms and he stood uncertainly in the middle of the room.

"Now, listen, boy," Lawson began, "forget those wild lies you've been telling us. Where did you hide?"

"I just went underground, like I told you."

The room rocked with laughter. Lawson went to a cabinet and got a bottle of whisky; he placed glasses for Johnson and Murphy. The three of them drank.

He felt that he could not explain himself to them. He tried to muster all the sprawling images that floated in him; the images stood out sharply in his mind, but he could not make them have the meaning for others that they had for him. He felt so helpless that he began to cry.

"He's nuts, all right," Johnson said. "All nuts cry like that."

Murphy crossed the room and slapped him.

"Stop that raving!"

A sense of excitement flooded him; he ran to Murphy and grabbed his arm.

"Let me show you the cave," he said. "Come on, and you'll see!"

Before he knew it a sharp blow had clipped him on the chin; darkness covered his eyes. He dimly felt himself being lifted and laid out on the sofa. He heard low voices and struggled to rise, but hard hands held him down. His brain was clearing now. He pulled to a sitting posture and stared with glazed eyes. It had grown dark. How long had he been out?

"Say, boy," Lawson said soothingly, "will you show us the underground?"

His eyes shone and his heart swelled with gratitude. Lawson believed him! He rose, glad; he grabbed Lawson's arm, making the policeman spill whisky from the glass to his shirt.

"Take it easy, goddammit," Lawson said.

"Yes, sir."

"O.K. We'll take you down. But you'd better be telling us the truth, you hear?"

He clapped his hands in wild joy.

"I'll show you everything!"

He had triumphed at last! He would now do what he had felt was compelling him all along. At last he would be free of his burden.

"Take 'im down," Lawson ordered.

They led him down to the vestibule; when he reached the sidewalk he saw that it was night and a fine rain was falling.

"It's just like when I went down," he told them.

"What?" Lawson asked.

"The rain," he said, sweeping his arm in a wide arc. "It was raining when I went down. The rain made the water rise and lift the cover off."

"Cut it out," Lawson snapped.

They did not believe him now, but they would. A mood of high selflessness throbbed in him. He could barely contain his rising spirits. They would see what he had seen; they would feel what he had felt. He would lead them through all the holes he had dug and . . . He wanted to make a hymn, prance about in physical ecstasy, throw his arm about the policemen in fellowship.

"Get into the car," Lawson ordered.

He climbed in and Johnson and Murphy sat at either side of him; Lawson slid behind the steering wheel and started the motor.

"Now, tell us where to go," Lawson said.

"It's right around the corner from where the lady was killed," he said.

The car rolled slowly and he closed his eyes, remembering the song he had heard in the church, the song that had wrought him to such a high pitch of terror and pity. He sang softly, lolling is head:

> Glad, glad, glad, oh, so glad
> I got Jesus in my soul . . .

"Mister," he said, stopping his song, "you ought to see how funny the rings look on the wall." He giggled. "I fired a pistol, too. Just once, to see how it felt."

"What do you suppose he's suffering from?" Johnson asked.

"Delusions of grandeur, maybe," Murphy said.

"Maybe it's because he lives in a white man's world," Lawson said.

"Say, boy, what did you eat down there?" Murphy asked, prodding Johnson anticipatorily with his elbow.

"Pears, oranges, bananas, and pork chops," he said.

The car filled with laughter.

"You didn't eat any watermelon?" Lawson asked, smiling.

"No, sir," he answered calmly. "I didn't see any."

The three policemen roared harder and louder.

"Boy, you're sure some case," Murphy said, shaking his head in wonder.

The car pulled to a curb.

"All right, boy," Lawson said. "Tell us where to go."

He peered through the rain and saw where he had gone down. The streets, save for a few dim lamps glowing softly through the rain, were dark and empty.

"Right there, mister," he said, pointing.

"Come on; let's take a look," Lawson said.

"Well, suppose he did hide down there," Johnson said, "what is that supposed to prove?"

"I don't believe he hid down there," Murphy said.

"It won't hurt to look," Lawson said. "Leave things to me."

Lawson got out of the car and looked up and down the street.

He was eager to show them the cave now. If he could show them what he had seen, then they would feel what he had felt and they in turn would show it to others and those others would feel as they had felt, and soon everybody would be governed by the same impulse of pity.

"Take 'im out," Lawson ordered.

Johnson and Murphy opened the door and pushed him out; he stood trembling in the rain, smiling. Again Lawson looked up and down the street; no one was in sight. The rain came down hard, slanting like black wires across the wind-swept air.

"All right," Lawson said. "Show us."

He walked to the center of the street, stopped and inserted a finger in one of the tiny holes of the cover and tugged, but he was too weak to budge it.

"Did you really go down in there, boy?" Lawson asked; there was a doubt in his voice.

"Yes, sir. Just a minute. I'll show you."

"Help 'im get that damn thing off," Lawson said.

Johnson stepped forward and lifted the cover; it clanged against the wet pavement. The hole gaped round and black.

"I went down in there," he announced with pride.

Lawson gazed at him for a long time without speaking, then he reached his right hand to his holster and drew his gun.

"Mister, I got a gun just like that down there," he said, laughing and looking into Lawson's face. "I fired it once then hung it on the wall. I'll show you."

"Show us how you went down," Lawson said quietly.

"I'll go down first, mister, and then you-all can come after me, hear?" he spoke like a little boy playing a game.

"Sure, sure," Lawson said soothingly. "Go ahead. We'll come."

He looked brightly at the policemen; he was bursting with happiness. He bent down and placed his hands on the rim of the hole and sat on the edge, his feet dangling into watery darkness. He heard the familiar drone of the gray current. He lowered his body and hung for a moment by his fingers, then he went downward on the steel prongs, hand over hand, until he reached the last rung. He dropped and his feet hit the water and he felt the stiff current trying to suck him away. He balanced himself quickly and looked back upward at the policemen.

"Come on, you-all!" he yelled, casting his voice above the rustling at his feet.

The vague forms that towered above him in the rain did not move. He laughed, feeling that they doubted him. But, once they saw the things he had done, they would never doubt again.

"Come on! The cave isn't far!" he yelled. "But be careful when your feet hit the water, because the current's pretty rough down here!"

Lawson still held the gun. Murphy and Johnson looked at Lawson quizzically.

"What are we going to do, Lawson?" Murphy asked.

"We are not going to follow that crazy nigger down into that sewer, are we?" Johnson asked.

"Come on, you-all!" he begged in a shout.

He saw Lawson raise the gun and point it directly at him. Lawson's face twitched, as though he were hesitating.

Then there was a thunderous report and a streak of fire ripped through his chest. He was hurled into the water, flat on his back. He looked in amazement at the blurred white faces looming above him. They shot me, he said to himself. The water flowed past him, blossoming in foam about his arms, his legs, and his head. His jaw sagged and his mouth gaped soundless. A vast pain gripped his head and gradually squeezed out consciousness. As from a great distance he heard hollow voices.

"What did you shoot him for, Lawson?"

"I had to."

"Why?"

"You've got to shoot his kind. They'd wreck things."

As though in a deep dream, he heard a metallic clank; they had replaced the manhole cover, shutting out forever the sound of wind and rain. From overhead came the muffled roar of a powerful motor and the swish of a speeding car. He felt the strong tide pushing him slowly into the middle of the sewer, turning him about. For a split second there hovered before his eyes the glittering cave, the shouting walls, and the laughing floor . . . Then his mouth was full of thick, bitter water. The current spun him around. He sighed and closed his eyes, a whirling object rushing alone in the darkness, veering, tossing, lost in the heart of the earth.

BIG BLACK GOOD MAN

THROUGH THE OPEN WINDOW Olaf Jenson could smell the sea and hear the occasional foghorn of a freighter; outside, rain pelted down through an August night, drumming softly upon the pavements of Copenhagen, inducing drowsiness, bringing dreamy memory, relaxing the tired muscles of his work-wracked body. He sat slumped in a swivel chair with his legs outstretched and his feet propped atop an edge of his desk. An inch of white ash tipped the end of his brown cigar and now and then he inserted the end of the stogie into his mouth and drew gently upon it, letting wisps of blue smoke eddy from the corners of his wide, thin lips. The watery gray irises behind the thick lenses of his eyeglasses gave him a look of abstraction, of absent-mindedness, of an almost genial idiocy. He sighed, reached for his half-empty bottle of beer, and drained it into his glass and downed it with a long slow gulp,

85

then licked his lips. Replacing the cigar, he slapped his right palm against his thigh and said half aloud:

"Well, I'll be sixty tomorrow. I'm not rich, but I'm not poor either . . . Really, I can't complain. Got good health. Traveled all over the world and had my share of the girls when I was young . . . And my Karen's a good wife. I own my home. Got no debts. And I love digging in my garden in the spring . . . Grew the biggest carrots of anybody last year. Ain't saved much money, but what the hell . . . Money ain't everything. Got a good job. Night portering ain't too bad." He shook his head and yawned. "Karen and I could of had some children, though. Would of been good company . . . 'Specially for Karen. And I could of taught 'em languages . . . English, French, German, Danish, Dutch, Swedish, Norwegian, and Spanish . . ." He took the cigar out of his mouth and eyed the white ash critically. "Hell of a lot of good language learning did me . . . Never got anything out of it. But those ten years in New York were fun . . . Maybe I could of got rich if I'd stayed in America . . . Maybe. But I'm satisfied. You can't have everything."

Behind him the office door opened and a young man, a medical student occupying room number nine, entered.

"Good evening," the student said.

"Good evening," Olaf said, turning.

The student went to the keyboard and took hold of the round, brown knob that anchored his key.

"Rain, rain, rain," the student said.

"That's Denmark for you," Olaf smiled at him.

"This dampness keeps me clogged up like a drainpipe," the student complained.

"That's Denmark for you," Olaf repeated with a smile.

"Good night," the student said.

"Good night, son," Olaf sighed, watching the door close.

Well, my tenants are my children, Olaf told himself. Almost all of his children were in their rooms now . . . Only seventy-two and forty-four were missing . . . Seventy-two might've gone to Sweden . . . And forty-four was maybe staying at his girl's place tonight, like he sometimes did . . . He studied the pear-shaped blobs of hard rubber, reddish brown like ripe fruit, that hung from the keyboard, then glanced at his watch. Only room thirty, eighty-one, and one hundred and one were empty . . . And it was almost midnight. In a few moments he could take a nap. Nobody hardly ever came looking for accommodations after midnight, unless a stray freighter came in, bringing thirsty, women-hungry sailors. Olaf chuckled softly. Why in hell was I ever a sailor? The whole time I was at sea I was thinking and dreaming about women. Then why didn't I stay on land where women could be had? Hunh? Sailors are crazy . . .

But he liked sailors. They reminded him of his youth, and there was something so direct, simple, and childlike about them. They always said straight out what they wanted, and what they wanted was almost always women and whisky . . . "Well, there's no harm in that . . . Nothing could be more natural," Olaf sighed, looking thirstily at his empty beer bottle. No; he'd not drink any more tonight; he'd had enough; he'd go to sleep . . .

He was bending forward and loosening his shoelaces when he heard the office door crack open. He lifted his eyes, then sucked in his breath. He did not straighten; he just stared up and around at the huge black thing that filled the doorway. His reflexes refused to function; it was not fear; it was just simple astonishment. He was staring at the biggest, strangest, and blackest man he'd ever seen in all his life.

"Good evening," the black giant said in a voice that filled the small office. "Say, you got a room?"

Olaf sat up slowly, not to answer but to look at this brooding black vision; it towered darkly some six and a half feet into the air, almost touching the ceiling; and its skin was so black that it had a bluish tint. And the sheer bulk of the man! . . . His chest bulged like a barrel; his rocklike and humped shoulders hinted of mountain ridges; the stomach ballooned like a threatening stone; and the legs were like telephone poles . . . The big black cloud of a man now lumbered into the office, bending to get its buffalolike head under the door frame, then advanced slowly upon Olaf, like a stormy sky descending.

"You got a room?" the big black man asked again in a resounding voice.

Olaf now noticed that the ebony giant was well dressed, carried a wonderful new suitcase, and wore black shoes that gleamed despite the raindrops that peppered their toes.

"You're American?" Olaf asked him.

"Yeah, man; sure," the black giant answered.

"Sailor?"

"Yeah. American Continental Lines."

Olaf had not answered the black man's question. It was not that the hotel did not admit men of color; Olaf took in all comers—blacks, yellows, whites, and browns . . . To Olaf, men were men, and, in his day, he'd worked and eaten and slept and fought with all kinds of men. But this particular black man . . . Well, he didn't seem human. Too big, too black, too loud, too direct, and probably too violent to boot . . . Olaf's five feet seven inches scarcely reached the black giant's shoulder and his frail body weighed less, perhaps, than one of the man's gigantic legs . . . There was something about the man's intense blackness and ungamely bigness that frightened and insulted Olaf; he felt as though this man had come here expressly to remind him how puny, how tiny, and how weak and how white he was. Olaf knew, while registering his reactions, that he was being irrational and foolish; yet, for the first time in his life, he was emotionally determined to refuse a man a room solely on the basis of the man's size and color . . . Olaf's lips parted as he groped for the right words in which to couch his refusal, but the black giant bent forward and boomed:

"I asked you if you got a room. I got to put up somewhere tonight, man."

"Yes, we got a room," Olaf murmured.

And at once he was ashamed and confused. Sheer fear had made him yield. And he seethed against himself for his involuntary weakness. Well, he'd look over his book and pretend that he'd made a mistake; he'd tell this hunk of blackness that there was really no free room in the hotel, and that he was so sorry . . . Then, just as he took out the hotel register to make believe that he was poring over it, a thick roll of American bank notes, crisp and green, was thrust under his nose.

"Keep this for me, will you?" the black giant commanded. " 'Cause I'm gonna get drunk tonight and I don't wanna lose it."

Olaf stared at the roll; it was huge, in denominations of fifties and hundreds. Olaf's eyes widened.

"How much is there?" he asked.

"Two thousand six hundred," the giant said. "Just put it into an envelope and write 'Jim' on it and lock it in your safe, hunh?"

The black mass of man had spoken in a manner that indicated that it was taking it for granted that Olaf would obey. Olaf was licked. Resentment clogged the pores of his wrinkled white skin. His hands trembled as he picked up the money.

No; he couldn't refuse this man . . . The impulse to deny him was strong, but each time he was about to act upon it something thwarted him, made him shy off. He clutched about desperately for an idea. Oh, yes, he could say that if he planned to stay for only one night, then he could not have the room, for it was against the policy of the hotel to rent rooms for only one night . . .

"How long are you staying? Just tonight?" Olaf asked.

"Naw. I'll be here for five or six days, I reckon," the giant answered offhandedly.

"You take room number thirty," Olaf heard himself saying. "It's forty kronor a day."

"That's all right with me," the giant said.

With slow, stiff movements, Olaf put the money in the safe and then turned and stared helplessly up into the living, breathing blackness looming above him. Suddenly he became conscious of the outstretched palm of the black giant; he was silently demanding the key to the room. His eyes downcast, Olaf surrendered the key, marveling at the black man's tremendous hands . . . He could kill me with one blow, Olaf told himself in fear.

Feeling himself beaten, Olaf reached for the suitcase, but the black hand of the giant whisked it out of his grasp.

"That's too heavy for you, big boy; I'll take it," the giant said.

Olaf let him. He thinks I'm nothing . . . He led the way down the corridor, sensing the giant's lumbering presence behind him. Olaf opened the door of number thirty and stood politely to one side, allowing the black giant to enter. At once the room seemed like a doll's house, so dwarfed and filled and tiny it was with a great living blackness . . . Flinging his suitcase upon a chair, the giant turned. The two men looked directly at each other now. Olaf saw that the giant's eyes were tiny and red, buried, it seemed, in muscle and fat. Black cheeks spread, flat and broad, topping the wide and flaring nostrils. The mouth was the biggest that Olaf had ever seen on a human face; the lips were thick, pursed, parted, showing snow-white teeth. The black neck was like a bull's . . . The giant advanced upon Olaf and stood over him.

"I want a bottle of whisky and a woman," he said. "Can you fix me up?"

"Yes," Olaf whispered, wild with anger and insult.

But what was he angry about? He'd had requests like this every night from all sorts of men and he was used to fulfilling them; he was a night porter in a cheap, water-front Copenhagen hotel that catered to sailors and students. Yes, men needed women, but this man, Olaf felt, ought to have a special sort of woman. He felt a deep and strange reluctance to phone any of the women whom he habitually sent to men. Yet he had promised. Could he lie and say that none was available? No. That sounded too fishy. The black giant sat upon the bed, staring straight before him. Olaf moved about quickly, pulling down the window shades, taking the pink coverlet off the bed, nudging the giant with his elbow to make him move as he did so . . . That's the way to treat 'im . . . Show 'im I ain't scared of 'im . . . But he was still seeking for an excuse to refuse. And he could think of nothing. He felt hypnotized, mentally immobilized. He stood hesitantly at the door.

"You send the whisky and the woman quick, pal?" the black giant asked, rousing himself from a brooding stare.

"Yes," Olaf grunted, shutting the door.

Goddamn, Olaf sighed. He sat in his office at his desk before the phone. Why did *he* have to come here? . . . I'm not prejudiced . . . No, not at all . . . But . . . He couldn't think any more. God oughtn't make men as big and black as that . . . But what the hell was he worrying about? He'd sent women of all races to men of all colors . . . So why not a woman to the black giant? Oh, only if the man were small, brown, and intelligent-looking . . . Olaf felt trapped.

With a reflex movement of his hand, he picked up the phone and dialed Lena. She was big and strong and always cut him in for fifteen per cent instead of the usual ten per cent. Lena had four small children to feed and clothe. Lena was willing; she was, she said, coming over right now. She didn't give a good goddamn about how big and black the man was . . .

"Why you ask me that?" Lena wanted to know over the phone. "You never asked that before . . ."

"But this one is *big*," Olaf found himself saying.

"He's just a man," Lena told him, her voice singing stridently, laughingly over the wire. "You just leave that to me. You don't have to do anything. *I'll* handle 'im."

Lena had a key to the hotel door downstairs, but tonight Olaf stayed awake. He wanted to see her. Why? He didn't know. He stretched out on the sofa in his office, but sleep was far from him. When Lena arrived, he told her again how big and black the man was.

"You told me that over the phone," Lena reminded him.

Olaf said nothing. Lena flounced off on her errand of mercy. Olaf shut the office door, then opened it and left it ajar. But why? He didn't know. He lay upon the sofa and stared at the ceiling. He glanced at his watch; it was almost two o'clock . . . She's staying in there a long time . . . Ah, God, but he could do with a drink . . . Why was he so damned worked up and nervous about a nigger and a white whore? . . . He'd never been so upset in all his life. Before he knew it, he had drifted off to sleep. Then he heard the office door swinging creakingly open on its rusty hinges. Lena stood in it, grim and businesslike, her face scrubbed free of powder and rouge. Olaf scrambled to his feet, adjusting his eyeglasses, blinking.

"How was it?" he asked her in a confidential whisper.

Lena's eyes blazed.

"What the hell's that to you?" she snapped. "There's your cut," she said, flinging him his money, tossing it upon the covers of the sofa. "You're sure nosy tonight. You wanna take over my work?"

Olaf's pasty cheeks burned red.

"You go to hell," he said, slamming the door.

"I'll meet you there!" Lena's shouting voice reached him dimly.

He was being a fool; there was no doubt about it. But, try as he might, he could not shake off a primitive hate for that black mountain of energy, of muscle, of bone; he envied the easy manner in which it moved with such a creeping and powerful motion; he winced at the booming and commanding voice that came to him when the tiny little eyes were not even looking at him; he shivered at the sight of those vast and clawlike hands that seemed always to hint of death . . .

Olaf kept his counsel. He never spoke to Karen about the sordid doings at the hotel. Such things were not for women like Karen. He knew instinctively that Karen would have been amazed had he told her that he was worried sick about a nigger and a blonde whore . . . No; he couldn't talk to anybody about it, not even the hard-bitten old bitch who owned the hotel. She was concerned only about money; she didn't give a damn about how big and black a client was as long as he paid his room rent.

Next evening, when Olaf arrived for duty, there was no sight or sound of the black giant. A little later after one o'clock in the morning he appeared, left his key, and went out word-lessly. A few moments past two the giant returned, took his key from the board, and paused.

"I want that Lena again tonight. And another bottle of whisky," he said boomingly.

"I'll call her and see if she's in," Olaf said.

"Do that," the black giant said and was gone.

He thinks he's God, Olaf fumed. He picked up the phone and ordered Lena and a bottle of whisky, and there was a taste of ashes in his mouth. On the third night came the same request: Lena and whisky. When the black giant appeared on the fifth night, Olaf was about to make a sarcastic remark to the effect that maybe he ought to marry Lena, but he checked it in time . . . After all, he could kill me with one hand, he told himself.

Olaf was nervous and angry with himself for being nervous. Other black sailors came and asked for girls and Olaf sent them, but with none of the fear and loathing that he sent Lena and a bottle of whisky to the giant . . . All right, the black giant's stay was almost up. He'd said that he was staying for five or six nights; tomorrow night was the sixth night and that ought to be the end of this nameless terror.

On the sixth night Olaf sat in his swivel chair with his bottle of beer and waited, his teeth on edge, his fingers drumming the desk. But what the hell am I fretting for? . . . The hell with 'im . . . Olaf sat and dozed. Occasionally he'd awaken and listen to the foghorns of freighters sounding as ships came and went in the misty Copenhagen harbor. He was half asleep when he felt a rough hand on his shoulder. He blinked his eyes open. The giant, black and vast and powerful, all but blotted out his vision.

"What I owe you, man?" the giant demanded. "And I want my money."

"Sure," Olaf said, relieved, but filled as always with fear of this living wall of black flesh.

With fumbling hands, he made out the bill and received payment, then gave the giant his roll of money, laying it on the desk so as not to let his hands touch the flesh of the black mountain. Well, his ordeal was over. It was past two o'clock in the morning. Olaf even managed a wry smile and muttered a guttural "Thanks" for the generous tip that the giant tossed him.

Then a strange tension entered the office. The office door was shut and Olaf was alone with the black mass of power, yearning for it to leave. But the black mass of power stood still, immobile, looking down at Olaf. And Olaf could not, for the life of him, guess at what was transpiring in that mysterious black mind. The two of them simply stared at each other for a full two minutes, the giant's tiny little beady eyes blinking slowly as they seemed to measure and search Olaf's face. Olaf's vision dimmed for a second as terror seized him and he could feel a flush of heat overspread his body. Then Olaf sucked in his breath as the devil of blackness commanded:

"Stand up!"

Olaf was paralyzed. Sweat broke on his face. His worst premonitions about this black beast were coming true. This evil blackness was about to attack him, maybe kill him . . . Slowly Olaf shook his head, his terror permitting him to breathe:

"What're you talking about?"

"Stand up, I say!" the black giant bellowed.

As though hypnotized, Olaf tried to rise; then he felt the black paw of the beast helping him roughly to his feet.

They stood an inch apart. Olaf's pasty-white features were lifted to the giant's swollen black face. The ebony ensemble of eyes and nose and mouth and cheeks looked down at Olaf, silently; then, with a slow and deliberate movement of his gorillalike arms, he lifted his mammoth hands to Olaf's throat. Olaf had long known and felt that this dreadful moment was coming; he felt trapped in a nightmare. He could not move. He wanted to scream, but could find no words. His lips refused to open; his tongue felt icy and inert. Then he knew that his end had come when the giant's black fingers slowly, softly encircled his throat while a horrible grin of delight broke out on the sooty face . . . Olaf lost control of the reflexes of his body and he felt a hot stickiness flooding his underwear . . . He stared without breathing, gazing into the grinning blackness of the face that was bent over him, feeling the black fingers caressing his throat and waiting to feel the sharp, stinging ache and pain of the bones in his neck being snapped, crushed . . . He knew all along that I hated 'im . . . Yes, and now he's going to kill me for it, Olaf told himself with despair.

The black fingers still circled Olaf's neck, not closing, but gently massaging it, as it were, moving to and fro, while the obscene face grinned into his. Olaf could feel the giant's warm breath blowing on his eyelashes and he felt like a chicken about to have its neck wrung and its body tossed to flip and flap dyingly in the dust of the barnyard . . . Then suddenly the black giant withdrew his fingers from Olaf's neck and stepped back a pace, still grinning. Olaf sighed, trembling, his body seeming to shrink; he waited. Shame sheeted him for the hot wetness that was in his trousers. Oh, God, he's teasing me . . . He's showing me how easily he can kill me . . . He swallowed, waiting, his eyes stones of gray.

The giant's barrel-like chest gave forth a low, rumbling chuckle of delight.

"You laugh?" Olaf asked whimperingly.

"Sure I laugh," the giant shouted.

"Please don't hurt me," Olaf managed to say.

"I wouldn't hurt you, boy," the giant said in a tone of mockery. "So long."

And he was gone. Olaf fell limply into the swivel chair and fought off losing consciousness. Then he wept. He was showing me how easily he could kill me . . . He made me shake with terror and then laughed and left . . . Slowly, Olaf recovered, stood, then gave vent to a string of curses:

"Goddamn 'im! My gun's right there in the desk drawer; I should of shot 'im. Jesus, I hope the ship he's on sinks . . . I hope he drowns and the sharks eat 'im . . ."

Later, he thought of going to the police, but sheer shame kept him back; and, anyway, the giant was probably on board his ship by now. And he had to get home and clean himself. Oh, Lord, what could he tell Karen? Yes, he would say that his stomach had been upset . . . He'd change clothes and return to work. He phoned the hotel owner that he was ill and wanted an hour off; the old bitch said that she was coming right over and that poor Olaf could have the evening off.

Olaf went home and lied to Karen. Then he lay awake the rest of the night dreaming of revenge. He saw that freighter on which the giant was sailing; he saw it springing a dangerous leak and saw a torrent of sea water flooding, gushing into all the compartments of the ship until it found the bunk in which the black giant slept. Ah, yes, the foamy, surging waters would surprise that sleeping black bastard of a giant and he would drown, gasping and choking like a trapped rat, his tiny eyes bulging until they glittered red, the bitter water of the sea pounding his lungs until they ached and finally burst . . . The ship would sink slowly to the bottom of the cold, black, silent depths of the sea and a shark, a *white* one, would glide aimlessly about the shut portholes until it found an open one and

it would slither inside and nose about until it found that
swollen, rotting, stinking carcass of the black beast and it would
then begin to nibble at the decomposing mass of tarlike flesh,
eating the bones clean . . . Olaf always pictured the giant's
bones as being jet black and shining.

Once or twice, during these fantasies of cannibalistic revenge,
Olaf felt a little guilty about all the many innocent people,
women and children, all white and blonde, who would have to
go down into watery graves in order that that white shark
could devour the evil giant's black flesh . . . But, despite
feelings of remorse, the fantasy lived persistently on, and
when Olaf found himself alone, it would crowd and cloud his
mind to the exclusion of all else, affording him the only revenge he knew. To make me suffer just for the pleasure of it,
he fumed. Just to show me how strong he was . . . Olaf learned
how to hate, and got pleasure out of it.

Summer fled on wings of rain. Autumn flooded Denmark with
color. Winter made rain and snow fall on Copenhagen. Finally
spring came, bringing violets and roses. Olaf kept to his job.
For many months he feared the return of the black giant. But
when a year had passed and the giant had not put in an appearance, Olaf allowed his revenge fantasy to peter out, in-
dulging in it only when recalling the shame that the black
monster had made him feel.

Then one rainy August night, a year later, Olaf sat drowsing
at his desk, his bottle of beer before him, tilting back in his
swivel chair, his feet resting atop a corner of his desk, his mind
mulling over the more pleasant aspects of his life. The office
door cracked open. Olaf glanced boredly up and around. His
heart jumped and skipped a beat. The black nightmare of terror and shame that he had hoped that he had lost forever was
again upon him . . . Resplendently dressed, suitcase in hand,

the black looming mountain filled the doorway. Olaf's thin lips parted and a silent moan, half a curse, escaped them.

"Hy," the black giant boomed from the doorway.

Olaf could not reply. But a sudden resolve swept him: this time he would even the score. If this black beast came within so much as three feet of him, he would snatch his gun out of the drawer and shoot him dead, so help him God . . .

"No rooms tonight," Olaf heard himself announcing in a determined voice.

The black giant grinned; it was the same infernal grimace of delight and triumph that he had had when his damnable black fingers had been around his throat . . .

"Don't want no room tonight," the giant announced.

"Then what are you doing here?" Olaf asked in a loud but tremulous voice.

The giant swept toward Olaf and stood over him; and Olaf could not move, despite his oath to kill him . . .

"What do you want then?" Olaf demanded once more, ashamed that he could not lift his voice above a whisper.

The giant still grinned, then tossed what seemed the same suitcase upon Olaf's sofa and bent over it; he zippered it open with a sweep of his clawlike hand and rummaged in it, drawing forth a flat, gleaming white object done up in glowing cellophane. Olaf watched with lowered lids, wondering what trick was now being played on him. Then, before he could defend himself, the giant had whirled and again long, black, snakelike fingers were encircling Olaf's throat . . . Olaf stiffened, his right hand clawing blindly for the drawer where the gun was kept. But the giant was quick.

"Wait," he bellowed, pushing Olaf back from the desk.

The giant turned quickly to the sofa and, still holding his fingers in a wide circle that seemed a noose for Olaf's neck, he inserted the rounded fingers into the top of the flat, gleaming object. Olaf had the drawer open and his sweaty fingers were now touching his gun, but something made him freeze. The flat, gleaming object was a shirt and the black giant's circled fingers were fitting themselves into its neck . . .

"A perfect fit!" the giant shouted.

Olaf stared, trying to understand. His fingers loosened about the gun. A mixture of a laugh and a curse struggled in him. He watched the giant plunge his hands into the suitcase and pull out other flat, gleaming shirts.

"One, two, three, four, five, six," the black giant intoned, his voice crisp and businesslike. "Six nylon shirts. And they're all yours. One shirt for each time Lena came . . . See, Daddy-O?"

The black, cupped hands, filled with billowing nylon whiteness, were extended under Olaf's nose. Olaf eased his damp fingers from his gun and pushed the drawer closed, staring at the shirts and then at the black giant's grinning face.

"Don't you like 'em?" the giant asked.

Olaf began to laugh hysterically, then suddenly he was crying, his eyes so flooded with tears that the pile of dazzling nylon looked like snow in the dead of winter. Was this true? Could he believe it? Maybe this too was a trick? But, no. There were six shirts, all nylon, and the black giant had had Lena six nights.

"What's the matter with you, Daddy-O?" the giant asked. "You blowing your top? Laughing and crying . . ."

Olaf swallowed, dabbed his withered fists at his dimmed eyes; then he realized that he had his glasses on. He took them off and dried his eyes and sat up. He sighed, the tension and shame and fear and haunting dread of his fantasy went from him, and he leaned limply back in his chair . . .

"Try one on," the giant ordered.

Olaf fumbled with the buttons of his shirt, let down his suspenders, and pulled the shirt off. He donned a gleaming nylon one and the giant began buttoning it for him.

"Perfect, Daddy-O," the giant said.

His spectacled face framed in sparkling nylon, Olaf sat with trembling lips. So he'd not been trying to kill me after all.

"You want Lena, don't you?" he asked the giant in a soft whisper. "But I don't know where she is. She never came back here after you left—"

"I know where Lena is," the giant told him. "We been writing to each other. I'm going to her house. And, Daddy-O, I'm late." The giant zippered the suitcase shut and stood a moment gazing down at Olaf, his tiny little red eyes blinking slowly. Then Olaf realized that there was a compassion in that stare that he had never seen before.

"And I thought you wanted to kill me," Olaf told him. "I was scared of you . . ."

"Me? Kill you?" the giant blinked. "When?"

"That night when you put your fingers about my throat—"

"What?" the giant asked, then roared with laughter. "Daddy-O, you're a funny little man. I wouldn't hurt you. I like you. You a *good* man. You helped me."

Olaf smiled, clutching the pile of nylon shirts in his arms.

"You're a good man too," Olaf murmured. Then loudly: "You're a big black good man."

"Daddy-O, you're crazy," the giant said.

He swept his suitcase from the sofa, spun on his heel, and was at the door in one stride.

"Thanks!" Olaf cried after him.

The black giant paused, turned his vast black head, **and** flashed a grin.

"Daddy-O, drop dead," he said and was gone.

THE MAN WHO SAW

THE FLOOD

When the flood waters recede,
the poor folk along the river
start from scratch.

AT LAST THE FLOOD WATERS had receded. A black father, a black
mother, and a black child tramped through muddy fields, leading a tired cow by a thin bit of rope. They stopped on a
hilltop and shifted the bundles on their shoulders. As far as
they could see the ground was covered with flood silt. The
little girl lifted a skinny finger and pointed to a mud-caked
cabin.

"Look, Pa! Ain tha our home?"

The man, round-shouldered, clad in blue, ragged overalls,
looked with bewildered eyes. Without moving a muscle,
scarcely moving his lips, he said: "Yeah."

For five minutes they did not speak or move. The flood
waters had been more than eight feet high here. Every tree,

blade of grass, and stray stick had its flood mark; caky, yellow mud. It clung to the ground, cracking thinly here and there in spider web fashion. Over the stark fields came a gusty spring wind. The sky was high, blue, full of white clouds and sunshine. Over all hung a first-day strangeness.

"The henhouse is gone," sighed the woman.

"N the pigpen," sighed the man.

They spoke without bitterness.

"Ah reckon them chickens is all done drowned."

"Yeah."

"Miz Flora's house is gone, too," said the little girl.

They looked at a clump of trees where their neighbor's house had stood.

"Lawd!"

"Yuh reckon anybody knows where they is?"

"Hard t tell."

The man walked down the slope and stood uncertainly.

"There wuz a road erlong here somewheres," he said.

But there was no road now. Just a wide sweep of yellow, scalloped silt.

"Look, Tom!" called the woman. "Here's a piece of our gate!"

The gatepost was half buried in the ground. A rusty hinge stood stiff, like a lonely finger. Tom pried it loose and caught it firmly in his hand. There was nothing particular he wanted to do with it; he just stood holding it firmly. Finally he dropped it, looked up, and said:

"C mon. Les go down n see whut we kin do."

Because it sat in a slight depression, the ground about the cabin was soft and slimy.

"Gimme tha bag o lime, May," he said.

With his shoes sucking in mud, he went slowly around the cabin, spreading the white lime with thick fingers. When he reached the front again he had a little left; he shook the bag out on the porch. The fine grains of floating lime flickered in the sunlight.

"Tha oughta hep some," he said.

"Now, yuh be careful, Sal!" said May. "Don yuh go n fall down in all this mud. yuh hear?"

"Yessum."

The steps were gone. Tom lifted May and Sally to the porch. They stood a moment looking at the half-opened door. He had shut it when he left, but somehow it seemed natural that he should find it open. The planks in the porch floor were swollen and warped. The cabin had two colors; near the bottom it was a solid yellow; at the top it was the familiar gray. It looked weird, as though its ghost were standing beside it.

The cow lowed.

"Tie Pat t the pos on the en of the porch, May."

May tied the rope slowly, listlessly. When they attempted to open the front door, it would not budge. It was not until Tom placed his shoulder against it and gave it a stout shove that it scraped back jerkily. The front room was dark and silent. The damp smell of flood silt came fresh and sharp to their nostrils. Only one-half of the upper window was clear, and through it fell a rectangle of dingy light. The floors swam in ooze. Like a mute warning, a wavering flood mark went high around the walls of the room. A dresser sat cater-cornered, its drawers and sides bulging like a bloated corpse. The bed, with the mattress still on it, was like a giant casket forged of mud. Two smashed chairs lay in a corner, as though huddled together for protection.

"Les see the kitchen," said Tom.

The stovepipe was gone. But the stove stood in the same place.

"The stove's still good. We kin clean it."

"Yeah."

"But where's the table?"

"Lawd knows."

"It must've washed erway wid the rest of the stuff, Ah reckon."

They opened the back door and looked out. They missed the barn, the henhouse, and the pigpen.

"Tom, yuh bettah try tha ol pump n see ef eny watah's there."

The pump was stiff. Tom threw his weight on the handle and carried it up and down. No water came. He pumped on. There was a dry, hollow cough. Then yellow water trickled. He caught his breath and kept pumping. The water flowed white.

"Thank Gawd! We's got some watah."

"Yuh bettah boil it fo yuh use it," he said.

"Yeah. Ah know."

"Look, Pa! Here's yo ax," called Sally.

Tom took the ax from her. "Yeah. Ah'll need this."

"N here's somethin else," called Sally, digging spoons out of the mud.

"Waal, Ahma git a bucket n start cleanin," said May. "Ain no use in waitin, cause we's gotta sleep on them floors tonight."

When she was filling the bucket from the pump, Tom called from around the cabin. "May, look! Ah done foun mah plow!" Proudly he dragged the silt-caked plow to the pump. "Ah'll wash it n it'll be awright."

"Ahm hongry," said Sally.

"Now, yuh jus wait! Yuh et this mawnin," said May. She turned to Tom. "Now, whutcha gonna do, Tom?"

He stood looking at the mud-filled fields.

"Yuh goin back t Burgess?"

"Ah reckon Ah have to."

"Whut else kin yuh do?"

"Nothin," he said. "Lawd, but Ah sho hate t start all over wid tha white man. Ah'd leave here ef Ah could. Ah owes im nigh eight hundred dollahs. N we needs a hoss, grub, seed, n a lot mo other things. Ef we keeps on like this tha white man'll own us body n soul."

"But, Tom, there ain nothin else t do," she said.

"Ef we try t run erway they'll put us in jail."

"It coulda been worse," she said.

Sally came running from the kitchen. "Pa!"

"Hunh?"

"There's a shelf in the kitchen the flood didn git!"

"Where?"

"Right up over the stove."

"But, chile, ain nothin up there," said May.

"But there's somethin on it," said Sally.

"C mon. Les see."

High and dry, untouched by the flood-water, was a box of matches. And beside it a half-full sack of Bull Durham tobacco. He took a match from the box and scratched it on his overalls. It burned to his fingers before he dropped it.

"May!"

"Hunh?"

"Look! Here's ma bacco n some matches!"

She stared unbelievingly. "Lawd!" she breathed.

Tom rolled a cigarette clumsily.

May washed the stove, gathered some sticks, and after some difficulty, made a fire. The kitchen stove smoked, and their eyes smarted. May put water on to heat and went into the front room. It was getting dark. From the bundles they took a kerosene lamp and lit it. Outside Pat lowed longingly into the thickening gloam and tinkled her cowbell.

"Tha old cow's hongry," said May.

"Ah reckon Ah'll have t be gittin erlong t Burgess."

They stood on the front porch.

"Yuh bettah git on, Tom, fo it gits too dark."

"Yeah."

The wind had stopped blowing. In the east a cluster of stars hung.

"Yuh goin, Tom?"

"Ah reckon Ah have t."

"Ma, Ah'm hongry," said Sally.

"Wait erwhile, honey. Ma knows yuh's hongry."

Tom threw his cigarette away and sighed.

"Look! Here comes somebody!"

"Thas Mistah Burgess now!"

A mud-caked buggy rolled up. The shaggy horse was splattered all over. Burgess leaned his white face out of the buggy and spat.

"Well, I see you're back."

"Yessuh."

"How things look?"

"They don look so good, Mistah."

"What seems to be the trouble?"

"Waal. Ah ain got no hoss, no grub, nothin. The only thing Ah got is tha ol cow there . . ."

"You owe eight hundred dollahs down at the store, Tom."

"Yessuh, Ah know. But, Mistah Burgess, can't yuh knock somethin off of tha, seein as how Ahm down n out now?"

"You ate that grub, and I got to pay for it, Tom."

"Yessuh, Ah know."

"It's going to be a little tough, Tom. But you got to go

through with it. Two of the boys tried to run away this morning and dodge their debts, and I had to have the sheriff pick em up. I wasn't looking for no trouble out of you, Tom . . . The rest of the families are going back."

Leaning out of the buggy, Burgess waited. In the surrounding stillness the cowbell tinkled again. Tom stood with his back against a post.

"Yuh got t go on, Tom. We ain't got nothin here," said May.

Tom looked at Burgess.

"Mistah Burgess, Ah don wanna make no trouble. But this is jus *too* hard. Ahm worse off now than befo. Ah got to start from scratch."

"Get in the buggy and come with me. I'll stake you with grub. We can talk over how you can pay it back." Tom said nothing. He rested his back against the post and looked at the mud-filled fields.

"Well," asked Burgess. "You coming?" Tom said nothing. He got slowly to the ground and pulled himself into the buggy. May watched them drive off.

"Hurry back, Tom!"

"Awright."

"Ma, tell Pa t bring me some 'lasses," begged Sally.

"Oh, Tom!"

Tom's head came out of the side of the buggy.

"Hunh?"

"Bring some 'lasses!"

"*Hunh?*"

"Bring some 'lasses for Sal!"

"Awright!"

She watched the buggy disappear over the crest of the muddy hill. Then she sighed, caught Sally's hand, and turned back into the cabin.

MAN OF ALL WORK

— Carl! Carl!

— Hunh.

— Carl, the baby's awake.

— Yeah? Hummnn . . .

— Carl, the baby's crying.

— Oh, all right. I'll get up. It's time for her bottle.

— Be sure and heat it to the right temperature, Carl.

— Of course. Put on the light.

— How is she?

— Fine. Ha, ha! What a pair of lungs! She's really bawling us out. O.K., Tina. I'm getting your bottle right now. Oooowaaa . . . Lucy, you kind of scared me when you called me.

— I know, Carl. You haven't had much sleep lately. You're jumpy. Both of us are. You want me to feed her?

— No, no. It's nothing. I'll heat the bottle now.

— I hear Henry coming.

— Papa, Papa!

— Henry, go back to bed.

— Papa, can't I see Tina? I heard her crying.

— Come in, Henry. Carl, let Henry see the baby.

— Oh, sure.

— Henry, while Papa is heating the bottle, you can look at Tina.

— But, Mama, she's still so little.

— She's as big as you were when you were a week old.

— I never looked like *that*.

— Yes, you did. Not a bit different.

— But I don't remember when I—

— Of course, you don't. And Tina won't remember either when she grows up.

— All she knows is how to eat.

— We're born with that know-how, Henry. Oh, Henry, you didn't put on your house shoes and robe. How many times must I tell you that. You'll catch cold on that bare floor.

— O.K., Mama. But why does she cry so loud?

— That's the way babies are supposed to cry. She's healthy. NOW, PUT YOUR SHOES AND ROBE ON IF YOU WANT TO WATCH PAPA.

— Yessum.

— Lucy, here's the bottle. Feel it and see if it's warm enough.

— Seems just right to me, Carl.

— Papa, don't give her the bottle. I want to see you feed her.

— Then hurry up, Henry.

— Carl, let me feed her. Hand her to me.

— No. You lie still, Lucy. You're tired. The doctor said for you to rest. I can give the baby the bottle.

— I'm coming, Papa. Lemme see you feed her.

— O.K., son. Now, watch. I lift her head up a bit, then put the nipple in her mouth. See? She's stopped crying.

— Mama, Tina's eating!

— Ha, ha! Of course, Henry. Now, go to bed.

— O.K. Good night, Mama. Good night, Papa. Good night, Tina.

— Good night, Henry.

— Good night, son.

— He sure loves his little sister.

— Yes, he does. To him she's a toy.

— How do you feel, Lucy?

— Oh, all right. You know . . . Sometimes I'm quite normal, then I feel faint, weak . . .

— Darling, don't worry. You're upset. Just let me take care of everything. Ha, ha! Good thing you married a professional cook, eh?

— Carl, I wouldn't be so worried if I knew that we weren't going to lose the house.

— Sh. Don't talk so loud. Henry'll hear you.

— I'm sorry. We mustn't let him know that we've got trouble.

— Children have a way of sensing what's going on.

— Is she taking her milk all right?

— Gulping it down a mile a minute. Greedy thing.

— Oh, Carl, what're we going to do?

— Lucy, stop worrying. The doctor said—

— I can't help but worry, Carl.

—But that's what's making you sick. After you had Henry, you weren't ill.

— I know. But everything was all right then. Now, all of our money's tied up in this house and we can't make the last two payments. Oh, Carl, we mustn't lose our house.

— Honey, don't worry. Something'll turn up.

— Carl, did you sleep some?

— No. I just dozed a bit. Did you?

— No.

— Lucy, the doctor said—

— I know, Carl. But I can't help but worry.

— I'll think of something. You'll see.

— If we both hadn't lost our jobs at the same time. Giving birth knocked me out of my job. And your boss had to close his restaurant. Hard luck comes all at once.

— Lucy, look . . . She's finished her bottle.

— All of it?

— Every drop.

— Can you burp her?

— Sure.

— No. Hand her to me, Carl.

— No. Look. I'll just lift her gently and lay her across my shoulder. Like that . . . Then I'll pat her back. Easy does it. There! Did you hear it?

— Ha, ha! You did it as well as I could.

— Why not? Burping a baby's no mystery. Ha, ha. She's gone to sleep again.

— That warm milk always knocks her out.

— Okay, Tina. To bed you go now.

— Let me take a peek at her, Carl.

— Don't get up, Lucy. I'll bring her to you. Just lift yourself upon your elbow . . . There.

— Aw, she's a doll. Is she dry?

— I felt her diaper. It's dry. But it won't be for long.

— It never is. She looks like you, Carl.

— No. She looks like you, Lucy.

— Oh, come on. She looks like both of us.

— That's natural. She'd better not look like anybody else.

— Ha, ha. Are you jealous?

— I'll tuck her in. I think she'll be all right till morning.

— Carl, come back to bed. You've been up twice tonight.

— It's nothing. What time is it?

— It's five o'clock.

— What's that?

— That's the morning paper hitting the front door. I'll get it.

— Oh, come to bed, Carl. Get the paper later.

— No. I want to take a look at the want ads.

— Carl, don't be so nervous. Later . . .

— Lucy, I've got to smell out a job somehow. We've got only two fifty-dollar payments to make on this house. And, if I live, we're not going to lose this house. You go to sleep.

— Poor Carl. He does all he can. This shouldn't've happened to him.

— Darling, you won't mind if I keep the light on, will you? I want to study these ads.

— No, Carl. I'll try to sleep.

— Turn away from the light, hunh? Aw, let's see here . . . Yeah. MALE HELP WANTED: Machinists. Bricklayers. Pipe fitters. Masons. Bookkeepers. Salesmen. Hunh. Not a single ad for a cook.

— Carl, stop fretting and get some sleep.

— Aw, Lucy, I've *got* to get a job.

— Don't talk so loud. You'll wake the baby.

— I'm sorry, honey.

— Carl, we must try to be calm.

— Yeah. I know. No jobs for men in this paper . . . But there're plenty of ads for domestic workers. It's always like that.

— Oh, Carl. If I were well, I'd get a cooking job.

— Hush, Lucy.

— Well, you mentioned jobs for women and—

— I wasn't hinting that you ought to go to work. You're ill. Now, don't talk rot.

— Carl, I—

— Lucy, don't cry! Everything's going to be all right.

— I wish I could do something.

— Lucy, I'll find a job. You'll see. Aw, here's a wonderful ad. Listen:

> Cook and housekeeper wanted. Take care of one child and small modern household. All late appliances. Colored cook preferred. Salary: fifty dollars a week. References required. 608 South Ridgeway Boulevard. Mrs. David Fairchild.

— Oh, Carl! That job would solve our problem.

— Yeah, but they want a woman, Lucy. Ha, ha. I'm an A-1 cook. I wish to God I could sneak in and get that job.

— Aw, Carl, stop getting so worked up. I'm turning out the light.

— Oh, O.K. Try to get some sleep, darling.

— Lucy.

— Humnnnn . . . Hunh?

— Look, Lucy.

— Yeah, Carl. W-what is it?

— Turn on the light, honey.

— All right. Just a sec, Carl. OHHHHHH! Who are you?

— Take it easy, Lucy. Don't yell.

— Who is that? Carl? Is that you, Carl?

— Yes, Lucy. Now, look, darling. Be calm.

— Oh, God! I thought you were somebody else. Oh, Carl,

what are you doing? Those are my clothes you got on. You almost scared me to death.

— Listen, Lucy. Now, I'm—

— Carl, what's the matter?

— Sh. Don't wake up the children. Darling, now I'm—

— Oh, Carl. No. Don't do that. Is this a joke? Pull off my dress!

— Lucy, listen to me. I'm—

— Carl, have you gone crazy?

— Hush and listen to me. I know how to handle children. I can cook. Don't stop me. I've found a solution to our problem. I'm an army trained cook. I can clean a house as good as anybody. Get my point? I put on your dress. I looked in the mirror. I can pass. I want that job—

— Carl! Go 'way! TAKE OFF MY DRESS! No, no!

— Lucy, I'm going for that job advertised in the paper. Nobody'll see me leave. Don't worry. I'm going out the back way across the vacant lot, see? I'll take the bus behind the church. I've got it all figured out. Trust me. I'm going to work as a maid for two months in that white family. That means two hundred dollars. Half of that money'll pay off the house. The other half will keep us eating. You just stay home. Have Henry help you a bit while I'm gone and—

— Oh, God, no! You're wild, Carl!

— Be quiet, Lucy, and listen.

— God, I'm trembling . . . C-c-can't you see that—Oh, no!

— Lucy, don't cry.

— Carl, you're foolish.

— I'm not. I'll get that job.

— No. They'll find out.

— How?

— Carl, people can l-look at you and s-see that you're a man.

— Ha, ha. No, Lucy. I just looked at myself in the bathroom mirror. I've got on a dress and I look just like a million black women cooks. Who looks that close at us colored people anyhow? We all look alike to white people. Suppose you'd never seen me before? You'd take one look at me and take me for a woman because I'm wearing a dress. And the others'll do that too. Lucy, colored men are now wearing their hair long, like mine. Isn't that true? Look at Sugar Ray Robinson's hair. Look at Nat King Cole's hair. Look at all the colored men in the Black Belt. They straighten their hair. It's the style.

— Y-yes, but—

— All right. I'm just about your size. Your dresses fit me. I'll take your purse. I'll wear low-heeled shoes. What's more I don't need any make-up. A cook isn't supposed to be powdered and rouged. I've shaved very, very closely. I'm taking my razor with me; if my beard starts to grow, I'll sneak a quick shave, see? All I have to do is say 'Yessum, No'm,' and keep my mouth shut. Do my work. My voice is tenor; nobody'll notice it. I'll get the money we need and we're saved.

— Oh, Carl! Have you been drinking?

— I'm not drunk. I'm going for that job.

— Oh, Carl, if they catch you, they'll put you in jail.

— They won't suspect anything.

— They will. You'll see.

— They won't.

— Suppose they get suspicious of how you walk?

— They won't. There isn't much difference between a man's walk and a woman's. Look. I'm leaving my suit in the coal house; when I come back, I'll change this dress for my suit before coming into the house, see? Nobody'll know but you. When you're cooking for a family like that, you usually stay until after dinner—to do the dishes. It's fall now; the days are getting shorter. When I leave their house, it'll be night. Nobody among our folks'll see me. Like I told you, I'll change my clothes in the coal house and come in through the kitchen . . . You keep Henry near you, see? He'll know nothing.

— Carl, you'll make me scream! This is crazy!

— Darling, don't shout.

— Carl, if you go out of that door like that, I'll scream.

— Lucy, let me try this.

— No, no. Of all the damnfool ideas!

— Lucy, when I was in high school, I acted in plays. When I was in the army, I was in company plays. I can act good enough to fool white folks. And it's just for two months. Then we're fixed. Think. After two months, the house is safe, is ours.

— Carl, I don't want to talk to you. Leave me alone. AND GET OUT OF MY DRESS! *Now!* You hear! *Please* . . .

— Lucy, listen . . .

— CARL, PULL OFF MY DRESS!

— Lucy, look at me. Take your face out of the pillow. Be sensible. I'm taking a chance, but it'll come out all right.

— I don't want to look at you.

— Come on. Be a sport.

— The police'll catch you walking around in a dress and will put you in jail for impersonating a woman. And, if that happens, I'll leave you and the children! I'll just walk out, I swear to you. If you go out of that door in that dress, I'M THROUGH!

— How will anybody know? Lift up my dress? Ha, ha. Lucy, don't be silly. It's easy to fool 'em.

— Carl, stop it! Stop it or I'll scream! I'll get up and scratch you! PULL OFF MY DRESS!

— Oh, O.K. O.K. I give up. I'll pull off your dress. I was

only joking. Now, be calm, stop crying. Turn off the light and go to sleep.

— All right, Carl. But don't ever do that again, please. Oh, God, you scared me.

— O.K.

— You're really going to pull that dress off, aren't you?

— Sure, darling. I'll be back in a sec.

— And, Carl, don't worry so much. We'll solve things some-how, hunh? Oh, God, poor Carl. What's got into him? What can I do? He's worried sick. I thought I was having a night-mare when I saw him in my dress. I almost passed out. It's a wonder I didn't scream.

— Hummnnn . . . Carl. Carl. *Carl!* Oh, God, where is he? He must be in the kitchen. It's almost eight o'clock. The baby needs feeding. CARL! CARL! Where's my robe? He didn't leave here. No, he wouldn't do that. But he's not in the kitchen. And he's not in the bathroom. CARL! *Oh, God, he's not in the house!* I've awakened the baby. Aw, my dress is gone. And my purse. AND MY SHOES! *Did he do that?* No, he wouldn't dare go out into the streets like that! Then where could he be? He's gone to that job, that crazy fool . . . He'll get into trouble. I know it. I know it.

— Mama.

— Yes, Henry.

— The baby's crying.

— Yes, I know, darling. Get back to bed. I'm fixing the baby's bottle.

— I'm hungry.

— I'll get you your breakfast in a minute. Just wait now.

— Where's Papa?

— He's gone out. He'll be back soon.

— Mama, why are you crying?

— Henry, go back to bed till I call you, you hear?

— Okay, Mama.

— That's a good boy . . . What is that crazy Carl doing? I feel I can't stand on my legs. I must lie down. THAT FOOL! Maybe I ought to try to catch him? Or tell the police? No, no. I've got to look after the children. What can I do? Poor Carl's worried sick. That's it. He's frantic.

— Who is it?

— Ma'am, I came for the job. I'm answering the ad you put in the paper. Can I speak to you a minute?

— Oh. Just a moment. Dave! There's a colored woman outside who says she came for the job.

— My God, what time is it?

— It's a bit after eight.

— I should've been up. All right, see what she looks like. But where did she come from at this hour of the morning? We only put the ad in last night.

— Well, I guess it appeared in this morning's paper.

— I'll ask her in. Anne, put on your robe and talk to her. Be stern. You picked a lemon last time. Remember?

— Who picked a lemon? She was doing all right till you started getting ideas about her.

— Aw, Anne. Don't start all that again. I'll let her in and tell her to wait for you, hunh?

— Yes, Dave.

— Good morning, sir.

— Good morning.

— Excuse me for coming so early, but I just wanted to be the first one. I really need that job, mister.

— Come in.

— Thank you, sir.

— My wife'll talk to you in a moment. What's your name?

— Lucy Owens, sir.

— How old are you?

— Thirty, sir.

— You live here in town?

— Yes, sir. Just a twenty-minute bus ride from here.

— You've done domestic work before? You can handle children?

— Oh, yes, sir. I've two children of my own.

— What ages?

— One's a year old and the other's six.

— Who looks after the young one when you work?

— My husband, sir. You see, he works at night in a lumber-mill and is at home during the day.

— Have you references?

— Oh, yes, sir.

— Well, Lucy, my wife'll speak to you in a moment. This is her department. Sit down and wait a bit.

— Yes, sir. Thank you, sir.

— Anne, you'd better talk to her. She doesn't live far from here. Seems clean, strong. Knows her place. Name's Lucy Owens. Got two children.

— I'll talk to her and check her references. Dave, if she drinks, I'll not hire her.

— Use your judgment, Anne.

— How does she look? How old is she?

— Didn't ask her. Didn't notice her.

— If you didn't, it would be the first time.

— Aw, Anne, cut it out. Hire the woman if you want her.

— I'll talk to her.

— I'll shave now. If you decide to take her, you might let her try to rustle up some breakfast.

— We'll see.

— Good morning, ma'am.

— You're Lucy Owens?

— Yessum.

— Now, Lucy, do you think you can handle a child of six and do the work in the house?

— Oh, that's nothing, ma'am. Give me a try. I love kiddies.

— Here's my little daughter, Lily, now. Lily, come here. This is Lucy. She wants to work for us.

— Hello, Lucy.

— Hello, Miss Lily. My, you're pretty. How are you?

— Fine. Lucy, can you cook cakes?

— Ha, ha! Lucy, you'd better answer Lily. She's the boss at the table.

— Miss Lily, I can cook the best food you ever tasted. I make fudge, cakes, ice cream—everything. I'll put some flesh on you.

— Now, run along, Lily. Lucy, what about your references?

— Well, ma'am, I have a good reference. But the trouble is that the folks I used to work for have gone to Europe and won't be back for two months. You won't be able to check on me with them. But there's Reverend Burke of the Pearl Street Baptist Church. You can phone him any time you want and ask about Sister Lucy Owens.

— I see. How long were you with your last family?

— Five years, ma'am.

— Lucy, I want to talk frankly to you. We had a girl here. But she was a disappointment to me. She seemed so nice.

But she drank. And when she did, her conduct was awful. Guess you know what I mean?

— Yessum. I think I know what you mean. But, ma'am, I don't drink. I'm a straight, God-fearing woman. I just want to give you an honest day's work. You see, ma'am, me and my husband's buying our own place. We're responsible people.

— I like that. One should own one's own place. Well, you seem clean, strong, quick.

— Oh, ma'am, you won't have any trouble from me.

— Well, Lucy, we said fifty dollars a week. You'll have to be here at seven in the morning; we're generally asleep. But by the time you get breakfast on the table, we'll be up and ready to eat. When we've gone, you take care of Lily, do the housework, do the wash when necessary, and prepare lunch and dinner. Generally, my husband's in every day for lunch. When I'm in the neighborhood, I drop in for lunch. Understand?

— Yessum. That's quite all right. You just keep to your schedule and tell me what you want done and I'll do it.

— That sounds good. Well, Lucy, I'm going to take a chance on you. You're hired. I just look at a person and something tells me that they ought to be all right.

— Thank you, ma'am.

— Now, Lucy, I'll show you around the house. This is the sun porch. As you see, this is the entry. There's the living room. Here's our bedroom. There's the bath. And here's Lily's room. And that's a guest room. Here's the dining room. And here's the kitchen.

— Oh, it's big, ma'am.

— To save trouble, we eat breakfast in the kitchen.

— I understand. Oh, what a pretty refrigerator.

— It's the latest. And there's the washing machine.

— I can handle 'em all, ma'am.

— The food's here in this pantry. Knives and forks and dishes are here. Soap powder. Mops. Brooms. There's the backyard where you hang up clothes to dry. But your main job's looking after Lily.

— Mama, does Lucy know about Little Red Riding Hood?

— Miss Lily, I know all about her.

— O.K., Lucy. Now, do you think you can rustle up some breakfast for us?

— I'll try, ma'am. What would you-all want?

— What do you specialize in for breakfast, Lucy?

— Reckon you all would love some pancakes? I cook 'em light as a feather. You can digest 'em in your sleep.

— Just a moment, Lucy. Dave!

— Yeah, Anne.

— Lucy wants to try her hand at some pancakes. She says she's good at 'em.

— Well, tell her to rustle some up. I haven't had any good pancakes since Heck was a pup.

— You've got your orders, Lucy.

— Ha, ha! Yessum. Pancakes coming up. Hot and with maple syrup and butter. Ha, ha!

— Breakfast is ready, everybody!

— O.K., Lucy. Come on, Lily. Lucy, Lily and I always eat breakfast together. Mrs. Fairchild's still in the bath and will eat later. She's on a strict diet and will only want a slice of toast and black coffee. She won't leave for work until a bit later.

— I understand, sir.

— Lucy, these pancakes are wonderful. Anne, you ought to try one, really. Lily, tell Mama how good they are.

— Mama, they're like cake.

— Hummmnnn . . . I want a stack of five of 'em.

— Dave, watch your waistline.

— Lucy, I haven't had pancakes like this in years. Hummnnn . . .

— Better eat your fill of 'em, Mister Dave.

— Lily, take some more.

— Sure, Papa. They're so good.

— Mister Dave, you want me to make another batch for you?

— Yeah. You'd better cook me another batch, Lucy.

— O.K. Another batch of pancakes coming up!

— Oh, Papa, she cooks real good.

— Sh. Don't talk so loud. We don't want to spoil her. That gal knows her onions. Don't know what she put in these cakes, but I'm taking a third stack of 'em. Anne!

— Yes, Dave.

— I'm downing these cakes. God, they're good.

— All right, Dave. Glad you like 'em. See you at lunch, maybe. And, Lily, I want you to be nice to Lucy, hear? You obey her. No screaming, no tantrums.

— Yes, Mama. I like Lucy. She's big and strong. Papa, may I have another pancake?

— Anne, Lily's already eating better.

— I'm sure happy about that.

— And, Anne, this coffee's good. Hummmnnn . . . It's good to have a solid breakfast before hitting those streets in the morning.

— Well, Anne, I'm off. Will I see you for lunch?

— If I can make it, Dave. Good-by.

— Good-by, Papa.

— Good-by, Lily. Run on back into the kitchen and stay with Lucy while Mama takes her bath.

— Yes, Papa.

— Hello, Lucy. What're you doing?

— Come in, Lily. I'm washing the dishes. Be through in a sec.

— Lucy, can you sing?

— Oh, yes. Why?

— Then sing something for me. Bertha used to sing all the time.

— Well, what do you want me to sing?

— Songs like your people sing.

— Ha, ha. I know. Oh, all right. Let's see.

> Swing low, sweet chariot
> Coming for to carry me home . . .
> Looked over Jordan and what did I see?
> A band of angels coming after me,
> Coming for to carry me home . . .

— That's pretty. Wish I could sing like that.

— You can. When you're a bit older.

— How'd you learn to sing that song?

— It was so long ago, I've forgotten, Lily.

— Lucy, your arms are so big.

— Hunh?

— And there's so much hair on them.

— Oh, that's nothing.

— And you've got so many big muscles.

— Oh, that comes from washing and cleaning and cooking. Lifting heavy pots and pans.

— And your voice is not at all like Bertha's.

— What do you mean?

— Your voice is heavy, like a man's.

— Oh, that's from singing so much, child.

— And you hold your cigarette in your mouth like Papa holds his, with one end dropping down.

— Hunh? Oh, that's because my hands are busy, child.

— That's just what Papa said when I asked him about it.

— You notice everything, don't you, Lily?

— Sure. I like to look at people. Gee, Lucy, you move so quick and rough in the kitchen. You can lift that whole pile of dishes with one hand. Bertha couldn't do that.

— Just a lot of experience, Lily. Say, why don't you play with your dolls?

— I just like to watch you.

— Oh, Lucy!

— Mama's calling you, Lucy.

— Yessum, Mrs. Fairchild.

— Did you find that bundle of wash there in the hallway?

— Yessum. I see it.

— That's today's wash, Lucy.

— Yessum. I understand. Lily, suppose you come with me on the porch while I put this washing in the machine, hunh? Now, we'll put this soap powder in. Then we'll run in the hot water . . . Now, I'll dump all the white clothes in. There. Wasn't that quick? Now, I'll throw the switch. There. The clothes are being washed.

— Gee, Lucy, you work like a machine.

— God, child, you do notice everything, don't you? But don't look too much or you might see things you won't understand.

— What do you mean? How? Why?

— Ha, ha. Nothing. Now, Lily, while I clean the house, what do you want to do? Watch me or play?

— I want to play in my sand pile.

— Where is it?

— In the backyard.

— Well, come on and show me.

— It's right by the fence. There it is.

— What a pile of sand. Child, you're lucky.

— Papa bought me a whole truck load of sand to play in.

— Suppose I build you a sand castle?

— Oh, that'd be fun.

— Well, let's see. First, we'll make the foundation, like this . . . Then we start the walls. That's right. Pat the walls smoothly. Take your time. Now, we'll try to make the doorway. About here, hunh?

— Oh, yes. Lucy, this is going to be a wonderful castle. I can finish it now. I know how.

— You really think so?

— Sure.

— Well, I'll get inside and start my work on the house.

— Lucy!

— Yessum. I'm coming.

— Come here, please!

— Yessum. On the way, ma'am.

— Lucy!

— Yessum. Where are you, Mrs. Fairchild?

— I'm here in the bathroom. Won't you come in? I want you to wash my back.

— Hunh?

— Come into the bathroom.

— Ma'am?

— Right here. I hear you. Open the door and come in. I want you to wash my back.

— Yessum.

— Lucy, can't you hear me?

— Yessum.

— Then open the door and come in.

— Er . . . Er, yessum.

— Well, what's the matter, Lucy? Why are you poking your head like that around the door? Come in. I want you to wash my back with this brush. Come on in. I haven't got all day, Lucy.

— Yessum.

— I don't want to be late for work. Well, come on. Why are you standing there and staring like that at me?

— Er . . .

— Don't you feel well, Lucy?

— Yessum.

— Then come here and wash my back.

— Yessum.

— That's it. Scrub hard. I won't break. Do it hard. Oh, Lord, what's the matter with you? Your arm's shaking. Lucy?

— Ma'am.

— What's come over you? Are you timid or ashamed or something?

— No'm.

— Are you upset because I'm sitting here naked in the bathtub?

— Oh, no, ma'am.

— Then what's the matter? My God, your face is breaking out in sweat. You look terrible. Are you ill, Lucy?

— No, ma'am. I'm all right.

— Then scrub my back. Hard. Why, your arms are like rubber. Well, I never. You're acting very strange. Do I offend you because I ask you to wash my back? Bertha always helped me with my bath . . .

— It's just the first t-t-time . . .

— Oh, I see. Well, I don't see why I should frighten you. I'm a woman like you are.

— Yessum.

— A bit harder, Lucy. Higher, up between my shoulder blades. That's it, that's it. Aw . . . Good. That's enough. Now, Lucy, hand me that towel over there. Where're you going? You're not leaving yet. I'm not through. Oh, I must be careful getting out of this tub. Tub's are dangerous things; you can have accidents by slipping in tubs . . . Lucy, give me the towel . . . WHAT IS HAPPENING TO YOU, LUCY? Why are you staring at me like that? Take a hand towel from that rack and wipe your face. Are you well? Maybe the doctor ought to take a good look at you. My brother-in-law, Burt Stallman, is a doctor. Do you want me to call him for you?

— It's just hot in here, ma'am.

— Hot? Why it's rather cold to me. I'm cold, you're hot. What's wrong with you? HAND ME THE TOWEL! Now, that box of talcum . . . Thanks. Now, Lucy, sit here on this stool a moment. There's something I must say to you and there's no better time than now, while I'm drying myself. I want to talk frankly to you, as one woman to another.

— Yessum.

— Now, I didn't tell you when you first came here why I had to get rid of my last maid. Now, look, my husband, Dave, likes to take a drink now and then—maybe a drop more than is good for him. Otherwise, he's perfectly sober, thoughtful, and easy to get along with. You know what I mean?

— Yessum. I think I know.

— Now, Bertha too did a little drinking now and then. And, when both of 'em started drinking—well, you can imagine what happened. Understand?

— Yessum.

— Now, Lucy, tell me: do you drink?

— No, ma'am. Not a drop.

— Good. As long as you don't drink, my husband won't

bother you and you can very well defend yourself. Just push him away. Now, as one woman to another, do we understand each other?

— Mrs. Fairchild, your husband isn't going to touch me.

— Well, I'm glad to hear you say it like that. Dave's not so much a problem, Lucy. He gets the way men get sometimes. Afterwards he's ashamed enough to want to go out and drown himself or something. Understand? Any strong-minded person can handle Dave when he's like that. But if you're like Bertha, then trouble's bound to come.

— Yessum. You can depend on me, Mrs. Fairchild.

— Oh, Lucy, I've just got to watch my figure. Don't you think I'm too fat?

— Ma'am, some folks are just naturally a bit heavy, you know.

— But my breasts—aren't they much too large?

— Maybe . . . a little . . .

— And my thighs, aren't they rather large too?

— Well, not especially, Ma'am.

— Lucy, you are too polite to tell me what you really think. I wish I were as slender as you. How do you manage it?

— Just working hard, I guess, ma'am.

— Really, Lucy, I like you very much. Ha, ha! You're like a sixteen-year-old girl. I'm surprised that you've had two children. Listen, Lucy, what I've discussed with you about my husband is just between us, see?

— Yessum. I won't open my mouth to anybody, Ma'am.

— How do you and your husband get along?

— Oh, fine, ma'am.

— Oh, yes, Lucy . . . For lunch I want spinach, lamb chops, boiled potatoes, salad, and stewed pears. Coffee. Tonight we eat out.

— Yessum. I'll remember.

— Lucy, hand me my brassiere there . . .

— Yessum.

— Lord, even when I don't eat, I get fat . . . Give me my panties, Lucy.

— Yessum.

— Well, that's all, Lucy. You can go back to your work.

— Ma'am, the coffee's still hot. You want some toast?

— I won't touch a crumb of bread. Just black coffee.

— Yessum. I'm going to see what little Lily is up to.

— That's right, Lucy. Keep your eye on her.

— Lily! Lily!

— I'm here, Lucy. Look at my castle.

— Well, you've almost finished it.

— Lucy, what's the matter? Your face is wet . . . You're shaking.

— Oh, nothing. I just want to sit here on the steps for a moment and get my breath. It was hot there in that bathroom.

— You look scared, Lucy.

— Sometimes I'm short of breath, that's all.

— Do you really like my castle?

— It's wonderful.

— Lucy!

— Yessum, Mrs. Fairchild.

— Good-by. Good-by, Lily.

— Good-by, Mama.

— Good-by, Mrs. Fairchild.

— Oh, Lily!

— Yes.

— Your lunch's ready. You must eat and then take your nap.

— I'm coming, Lucy.

— No, Lily. You must come right now, while your food's hot.

— Oh, all right.

— Did you wash your hands?

— Yes.

— Sit down. Tuck your napkin in. Here's some nice spinach.

— I don't like spinach.

— It's good for you. Eat it. There's ice cream for dessert.

— What kind?

— Chocolate.

— I like vanilla.

— All right, now. Open your mouth and eat. Let's go.

— Lucy, your face is hard.

— Hunh?

— And very rough.

— Ha, ha. I've been working hard all my life, Lily. That's why. Why are you always staring at me so? Don't look at me. Eat.

— Papa's lunch is ready?

— Yes, lunch is ready for your papa and your mama.

— Is Mama coming to lunch?

— Don't know. Now, eat your food. Stop talking.

— Lucy, are you going to be like Bertha?

— What do you mean?

— Are you going to wrestle with Papa too?

— Hunh? Ha, ha. No, not me, Lily.

— Ha, ha. Bertha was always wrestling with Papa, running from room to room.

— What happened?

— I don't know. But it was funny. I could hear Bertha hollering. They'd make so much noise I couldn't take my nap. And Papa'd give me a dime not to tell Mama.

— I won't wrestle with your papa. You'll be able to sleep.

— Aw, but Papa is quick and strong.

— I can outrun him.

— He'll catch you like he did Bertha and make you wrestle with him.

— Stop talking, Lily, and eat your lamb chop.

— I'm eating, Lucy.

— Unless you eat faster, you won't be in bed by the time they come.

— You want me in bed, when Papa comes?

— I didn't say that.

— Bertha always made me eat fast so I would be sleeping when Papa came.

— Hummnnn . . . Say, tell me a bit more about how Bertha wrestled with your papa.

— They just wrestled.

— Did it happen often?

— Almost everyday. Then Bertha left.

— Why?

— Mama said it was not nice for a lady to wrestle with a man.

— That's right, Lily.

— Lucy, don't you ever wear lipstick, like Mama?

— Oh, when I need to. Come on, Lily. Open your mouth and eat. Stop playing around. Oh, what's that whistle?

— That's the mailman.

— Now, you just eat. I'll go to the door and get the mail.

— He's Bertha's friend. He's colored, you know.

— Oh.

— Bertha used to invite him in. Are you?

— No. Now, you eat. I'll get the mail.

— Any mail, Lucy?

— Just one letter for your father.

— Did you see the mailman? Talk to him?

— No. He was leaving the door and I didn't call him.

— Bertha always did.

— I'm not Bertha.

— But isn't he your friend too?

— No.

— Don't you know his name?

— No, Lily. What is it?

— His name is Kirkby Rickford.

— Oh, yeah. I've heard of him.

— Bertha used to invite him in.

— Well, I won't.

—And Bertha used to give him a drink out of Papa's bottle.

— Now, Lily, here's your dessert. While you're eating it, I'll set the table for your mother and father, hear?

— O.K., Lucy. But you're not at all like Bertha—

— Hello! Hello! Anybody in?

— Oh, Papa! Lucy, Papa's come home.

— Hello, Lily. Are you still eating?

— I'm almost through, Papa.

— I always told you to be in bed when I came—

— I was talking to Lucy, Papa.

— Oh, hello there, Lucy.

— Hello, Mr. Fairchild.

— Is everything all right, Lucy?

— Yessir. Everything's fine, sir.

— Did she eat all right, Lucy?

— Oh, so-so, Mr. Fairchild.

— Here, Lily, let me feed you this ice cream.

— I don't want it. Papa, is Mama coming to lunch?

— I don't know.

— You're going to eat by yourself?

— Maybe.

— Papa, where did Bertha go?

— I don't know. And stop talking about Bertha. Finish your ice cream.

— Ooowwa . . . Papa, don't be angry with me . . .

— Aw, come on, Lily. It's bedtime, *now*.

— You always want me to go to bed when you come home. I know. You want to talk to Lucy.

— Will you shut your mouth and eat! Now, let me see where in hell did Anne hide my bottle. She's always trying to keep it from me. Have you seen my bottle around, Lucy?

— What kind of a bottle, sir?

— You know. My bottle of whisky. I need a little nip.

— No, sir. I haven't seen it.

— Oh, here it is. I hid it so well that I hid it from myself. Say, Lucy?

— Yessir.

— Would you like a little nip?

— Oh, no, sir. I don't drink at all.

— That's a shame. A nip never hurt anybody. There's nothing better than a good drink before lunch to get your food down.

— No, sir. It's for those who like it, sir.

— Whisky's a lot of fun, Lucy.

— I wouldn't know, sir.

— I like my whisky, Lucy.

— Papa, did you bring me something?

— Hunh? No, darling. I never bring you anything at noon. I'll bring you something tonight. Now, finish eating.

— What'll you bring me?

— Oh, that'll be your surprise. Aw, that was a good shot . . .
Lily, finish eating. Say, Lucy, Lucy! Where'd she go?

— She's in the kitchen, Papa.

— Lucy!

— Yessir.

— What're you doing there in that kitchen?

— Putting the lamb chops on, sir.

— Sure you won't have a nip?

— No, sir. Thank you, sir.

— Too bad.

— I'm through now, Papa. Do I take my nap?

— Yes, right away. Lucy, come and put Lily to bed . . .

— Yessir. Come on, Lily. Go right into your room and get
your dress off. That's it.

— You're going to play with Papa, Lucy?

— Shut up and take off those sandals.

— O.K.

— Lucy, did Lily obey you?

— Oh, yessir. Now, Lily, climb right into bed. That's it.
Pull the blanket over you lightly. That's right. Now, take a
nice nap. I'm closing the door.

— You sure know how to handle people, Lucy.

— Oh, I manage, Mr. Fairchild.

— Lucy, come on and have a drink with me.

— Never drink, Mr. Fairchild.

— Where're you going now?

— I've got to tend to the lamb chops, sir.

— Lucy, you're such an A-1 cook, I want to see how you do
it.

— Just ordinary cooking, sir.

— Aw, Lucy. Huumnnnn . . .

— Take your hand away, Mr. Fairchild.

— Aw, come on.

— Take your hand off, Mr. Fairchild.

— Is your old man good to you, Lucy?

— Mr. Fairchild, you're going to make it impossible for me to work here.

— Lucy, I bet your old man's no good to you.

— Mr. Fairchild, don't touch me. Let me work.

— Gosh, you're cheeky. Not like Bertha, hunh? I just want to make you feel good.

— Take your hand away!

— Don't shout, Lucy. I'm only playing—

— If you touch me again, I'll grab you, Mr. Fairchild.

— Look who's threatening. You're going to grab me, hunh? Baby, that's just what I want. Aw, come on . . .

— I told you to stop.

— Goddamn, you're a strong bitch, eh? I can't hold you, hunh?

— Leave me alone, Mr. Fairchild!

— Goddamn, you're as strong as a man. Well, we'll see who's the stronger. I'll set my drink down and test you out, gal.

— Keep away, Mr. Fairchild.

— Damn, you've got guts. You're spry, like a spring chicken. Come here.

— I've got hold of your arm, Mr. Fairchild. If you move, I'll twist it!

— Goddamn, this nigger woman says she'll lick me. We'll see!

—Ooooow! Mr. Fairchild, it's your fault. You made me push those dishes over.

— Keep still, Lucy. You're crazy if you think you can handle me.

— I'm warning you, Mr. Fairchild!

— Damn, if you're not like steel. Let my hands go. I'll teach you.

— Stop, Mr. Fairchild. I'll pick you up and throw you.

— Godammit, I dare you, I double dare you!

— I'm asking you once more to get away from me!

— You're a sassy nigger bitch, aren't you?

— Let me go, Mr. Fairchild. Your chops are burning!

— Papa, what's happening?

— Go back to bed, Lily!

— Oh, Papa's wrestling Lucy like he wrestled Bertha.

— Lily, I said go back to bed.

— Yes, Papa. But—

— Get away, Mr. Fairchild.

— I'm going to teach you a lesson, Lucy.

— Oh, Papa! You knocked the table over!—Oh, Lucy, you!—

— You black bitch, you hit me!

— Papa, you're hurt? Lucy, you knocked Papa down.

— I got you, Mr. Fairchild. I'll let you up if you promise to leave me alone.

— I'll get up from here and break your neck. Turn my hands loose! Turn me loose or I'll kick you in the stomach!

— Promise you'll leave me alone?

— O.K., Lucy. Let me up.

— You'll let me cook?

— Yeah. Let me up.

— There, Mr. Fairchild. Now, leave me alone.

— Lily, get back to bed.

— Yes, Papa. You're hurt, Papa?

— No. Goddamn, Lucy, I don't believe you're that strong. I'm coming after you.

— Mr. Fairchild, you're crazy. Stay away from me. I'll hit you!

— Haw. We'll see.

— I'm warning you. Stay away.

— Now, I got you!

— Turn me loose, Mr. Fairchild.

— Give up, Lucy.

— I'm telling you but once.

— Arrrrk! Jesus . . .

— Don't kill Papa, Lucy!

— I told you, Mr. Fairchild. Now, I'll hit you again if you —No, no! Turn my leg loose! If I hit you again, I'll knock you out.

— Naw, Lucy! Goddammit, you're as strong as a mule!

— Oh, there's Mama!

— DAVE! OH, MY GOD! WHAT'S HAPPENING HERE?

— Mama, Papa's wrestling Lucy . . .

— Mrs. Fairchild, it's not my fault. Mr. Fairchild was drunk and he kept bothering me.

— You bitch! You're lying . . . Pay no attention to her, Anne.

— Mrs. Fairchild, he got drunk and kept making passes at me.

— You got drunk on my whisky, Lucy. It was you who kept—

— That's not true, Mr. Fairchild.

— I tried to get you off me and you scratched me . . . Anne, I swear, it wasn't my fault.

— DAVE, OH, DAVE . . . YOU DRIVE ME CRAZY! EVERY TIME I TURN MY BACK THIS HAPPENS! AND YOU SWORE TO ME IT'D NEVER HAPPEN AGAIN! AND I THOUGHT I COULD TRUST YOU, LUCY! I'M SICK AND TIRED OF THIS! THIS IS THE END!

— Mama, don't cry . . .

— O.K., Anne. Send this bitch away, right now. Let's send her packing.

— No. Don't speak to me, Dave. I've got a better idea. Just wait.

— You see, Lucy. My wife saw what you were doing.

— You goddamn rotten white man.

— Lucy, get your damned things together and get the hell out of here. Be gone before my wife comes back in.

— O.K. I go. Let me pass—

— Aw, no! You're not getting off that lightly, Lucy.

— Aw, Mama's got a gun!

— ANNE, PUT THAT GUN DOWN!

— Get out of my way, Dave. I ought to kill the both of you.

— ANNE, I SAID PUT THAT GUN DOWN! DON'T BE A FOOL!

— Get out of my way, Dave. I'll be made a fool of no longer. For all I know, you might have sent this black bitch here to work . . . No wonder she came so early in the morning. Now, I'm going to kill her.

— Mrs. Fairchild, I didn't do anything. I swear before God. I couldn't. You don't understand.

— Yes. That Bertha said the same thing. Dave, get away. I'm going to shoot. I'll hit you, if you don't move!

— ANNE, ANNE, DON'T BE A FOOL! PUT THAT GUN DOWN!

— Stay away from me, Dave.

— ANNE, GIVE ME THAT GUN!

— No!

— I'll take it from you! Oh, God! No, no . . . Anne, you shot her . . .

— Mama! Papa, Lucy's been killed . . .

— Go away, Lily! Don't go near your mama.

— Oh God . . . Dave, what did I do? I shot her . . . Oh, Dave, it's all your fault. You promised you'd never let me

find you doing that again. Now, I've killed somebody. Oh,
Lord! Dave, you made me do it. I'm sure I've killed her.

— Mama, there's blood on the floor . . .

— Anne, drop that gun.

— I want to kill myself . . . Dave, you've spoiled my whole
life . . . I'll kill us all . . . Then my misery is over . . .

— Anne, drop that gun! Don't pull that trigger again. You'll
hit me or Lily if you do!

— Here, Dave . . . Take the gun . . . Oh, God, Dave . . .
Look what you made me do! You've driven me crazy with
your drinking . . . What can I do now?

— Anne, get into your room. Take Lily with you. We've got
to talk. We're in trouble now.

— Mama, don't cry. Please, Mama . . .

— Dave, is she dead?

— I don't know . . . Lily, stop crying. Listen, Anne . . .

— Oh, Dave . . . What can we do? I want to kill myself . . .
They'll take me to jail, won't they?

— Oh, Jumping Jesus . . . Anne, get hold of yourself and
listen. I'm sorry. Honey, I was only fooling around.

— But, Dave, you promised me . . .

— I started drinking this morning. I didn't know what I was
doing.

— You always say that.

— Mama, is Lucy dead?

— Hush, Lily. Anne, we must call a doctor. We've got to
do something.

— Oh, God. I guess so. This is the end for me. Dave, see if
she's dead.

— I'll call Burt Stallman. He's your brother-in-law. He's
our friend. Maybe he can advise us. A bullet wound has to be

reported. Perhaps he'll find a way out for us, hunh? I'll call now. I'll dial . . .

— See if she's dead first, Dave.

— No. I'll phone Burt.

— Dave, I'm so sorry, but it's all your fault. I didn't mean to shoot her.

— Hush, Anne. Sh, Lily . . . That you, Burt? This is Dave speaking. Listen, Burt, you've got to get over to the house at once. Something awful has happened. I can't say it over the phone. Somebody's hurt bad. You got to come and help us. We're in trouble. Somebody's been shot, Burt. Yeah. It's a woman. A colored maid. She's bleeding. It just happened. I shot her, Burt. She's lying on the kitchen floor. I don't know if she's dead or not. Yes, Anne's all right. Sure. Lily's fine. You're coming right away? Good. Thanks, Burt. Ohhh . . . Anne, he's on the way. I told 'im I shot her, Anne.

—No, Dave. We must tell 'im the truth. If you don't, I will.

— Honey, let me handle this. It's all a mistake.

— Mama, is Lucy dead?

— Dave, see if she's still breathing.

— O.K., stay here, both of you.

— Mama, why did you kill her?

— Oh, Lily, I'm so sorry that you have to see and hear all of this. But it's not poor Mama's fault. If I get you out of this, I'm taking you and we're going far, far away. Er, ooaww . . .

— Anne, she seems in a bad way. She's still lying there and there's blood all over the kitchen floor.

— Oh, God . . . I hope she doesn't die . . . Dave, what happened to your hands?

— Oh, that gal scratched 'em. I hadn't noticed . . .

— Dave how could you do this to me? I want to die . . . I should've shot myself, rather than that poor fool of a gal!

— Take it easy, Anne. Look, I did the shooting, see? I'll take the blame. I found her stealing and I asked to halt. She ran. I shot her.

— No, no. I won't lie, Dave. I've been lying for you for years. Now, I stop, no matter what happens.

— Anne, don't be a fool. Let's get our story straight. We can depend on Burt to help us. Now, look, I shot her, see?

— I won't lie again, Dave. I shot her, I killed her . . .

— Anne, maybe one of us'll have to go to jail. I'll go. Then you look after Lily.

— Oh, God, I don't know. I want to die. You made me murder. I ought to have shot you, you fool! You rotten, low-down fool! You drunk—

— Sh. Here's Burt. Anne, remember, I shot her, see?

— Hy, Anne. Hy, Dave. Hey, what's going on?

— Come in, Burt. So glad you came. Look, we caught the maid stealing, see? I shot her . . .

— My God!

— It's a lie, Burt. *I* did it.

— Shut up, Anne.

— But where's the maid?

— She's lying on the kitchen floor, Burt.

— Let's take a look at her. Stay here. I'll do it. This is serious.

— Anne, why in hell can't you let me handle this?

— I'm not going to lie, Dave.

— Mama, will we all go to jail?

— Don't talk, Lily.

— Anne, forgive me. I was drunk. I didn't know what I was doing.

— Don't talk to me, Dave.

— Mama, is Lucy dead?

— We don't know, Lily. Be quiet, darling.

— Sh. Here comes Burt.

— I'm phoning my office to bring material for a blood transfusion.

— Is she hurt bad, Burt?

— Don't really know, Anne. There's been a terrific loss of blood.

— O.K., Burt. Do what you can for her. But remember I shot her.

— Er . . . You shot *her*?

— Yeah, Burt.

— Why, Dave?

— It's a long story, Burt. But try to save her.

— He's lying, Burt. I shot her. And I'll tell why in any courtroom.

— Aw, Anne, keep your mouth shut! Let me do the talking here, will you!

— Listen, you all . . . Let me attend to that transfusion. Stay here. I must talk to you. I don't understand this . . .

— Will she die?

— Don't know, Anne. Maybe not, if we work fast.

— Thank God. If anybody deserves to die, it's me.

— Anne, I beg you to keep quiet. I'll handle this.

— Dave, don't talk to me!

— Come in.

— Anne, Burt, the transfusion has been given.

— Is she living? Will she pull through?

— Er . . . The patient has a chance.

— Where is she?

— I put the patient on your living-room couch.

— Burt, what do we do now? Remember it was all my fault. Anne had nothing to do with shooting her . . .

— Don't lie, Dave! Burt, I shot her—

— Listen, I must ask you two a few questions.

— Yeah. I'm responsible, Burt. Not Anne.

— Where did you find this servant?

— She came this morning in response to an ad we put in the paper.

— Had either of you ever seen her before?

— No.

— Oh, Burt . . . Listen, I wouldn't put it past Dave to have asked her to come here for that job. He wants a black mistress. Aw, maybe that was why she came so early.

— Anne, don't be a goddamn fool! Shut your mouth!

— Listen, Burt . . . It's no longer a secret. Dave has been drinking. For ever so long . . . We can't keep a maid because of it.

— Anne, for God's sake. Think of our child . . .

— Let me talk, Dave.

— Stop, both of you. This is far more complicated than you think. The bullet wound is not so serious. A flesh wound in the thigh. A great loss of blood, but, with care, the patient will be all right.

— Thank God.

— You see, Anne, everything'll be all right.

— But there's something wrong here . . .

— What do you mean, Burt? Give it to us straight. Anne and I can take it. I'm responsible for everything that's happened.

— Well, did you, for some reason, *make him wear that dress?*

— What are you talking about, Burt?

— I don't understand, Burt.

— Didn't you know that . . . that . . . Well, hell, dammit, it's a man you shot.

— Good God, Burt! What are you talking about?

— Burt, I don't get you.

— Who shot that servant is up to you two. But what I'm trying to tell you is that your female servant is a man wearing a woman's dress.

— You're kidding.

— No, Dave. This is straight.

— Lucy is a man?

— Yes, Anne. A man.

— Ooww!

— Don't scream, Anne. Good God, Burt, is this true?

— It's true. He admits it.

— Oh, Dave . . . How is that possible? Aren't you mistaken, Burt?

— Ha, ha. Look, I'm a doctor. The most elementary thing I know is the difference between a man and a woman. That servant lying in your living room is a man—

— Oh, that is why she was so scared this morning in the bathroom . . .

— What're you saying, Anne? Was he with you in the bathroom?

— She . . . he . . . She was sweating, trembling . . .

— Jesus! This makes it simple . . . Did he bother you, Anne?

— Anne, Burt, listen . . . I've got it solved. It's simple. This nigger put on a dress to worm his way into my house to rape my wife! Ha! *See?* Then I detected 'im. I shot 'im in self-defense, shot 'im to protect my honor, my home. That's our answer! I was protecting white womanhood from a nigger rapist impersonating a woman! A rapist who wears a dress is

the worst sort! Any jury'll free me on that. Anne, that's our
case.

— Anne, did this man molest you in any way in that bathroom?

— No, Burt. I'm tired of lying. No, he didn't touch me. If
she is a man, she was scared to death, could barely move. Oh,
I see it all now . . .

— What?

— That's why she was so scared . . . I told her to wash my
back and she could scarcely—

— Then he did touch you! Burt, here's our defense!

— No, Dave. I'll not lie about this. You can't make me
lie.

— Burt, can we find a way of keeping this quiet? Anne won't
help me to do this thing right. Help us to get out of this.
You're our friend. This scandal'll ruin me at the bank.

— I'm a doctor. Normally, I'm required to report things of
this sort.

— But, Burt, this is kind of in the family, see?

— But suppose he reports that he was shot, Dave? Where
does that leave you, and me, and Anne?

— Of course, Burt. You must report it.

— Anne, goddammit, keep your damned mouth shut! Burt,
this nigger came into my house under false pretenses.

— That's true.

— And I defended myself against him!

— Dave, listen. I'm only a doctor. If this man talks to the
police, then you're in a scandal. And I'm in trouble because I
failed to report a gunshot wound. See?

— Burt, talk to 'im. Find out why he's running around in a
woman's dress.

— You want me to try and make a deal with 'im?

— Right. Do that. See how he reacts.

— No, Burt. I'll not lie.

— Shut up, Anne. Let Burt see what he can do.

— O.K., you two stay right here. But, listen, this means my career if it gets out that I did not report it, see?

— Rely on us, Burt.

— Anne, for Christ's sake, stop sobbing like that. Bear up and help me to bail us out of this jam.

— Dave, it's all such a sordid mess. That's all my life's been with you. I don't want to pretend any longer.

— Mama, I'm scared. Will the police come for us?

— Hush, Lily. I wish I had somebody to take you away from all this.

— If you stopped crying, Lily'd be all right, Anne. Burt's doing all he can for us.

— Settle it any way you like, Dave. But I'm not going to lie if anybody asks me any questions. I'M TIRED OF LYING!

— Anne, honey, I'll never touch another drop of whisky.

— You've said that a thousand times, Dave.

— This time I mean it, so help me God.

— Mama, will Lucy die?

— No, thank God.

— Mama, why did you shoot her?

— Lily, don't ask poor Mama any more questions, please . . .

— No, Lily. The police are not coming for anybody. Lucy is all right. Papa was just playing. Anne, stop being morbid with the child.

— Papa, Uncle Burt's knocking at the door.

— Come in, Burt.

— Well, I've tried. Don't know if it'll work or not. Now, you two sit down and listen to me. I don't know if I'm a good judge of character or not. Now, I've talked to this boy. He seems straight, if a man wearing a dress can be described as straight. Now, here's the story he tells me and he tells it in a way that makes me believe 'im. It seems that his wife has just had a baby. He was out of work. The wife could not work because she was sick. They were about to lose their home. He was desperate. He saw your ad. He put on his wife's dress, her shoes, took her purse, assumed her name, and came here. Then this happened.

— But he violated the law when he did that, Burt.

— True, Dave. But you said that you didn't want any publicity, didn't you? Anne says that she's not going to say that he bothered her.

— Right, Burt. I won't lie.

— O.K., Burt. I'm reasonable. Burt, what would that nigger take to forget all this?

— I've already asked him that. He says if you pay his doctor's bill and give him two hundred dollars, he'll forget it. That is, if Anne doesn't wish to prefer charges against him.

— I don't. He did not touch me.

— Burt, will that nigger sign a paper to that effect? Will he accept two hundred dollars for being shot?

— He's signed it. Here it is. But I'll not give you this paper unless you give me your check.

— Hell, yes. Right now. I'll write it out. See, Anne? It's all over.

— It's not over for me.

— Aw, honey, don't be like that . . . Here, Burt, give 'im that check and get 'im out of the house, quick. That settles it, hunh?

— Right. But he insists on borrowing a suit of your clothes

to go home in. He can't walk. His suit is hidden in his coal house.

— Oh, O.K. give 'im something from my clothes closet. But get 'im out of here quick.

— Right. Be right back, in about an hour. I'm taking him to his house.

— Thank God, Burt. Anne, it's all over. Baby, forgive me. I'm sorry.

— Dave, I can't go on like this.

— Aw, hell, Anne. Come on; be a sport.

— I've been a sport for eight years with you. I'm tired. This is the end.

— Anne, darling, I need your sympathy now. We weathered it. Everything came out all right. Think of the danger you were in with a nigger man wearing a dress in the house.

— Nothing's all right, Dave. I'm going to my mother. I'm taking Lily.

— Anne, you just can't leave me like that.

— I'm leaving, Dave.

— No, Oh, God, no, Anne. Don't say that.

— I can't help it, Dave.

— If you leave me, I'll get plastered and stay plastered for a month.

— Oh, Dave.

— Say you'll stay, Anne.

— Oh, God . . . I'll have to stay, I guess.

— Good girl. I'll change. You'll see. Sh. Look, there's Burt leading that nigger to his car. He looks pretty weak to me. Hope he doesn't die. There. They're driving off. Thank God, it's over, Anne.

— It's not over for me, Dave. Not as long as you drink, it'll never be over.

— Baby, I swear I'm on the wagon from now on.

— You always say that.

— Who is it?

— Open the door. We've got your husband here.

— Oh, God! What happened? CARL! CARL! You're sick . . .

— Now, Lucy, take it easy. I'm all right.

— You're hurt. What happened?

— You'd better get your husband in bed right away. He's been wounded.

— Who did it? How'd it happen?

— He'll tell you about it. First, let's get him to bed.

— Come in, come in.

— Oh, Papa.

— Hi, Henry.

— You're sick, Papa?

— No, Henry. Just hurt a bit. Nothing to worry about.

— Right through that door, sir.

— O.K. Now, let's ease him onto the bed. That's it. O.K. boy?

— I'm all right.

— Have you any pain?

— No, sir.

— Now, keep in bed for at least a week. And if you get any temperature, have your wife phone me, see?

— Yes, sir.

— Now, my friends are depending upon you to do what you promised. I'll come whenever it's necessary. You'll be up and about soon.

— Yes, sir. Thank you, sir.

— If you can't sleep, then here's some pills. Take one every two hours.

— Thank you, sir.

— I'll pass by and take a look at you tomorrow.

— Yes, sir. Thank you, sir.

— And, boy, never do that again. This time you were lucky.

— No, sir. It'll never happen again. Lucy, go to the door with the doctor.

— Yes, Carl. Do we owe him anything?

— You owe me nothing. Just keep your husband quiet.

— Yes, sir.

— You feel better, Papa?

— Sure, Henry. I'm fine. How're you?

— All right, Mama was crying—

— I know. How's the baby?

— She's sleeping, Papa. Are you hurt bad, Papa?

— No. It's nothing, son. Have you been helping Mama?

— Sure. We—

— Carl, I *told* you not to do it.

— What did Papa do, Mama?

— It's none of your business, Henry. Now, Carl, what happened?

— Listen, Lucy, don't ask me any questions. I'm not going to tell you anything. I'm all right. Everything's all right. Look. Here's the money to pay for the house. Our problem's solved. Two hundred dollars.

— Oh, God! But, Carl, where'd you get it from?

— It's a gift.

— You robbed something or somebody? You can tell me . . .

— No, no. Lucy, for once, I'm asking you not to ask me any questions. I gave my word I wouldn't talk. So don't ask me anything. In the morning, you take that check to the bank and get it cashed.

— I don't understand.

— You don't need to. The house is saved. We can eat.

— What did you do?

— I said not to ask me anything!

— But the police will come for you!

— No, they won't.

— I knew something bad would happen when you left—

— Nothing bad's happened. I just hurt my leg, that's all.

— But how did you hurt it? Where? When?

— Lucy, shut up now.

— Did you really wear my dress?

— Er, yeah. But forget that.

— Then where is it?

— Oh, I don't know. I lost it—

— What happened?

— Stop hammering at me, honey. I'll buy you another dress.

— Carl, is this check real? Is it good?

— It's as good as gold. Now, what are you crying for? Aw, Lucy . . . Now, Henry, stop that bawling. Look, you've gone and awakened the baby and she's crying too. Goddammit, everybody's crying. Stop! I tell you, stop! Aw, Lucy . . . Goddammit, I can't help but cry too if all of you are crying . . . Oooouaw . . .

— I'm sorry, Carl. Henry, see about the baby and stop crying. We'll make Papa sick like that.

— Y-yessum, Mama.

— Carl, why did somebody give you two hundred dollars?

— I worked for it.

— Cooking?

— Lucy, it was all kinds of work.

— In a home?

— Yeah.

— The wife was there?

— Lucy, don't ask me any more questions!

— Was she pleased with your work?

— Oh, hell, Lucy! Yes, yes! Everybody was pleased! . . . That's why I got those two hundred dollars! Now, stop questioning me.

— Well, if you don't want to tell me, what can I do? But there's one thing I know: wearing that dress got you into trouble, didn't it?

— Yep. In a way, yeah.

— Carl, never—Promise me you'll never do anything like that again.

— Ha, ha, Lucy, you don't have to ask. I was a woman for almost six hours and it almost killed me. Two hours after I put that dress on I thought I was going crazy.

— But, Carl, I warned you. It's not easy for a man to act like a woman.

— Gosh, Lucy, how do you women learn it?

— Honey, it's instinct.

— Guess you're right. I didn't know it was so hard.

— Carl, never let me see you in a dress again. I almost died when I awakened and found you gone.

— You don't have to beg me, darling. I wouldn't be caught dead again in a dress.

— I was on the verge of going to the police to tell 'em.

— Oh, God! Glad you didn't do that.

— Mama, Tina's crying for her bottle.

— Carl, you could've been killed.

— Lucy, now don't go crying like that again!

— Papa, why is Mama crying so?

— Henry, don't you go crying now. Aw, God! The whole bunch of you are crying . . . Lucy, Henry . . . Aw, Christ, if you all cry like that, you make me cry . . . Oooouuwa!

MAN, GOD AIN'T

LIKE THAT . . .

— John, look! We're entering the jungle! We're surrounded by solid walls of green choked with twisting creepers . . .

— Nature's God here, Elsie.

— What was that? I heard a scream.

— Some wild animal, I guess.

— Lord, I'd hate to be caught in that jungle at night.

— Elsie, the sun can't get down through those leaves, so it's always night in the jungle . . . Listen. Hear those tom-toms?

— Aw, John, it's so romantic and . . . mysterious! Darling, what does living in a jungle do to people?

— My guess is that this jungle is to black folks what the Place de la Concorde is to us in Paris.

— John, darling.

— Yes, Elsie.

— Aren't you glad we left Paris?

— Oh, of course, honey.

— You don't say that like you mean it.

— Look. We agreed we wouldn't argue—

— I'm not arguing, sweet. But, John, I *must* know. I took you away from that awful Odile Dufour woman and pestered you to come out here. Are you glad? Do you feel you'll be able to paint?

— I guess so. We're together. Isn't that enough?

— I love you, John.

— Sure, honey. Hmnn . . . Be careful! I can't drive when you kiss me . . .

— Hmnnn . . . Look. The sky's getting dark.

— Yeah. Seems like rain. This weather changes every quarter of an hour . . . Look at those Africans covered with calico cloths walking barefooted at the edges of the road. Oh, I'll paint here!

— Where do you think they're all going, John?

— Shopping. Visiting. Maybe boy calling on girl. Gosh, it's getting pitch-black. Better put on my headlights.

— That clap of thunder broke just above the car.

— Oops! There's the rain! A waterfall! Better put on my windshield wipers. Look at that lightning! . . .

— Not too fast, John! There're people at the side of the road . . .

— Damn! It's slippery; the road's turning to mud before my eyes! Hell, I'm skidding. We don't want to land in a ditch—

— You mean the Africans'll catch us and eat us?

— No, honey. Ha ha! Elsie, these savages think we're gods.

— John, be careful! We're skidding! Are we far from Kumasi?

— About twenty miles or so.

— This is like flying through a storm of water!

— Honey, you said you wanted to see Africa. Well, **this is** it.

— John, do be careful. You are off the road! There're people out there . . . Darling, pull up and wait till the rain stops . . .

— It's all right. The air's clearing a bit now. I can pick up speed—

— John, stop! You *hit* somebody!

— Oh, goddamn!

— Stop! We hit a man! He's lying in the ditch! Oh, God!

— I'm skidding . . . All right, Elsie. Take it easy. You can't hurt these baboons . . . You stay in the car and I'll get out and see how he is . . . No! Don't get out, Elsie!

— But suppose he's hurt?

— Stay in the car! You'll get soaked to the skin in this storm! Oh, all right . . .

— John, he's not moving! He's bleeding!

— His head's gashed . . . Say, boy! Did I hit you? Can't you hear me? Are you hurt?

— Aaaaooooow . . . My head, Massa!

— Can you stand? No? I'll lift you. Elsie, we've got to get 'im to a doctor.

— Is he badly hurt, John?

— How do I know? Let's get 'im into the car, Elsie. Easy there, boy. Lie down. There. Feel better?

— Aw, so sorry, Massa.

— Hunh? Sorry? Sorry about what?

— So sorry my head hurt Massa's car.

— What? Ha ha!

— Is he delirious, John?

— No. Ha ha! You can't hurt these monkeys. Let's get to

Kumasi. Bet he dented my fender more'n he did his thick skull.

— John, I'm shaking . . . Those damn tom-toms!

— The rain's almost stopped. I'll step on it.

— Not too fast, John!

— Elsie, let me drive! If you hadn't been yapping at me, I wouldn't've hit that goddamn nigger!

— Don't be nervous, darling. Shh! What's he saying?

— Ha ha! He's singing . . .

> *I belong to Jesus;*
> *I am not my own;*
> *All I have and all I am,*
> *Shall be His alone . . .*

— You see, Elsie? I told you that baboon wasn't hurt.

— What a voice he's got, John!

— How's your skull, boy?

— It fine, Massa. Just bleeding a little.

— O.K. We're taking you to a doctor. Sing some more . . .

— Yessar, Massa.

> *I belong to Jesus;*
> *He is Lord and King,*
> *Reigning in my inmost heart,*
> *Over ev'rything . . .*

— Where'd you learn to sing that, boy?

— Mission church, sar. Massa, my blood's dirtying up your fine car.

— Ha ha! Don't worry. It'll wash out.

— John, hurry. He's bleeding like a stuck pig.

— Elsie, listen . . . He's singing again.

> *Sin no more, thy soul is free,*
> *Christ has died to ransom thee;*

Now the power of sin is o'er.
Jesus bids thee sin no more . . .

— John, his singing blends with the jungle tom-toms!
— Ha ha! He's fantastic. Say, boy, where do you live?
— Got no home, Massa. Go Kumasi looking for work.
— What kind of work do you do?
— Cook, houseboy, yardboy, Massa.
— Still dirtying up my car?
— Yessar. So sorry, Massa.
— O.K. You know a doctor in Kumasi?
— Massa find juju man. Juju man cures folks.
— But I thought you were a Christian . . .
— I is, Massa.
— All right. Sing some more for us, boy . . . Did he pass out?
— John, his eyes are closed. He's lying in a pool of blood. You think he's dead?
— We're in the city now. We'll find a doctor for our black-bird. Look! There's a doctor's sign . . . Elsie, stay in the car while I—
— No! I'm coming with you, John. I won't stay with that dead thing!
— Aw, Elsie, he's not dead. Better feel for his pulse. Never felt for a nigger's pulse before . . . Yeah; here it 'tis . . . He's O.K., Elsie. Just passed out. Now, you stay in the car while I—
— I'm coming with you, John!
— Oh, all right. If you insist.

— You think he'll be all right, Doctor?
— Well, I took ten stitches in his scalp. Maybe he's got a slight concussion, but I'd have to X ray 'im to be sure. Put 'im

to bed for a few days. You can take 'im to your car now; my yardboy cleaned it out. That'll be two pounds, please.

— Here you are, Doctor. Gosh, niggers are expensive—

— So sorry, Massa. Pay Massa back . . .

— Good-by, Doctor. Come on, boy. By the way, what's your name?

— They call me Babu, Massa.

— John, are we going to take 'im to a hospital?

— No, Elsie. They'd report us to the police. There'd be complications. We'll have to take him with us.

— We can put 'im up at Dupree's. Dupree's boys can wait on 'im.

— Here's the car, boy. Lie down on the back seat. Don't talk.

— Yessar, Massa.

— What luck! I got a whole, live nigger to look after . . .

— Paint 'im, John! Make 'im pay his way, pose for you!

— Never painted a nigger before . . . He said he could cook. Say, maybe he'll come in handy. Goddamn . . . He's singing again.

> I am coming to the cross;
> I am poor and weak, and blind;
> I am counting on the cross,
> I shall full salvation find . . .

— I think he'll pull through, John.

— We've got the white man's burden, Elsie. Ha ha!

— Hold still, Babu. I'm almost through . . . I know it's hard to pose like that. But when the sun's full in your face, I see the *real* color of your skin. It's strange . . .

— Babu black, Massa.

— . . . and red and blue and green and yellow . . .

— Yessar, Massa. Ha ha!

— What're you laughing at, Babu?

— Babu wonder how black folks look to Massa.

— Oh . . . Well, Babu, when I first came here, your people looked odd to me. But now, by God, they all look *white*.

— Ha ha! Babu understand, Massa. Sometime Babu like to see white man's land.

— Hmmnnn . . . Maybe you will some day. But why?

— White man, he powerful, Massa.

— Don't move, Babu . . . There's a shade of yellow on your nose. I paint you like you sing, Babu. Sing; keep time with the tom-toms . . .

> *Alas! and did my Savior bleed,*
> *And did my Sovereign die?*
> *Would he devote that sacred head*
> *For such a worm as I?*

— Somebody knocking, Massa.

— It's me, John. Elsie.

— Come in, darling. I'm almost through.

— John, it's the most dazzling thing you've ever created!

— . . . must put a touch of green on Babu's cheek. Sing, Babu! It helps me . . .

> *At the cross, at the cross,*
> *Where I first saw the light,*
> *And the burden of my heart rolled away,*
> *It was there by faith I received*
> *   my sight,*
> *And now I am happy all the day . . .*

— There. Finished. How do you feel, boy? Tired?

— Nawsar, Massa. But Babu's neck ache.

— How do you like your portrait, Babu?

— Missus, Massa make Babu look like black burning rose!

— Ha ha! Babu you sound like an art critic . . . Goddammit, I'm pooped . . . I could eat a cow. How's chop, Babu?

— Chop quick, Massa.

— I hope you didn't cook that roast beef too much.

— Ha ha! No roast beef, Massa. Chicken chop for lunch.

— No! Goddammit! I told you *not* to buy chicken! I asked for roast beef! Did you forget, you blockhead?

— Nawsar, Massa. Babu no forget.

— Then why in hell did you buy chicken?

— Sorry, Massa. Babu's fault. It's Babu's religion, Massa.

— Religion? Your religion won't let you buy roast beef?

— Babu buy chicken for Babu's dead papa.

— Oh, God! What in hell has your dead papa to do with it?

— Babu buy chicken to make little sacrifice for dead papa.

— Oh, Lord, John . . . it's juju, jungle religion.

— Babu sorry, Massa. But it Massa's fault—

— My fault? Did I make you buy chicken, you ape?

— Babu's head hit Massa's car. Babu's blood make sacrifice to Massa and Massa ask Babu to work. Babu then buy chickens and cut chickens' throats and let blood run to Babu's dead papa to say thanks to God. Babu bless Massa with blood.

— Aw, John, this'll drive me crazy!

— Ha ha! Why in hell didn't you tell me this, boy?

— Sacrifice chicken good to eat. Massa come to chop?

— Get that damned chicken on the table, and quick!

— Yessar, Massa.

— Ha ha! I buy the chickens and he sacrifices them to thank me for my car hitting 'im; then he makes me eat chicken every day so that he can tell his dead papa to tell God that he was grateful for my car hitting 'im . . . Jungle logic! Ha ha! Well, honey, how do you like my show?

— You mean that you're through, John?

— Finished. I've done my black period.

— John, it's a choir of holy color!

— Elsie, you're looking at my Paris show. And, honey, look at *your* portraits. Isn't that a marvelous light falling on your breasts . . . Truth's beauty and beauty's truth; that's all I know and all I need to know. Thanks to you, darling.

— And Babu? Remember you came here only to paint landscapes. You hit Babu . . . Then you started painting black people . . .

— Out of Babu's songs and black skin I've produced forty paintings.

— John, Paris will go wild when they see how you painted black people—

— Telegram for Massa.

— Thanks, Babu. Is that chicken about ready?

— Wait small, Massa. Chop ready quick.

— Goddamn you, Babu. You brought me luck. Look at my work . . .

— That's 'cause Massa like Jesus.

— Why in hell do you say that?

— Massa got red beard and blue eyes like Jesus.

— But how do you know Jesus had a red beard and blue eyes?

— Babu see Jesus picture in Sunday school book, Massa.

— Ha ha! O.K., Babu. Get that sacrifice on the table.

— Yessar, Massa.

— Tom-toms and chickens'll be the death of us. What's in this telegram? Elsie, Dupree's due here right after lunch!

— No! I thought he was in London?

— Business brought 'im back. Honey, our stay is over . . . We'll have to move. Damn glad my work's finished.

— But what're we going to do, John? Go to a hotel?

— Honey, I want to confess I have a longing for Paris—

— Oh, yes! John, I've had enough of the jungle! Let's go!

— Then that settles it. We're Paris bound. I'll have my show in September. We'll ship the car by freight and take a plane from Accra . . . Elsie, I've got a wild idea . . .

— What is it, John?

— Let's take Babu back to Paris with us.

— What're you talking about? Take *Babu?*

— Sure. It's a whim. But why not?

— But what'll Babu do in Paris?

— He'll work for us. Cook, clean, like he does here. He's cheap, honest. He sings and he'll be loads of fun with his rainbow robe and wild religion—

— But, John, suppose he starts sacrificing chickens in Paris?

— Ha ha! That'd be a *sensation!*

— Aw, John . . . I . . . don't know.

— Come on, Elsie. Don't be a kill-joy. I didn't buck you when you wanted me to leave Odile Dufour . . . Let's take Babu to Paris.

— But Babu's blood religion frightens me—

— He's just a child, honey. Listen. Babu once worked in the Ivory Coast and he jabbers a bit of French. He'll be at home in Paris. And, honey, imagine Babu answering the door and serving cocktails in his robe . . . Ha ha!

— Well . . . You think Babu'd want to go?

— Ha ha! Babu'd follow us to the end of the world.

— I admit he'd solve our servant problem. He'd be a lot cheaper than those sassy French maids.

— Chop ready, Massa, Missus!

— Let's eat. I'll ask 'im at lunch, hunh? Ha ha!

— You can serve the coffee now, Babu. And, right after lunch, I want you to pack up all our things.

— Massa go 'way?

— That's it. We're leaving this afternoon.

— Aw, Massa . . . Babu so sorry. 'Scuse me, Massa . . .

— John, he's crying like a baby . . .

— What're you bawling about, boy?

— Babu want to work for Massa and Missus.

— You really mean that, boy?

— Yessar, M-m-massa . . .

— All right. How'd you like to come to Paris with us?

— M-m-massa . . . Oh . . . Ohhh . . .

—Watch out, you monkey! You're spilling that coffee!

— So sorry, Massa. Aw, Massa, Babu thank you! Babu thank papa! Papa, oh, thank you!

— What're you talking about, Babu?

— Babu thank his dead papa 'cause Babu ask papa to ask Massa to take Babu when Massa go—

— John, he's been praying to go with us.

— Massa, Babu want to ask small favor.

— What do you want, boy?

— Babu want five shillings—

— What for?

— Babu buy chicken to make thanks to dead papa—

— Ha ha! All right, boy. Now, listen . . . In Paris you work for us just like you work here. Tomorrow I'll fix up your passport and ticket. O.K.? Now, start packing.

— Yessar, Massa.

— John, darling. I . . . You really think we ought to? His religion makes me shudder . . .

— It's nothing. I'll cure 'im of that. Listen. He's singing . . .

Oh! clap your hands, mountains,
Ye valleys, resound!

Oh! leap for joy, fountains,
  Ye hills, catch the sound . . .

— How're you doing, Babu?

— Babu fine, Massa.

— We're in the air now. You can unbuckle your seat belt.

— Babu keep belt so Babu won't fall, Massa.

— Ha ha! All right. If it makes you feel better.

— John, he's terrified. Try to calm him a little . . .

— Babu, look out of your window. See all that jungle?

— Yessar, Massa. Black man's country. Babu's home. Babu see mud houses black people live in.

— Now look 'way over there . . . See that sparkle? We're coming to the Sahara. Relax, Babu. You're safe now.

— Babu fine, Massa. Babu up near God. Babu feel like Him.

— Yeah? Ha ha! What does He feel like, Babu?

— He make Babu scared. That's how Babu know He up here. Massa, Babu want to ask small question.

— Yes? What is it, Babu?

— There one God for everybody, Massa?

— Of course, Babu. There's only *one* God.

— And He white, Massa?

— Well, Babu, God really has no color—

— But Sunday school book show God white, Massa.

— Babu, yellow folks say God's yellow; black folks say He's black; brown folks say He's brown; and white folks say He's white . . .

— But He *really* white, ain't He, Massa? White like Massa?

— Why do you say that, Babu?

— White God powerful. He let white man fly.

— But you *believe* in Him, don't you, Babu?

— Yessar, Massa. God real, like you, Massa.

— No. Babu. You can't see God.

— People saw Jesus, Massa. They killed 'Im and He rose from the dead.

— Yes. But that was just *one* time. God's not on earth now . . . Go to sleep, Babu.

— Babu no sleepy, Massa. Babu look at God's big world . . .

— John, I see the Tour Eiffel!

— We're over Paris now. We'll land soon. Tired, Babu?

— Babu fine, Massa.

— Now, Babu, friends are meeting us. You come home with us. You'll have a room high up in the top of the house, near God—

— Oh, John! Stop teasing him!

— Just be calm, Babu, like you were in Africa. You'll have a stove and a little bed—

— Aw, Massa, that like Heaven!

— We're coming down. Fasten your seat belt, Babu.

— Belt already fastened . . . Massa! Plane falling!

— Sh! It's nothing. We're hitting air currents; that's all.

— God scares Babu!

— Babu, Missus wants you to always wear your lovely robe in Paris.

— Y-yessum, M-missus.

— Elsie, Babu's your pet. Take over his training—

— Sh! He'll hear you. Babu, whisper—hum us a song . . .

> Repeat the story o'er and o'er,
> Of grace so full and free;
> I love to hear it more and more,
> Since grace has rescued me . . .

— John! Elsie!

— Hi, Marcel! It's good of you to meet us!

— I got your cable this morning. But you're back early.

— Yes. John'll tell you all about it . . .

— That African sun burnt you both *brown!* Had a smooth flight?

— Wonderful, Marcel. I've got a crate of forty paintings—

— You monster! Africa really hit you, hunh?

— *Monsieur sont-ce là vos baggages?*

— *Oui, monsieur. Merci.* Say, Marcel, we brought an African friend back with us . . . Marcel, meet Babu . . .

— You . . . *Oh!* You think you'll like Paris, boy?

— Ha ha! Yessar, Massa. Paris God's city.

— *Mon Dieu* . . . Wait 'til you see what happens in this town. Your first time out of the bush?

— Yessar, Massa. Babu glad to see white man's land.

— Well, come along and watch your step.

— Marcel, what do you think of his robe?

— Elsie, he looks like the sunrise . . . He'll stop the traffic. Say, John, I haven't room in my car for you, Elsie, that boy, your suitcases and your crate . . . What'll we do?

— I'll send Babu by taxi. Babu?

— Yessar, Massa.

— Here's a thousand francs. You'll have to take a cab. Bring the crate along.

— Yessar, Massa.

— Taxi! Here's one . . . Hop in. Hang onto that crate, boy. *Monsieur, c'est 25 rue de Rennes . . . Laissez-le descendre là bas.*

— *Très bien, monsieur.*

— John, Babu's scared to death . . .

— He'll be all right. We're following you in the car, Babu. When the driver lets you out, pay 'im and wait for us on the sidewalk.

— Yessar, Massa. Massa coming quick?

— Yes. We'll be right behind you. Take care of that crate! Marcel, the taxi's pulling out. Come on; let's follow it . . .

— Aw, hell! That red light caught me.

— That's nothing. Babu'll be waiting.

— My friends, where in hell did you find *him?*

— Ha, ha! Smack in the middle of the jungle. It's a long story, Marcel.

— But what are you-all going to do with 'im?

— He's going to work for us: cook, clean, wash . . .

— If you're so keen on excitement, why didn't you bring back a crocodile?

— Ha ha! Marcel, crocodiles are dangerous. Babu's got tom-toms in his heart and you should hear 'im sing. He sends you. And, Marcel, he sacrifices chickens to his god—

— No!

— I swear. Ask Elsie.

— John, tell Marcel how we met Babu.

— We were driving through a storm one afternoon in the jungle . . . God, I can still hear those tom-toms . . .

— Here we are, John. But where's your boy? I don't see 'im.

— His taxi got stuck in the traffic, no doubt.

— Good Lord, John! He's got your paintings!

— Oh, he'll be along, Elsie. Let's take the suitcases out . . . All the same, where the hell is that Babu?

— John! John! The crate's here in the lobby!

— What? By God, you're right . . . Then where's that boy? Marcel, ask the *concierge* if she's seen him.

— Sure. *Madame! Madame!*

— *Aw, bonjour, messieurs, dame! Avez-vous eu un bon voyage?*

— *Oui, madame.* Did you see a black boy around here wearing a robe?

— *Oui, monsieur.* He was here; he left this crate. He was funny . . . He stood on the sidewalk in his red robe singing—

— Aw, John, it *starts* . . . *We shouldn't've brought 'im!*

— Goddammit, Elsie! Stop nagging me! You heckle every step I make . . . To please you, I left Odile. Now, you don't want me to hire Babu . . .

— Forgive me, John. Don't be nervous . . .

— *Madame,* how long has that boy been gone?

— Oh, about ten minutes, I think.

— John, listen . . . You and Elsie take your things up. I'll look in the bar next door. I'll bet that boy's having a drink . . .

— Thanks, Marcel. Elsie, where do you reckon that fool went?

— He he! Maybe a woman picked 'im up.

— Don't be stupid, Elsie. Babu's too religious for that.

— The police'll be sure to grab a black man singing hymns in a bright robe . . .

— That's Marcel at the door. Come in, Marcel. You see 'im?

— No sign of hide or hair of 'im.

— What could've happened? You remember the number of that taxi?

— No. Ha ha! I warned you. You should've brought a crocodile!

— Marcel, this is serious . . . John, if Babu's not here in two hours, we should call the police.

— Oh, don't be hysterical, Elsie!

— Say, John, how does this boy act?

— Well, Marcel, he talks religion, sings hymns . . . Give 'im a chance, and he'll sacrifice a chicken—

— You wanted excitement. Well, you got it. Ha ha!

— Stop joking, Marcel! That boy's lost . . .

— Look, my friends . . . If that boy's got a taste for blood, then you'd better call the police and report him missing if he doesn't show up soon . . .

— Sit down, please, sir. Any news of Babu?

— *Merci, monsieur, dame* . . . No, there are no new developments in the Babu case since you last talked to us three days ago. No hotel register has his name; we've scoured the Latin Quarter bars and cafés, and the hangouts of Arabs and foreigners. He's in no hospital, neither is he in the morgue. You told us that he was deeply religious; well, we've had all the churches in the city, both Catholic and Protestant, watched, but he's not been seen in any of them. We've interviewed women of the streets, but none of them recalls having had such a customer. We've telegraphed cities far from Paris without results. A check of air and shipping lines reveals that he has not left the country. And you have his passport . . . The only thing left is to dredge the Seine; maybe he was robbed, slain, and tossed in; or maybe he fell or jumped in . . .

— Oh, God! Poor Babu! John, what can we do?

— Elsie, you were right. I shouldn't've brought 'im here.

— *Monsieur,* did he leave any belongings behind?

— Just a cheap suitcase. You want to see it? I'll get it.

— Mr. Officer, my husband's an artist. He's been so worried about this boy's disappearance that he's neglected his art show—

— Aw, *monsieur* is an artist?

— Here's the suitcase. Shall I open it, sir?

— Yes.

— Well, here're his robes, a bottle of palm wine, a Bible,

hymn books, and a big knife. What's this? A skeleton! Good Lord! Here's the skull . . . Ughh!

— *Monsieur*, let me see those bones. They're *human!*

—John, do you think Babu's killed anybody?

— Did he bring these bones with him from Africa, *monsieur?*

— I don't know. We never saw 'em before.

— *Monsieur, dame* . . . what religion did this boy profess?

— Well, he said he was a Methodist. But he practiced his tribal religion too.

— John, why did you insist upon bringing him here?

— Shut up, Elsie. We've got to find 'im—

— Did this boy kill any goats or chickens when he worked for you in Africa?

— Well, yes. He sacrificed chickens—

— Aw, *monsieur, dame,* I'm willing to hazard a guess. These are the bones of the boy's dead father.

— Oh, how horrible!

— You see, *monsieur*, the boy's father's not really dead for him. He prays and makes sacrifices to these bones. We've had cases like this before.

— John, get those bones *out* of here!

— Elsie, stop shouting! But, *monsieur,* do you think Babu makes human sacrifices too?

— I don't think so . . . People'd be missed, you see. These bones put an entirely different aspect on this case.

— I don't understand.

— If he's alive, he'll return to this suitcase. These bones are his most precious possession.

— I wish that black creature'd never return!

— Elsie, for God's sake, shut up!

— John, send Babu back to Africa the moment you find him!

— Now, wait a minute—

— Either he goes or I go!

— *Monsieur, dame,* I must make my report. Give us a ring the moment he returns. I'm sure he will.

— We shall. Good-by, sir.

— *Au revoir, monsieur, dame.*

— John, listen—

— Stop plaguing me! You're nuts! These bones are the playthings of a child! There's nothing to be upset about—

— But old bones are dangerous! Think of the germs—

— No! They're clean as a whistle. Seems they've been waxed and polished.

— I don't care. You buy Babu's ticket at once!

— Elsie, I'm responsible for that boy! I can't send him packing unless I give 'im a few months' pay, and I haven't got it . . . Be reasonable. I'll send 'im off, but I must see that he's taken care of . . . Ha ha! Wait 'til Marcel hears about *this.*

— John, you've got to get rid of 'im.

— Aw, Elsie, this is *fun!* Ha ha!

— It's not my kind of fun!

— Darling, another slice of meat?

— No, thanks, Elsie. I'm not really hungry.

— There's some marrow in that bone—

— Elsie, stop being morbid . . . Goddamn that Babu . . . I'll never hear the last of 'im. It's been a month since he vanished.

— Darling, your show opens in an hour. Let's not talk of Babu. Some salad?

— No.

— But, darling, you're not eating . . .

— Just give me a cup of black coffee, Elsie. I'm all unstrung. I work like hell to create a show, then the critics must sit in judgment on me. Those critics have no notion of how I sweated to create those paintings in that jungle. They come to my work from the *outside*, and what they say can make or break me. It's not *fair!*

— John, your work'll stun the critics. You mark my word.

— I dunno. Critics stand outside of your world—how can they know the meaning of what one does? Critics are cruel . . . I'm in *one* world and they're in *another* . . . Shhh!

> *My hope is built on nothing less*
> *Than Jesus' blood and righteousness;*
> *I dare not trust the sweetest frame,*
> *But wholly lean on Jesus' name . . .*

— Open the window, John!

— Good Lord! Sounds like—!

> *On Christ, the Solid Rock I stand;*
> *All other ground is sinking sand,*
> *All other ground is sinking sand . . .*

— It's that crazy Babu!

— John call 'im and give 'im his passport and ticket, now!

— People are opening their windows . . . BABU!

— Yessar, Massa!

— *Come up here at once!*

— Yessar, Massa!

— John, listen . . . Don't be sentimental. Don't let 'im sway you. Send 'im off, quick! Your show's opening . . .

— Right, Elsie.

— Here he is . . . Come in, Babu.

— Thank you, Missus. How you, Massa?

— Babu, where in hell have you been?

— Babu sorry, Massa. Babu been about papa's business—

— Don't let 'im snare you with that crazy talk, John!

— Boy, don't you know the police are looking for you?

— Police? Babu ain't bad, Massa. Babu Christian.

— Get your suitcase, you black rascal, and get out!

— You worried us sick, Babu. Where did you hide?

— Babu no hide, Missus. Babu walk streets—

— Where's your robe? How'd you buy that suit you got on?

— Babu got little money—

— You're lying! You've been missing a month! Why did you run off?

— Babu no run, Massa. Babu went into white man's jungle—

— Stop that goddamn baby talk! How'd you eat? Where'd you sleep? You weren't in a hotel . . .

— Babu got money saved from Africa, Massa. Babu no wear African clothes now. Babu Christian—

— The police said that you weren't in a hotel!

— Babu sleep in movies, Massa. Babu look at white man's Heaven . . .

— You batty ape! You'll drive me crazy . . . Elsie, my show's opening now. Get along and tell Fineberg I'll be there in a minute. I've got to settle with Babu now.

— All right, John. But hurry. Do what you promised, huh?

— Sure, honey.

— Good-by. Babu, go home. Obey Massa.

— Good-by, Missus. But Babu home—

— Oh, God! Get rid of 'im. John!

— Sit down, Babu.

— Yessar, Massa.

— What in hell are you grinning at me for?

— Everything all right now, Massa. Babu see real good.

— Hell, we thought you were dead, boy.

— Babu no die now, Massa. Babu understand now.

— Are you trying to make a joke? Or make fun of me?

— Nawsar, Massa. Babu real serious. Babu man now. Babu got deep faith. Babu tell Massa everything—

—Are you sure you haven't stolen anything from anybody?

— Oh, Massa. Babu no steal. Babu Christian.

— Were you with a woman?

— Nawsar, Massa. Babu like saint. Babu look at God's city.

— Stop that jabbering! WHERE WERE YOU? Don't you know that I'm responsible for you?

— Babu know God loves us all—

— Shut up, you addled-brained fool! Listen . . . I've got to tell you something. It's going to be hard on you. I was wrong to bring you here . . . STOP GRINNING AT ME! What I'll tell you will wipe that grin off your black face!

— Babu know Massa never drive Babu 'way.

— Oh! You're cocky, eh? Well, I'm shipping you home!

— Babu ready for test, Massa.

— What test? Are you crazy? What're you talking about?

— Babu found God, Massa. And Babu can prove it.

— Ha ha! Forget your black magic. Your jungle juju won't work on me . . .

— Babu got white magic now, Massa. Babu Christian.

— You're lying! Your suitcase is full of human bones—

— Babu no need bones now, Massa.

— Whose bones are they? Your dead papa's?

— Yessar, Massa. But they no good now. Babu see real God—

— You pray and make sacrifices to those bones, don't you?

— Babu used to, Massa. But not now.

— You liar! You still do it! I see it in your face!

— Babu no lie. Babu found true God. Babu serve Massa now.

— You're trying to flatter me. That's how you hooked me into bringing you here in the first place, always bowing, grinning—

— Babu wait for test, Massa.

— You can't make me change my mind. Here's your ticket and passport. There's a plane at—

— Babu believe in Massa!

— Shut up! Take your bones and catch that night plane!

— Babu no leave! Babu prove God!

— Get out or I'll call the police!

— Babu tell Massa what Babu found in God's city when Babu walk night and day. But, Massa, Babu first want to ask question.

— I see. I have to humor you like a child. Be quick. I've got to get to my show.

— Babu went to Massa's Chambre des Députés . . .

— What? Ask your question . . .

— Babu went to Massa's Palais du Sénat.

— Aw, I understand now why the police couldn't find you . . .

— Babu went to Massa's Versailles.

— Why are you telling me all this?

— Now, Babu want to know where white man get all those fine buildings—

— You fool! You're wasting my time! You're a grown-up child, that's all. The white man *built* those buildings.

— No. Massa no tell Babu truth.

— Why are you grinning at me? I am telling you the truth.

— Massa fooling Babu!

— You're out of your mind. You wouldn't know the truth if you heard it.

— Massa tease Babu. Test Babu, Massa. Babu ready.

— All right, you monkey. Perhaps you'll tell me where the white man got his buildings from . . .

— Black man live in mud hut in jungle. White man live in stone building in city. Why, Massa?

ou, you can't understand all this. It's too much for
Go home. You'll be happy there. I'll take you to the
ne—

— Babu no leave Paris till Babu pass test. Now, Massa,
tell Babu about the buildings.

—Get out of here!

— Babu no move, Massa!

— Babu, listen . . . Architects built the buildings for the
white man. Now, you know. Get going!

— No, Massa!

— Then who built the buildings?

— God built the buildings, Massa. Babu know.

— Well, yeah . . . Ha ha! In a way, He did. You see, Babu,
God gave the French people, the English people—all the white
people schools. In those schools science was taught. We began
to make small buildings—

— No, Massa!

— You sassy dope! Listen to me . . . You were living in
trees when the white man was building Notre Dame.

— Massa no tell Babu the truth!

— Are you calling me a liar, you baboon?

— Babu know Massa testing Babu. God gave buildings to
white man! Babu know!

— All right, stupid. Ha ha! Now, get out of here!

— But, Massa, why God give white man buildings and He
no give black man same?

— Hunh? Poor Babu . . . What're you trying to say?

— Black man live in jungle. White man live in stone house.
Why God do that, Massa? God ain't like that, Massa.

— Maybe a missionary could help you, boy. I can't.

— Babu know Massa wants test now.

— What test is this you keep yapping about?

— Massa wants to see if Babu got faith, if Babu really believes.

— Boy, have you been drinking?

— Babu no drink palm wine now, Massa.

— But why are you glaring at me like that? Are you crazy? Why are you coming at me? Go 'way! What's that in your hand?

— God's picture, Massa. Massa hide it. Babu find it.

— Let me see that picture . . . Oh, yes! That's *my* picture . . . Listen . . .

— Babu found picture of God!

— Oh no, no! You sorry fool! Where did you get that picture?

— Babu find picture where they sell books on river bank.

— You're all mixed up . . . Let me explain, Babu. When I was a young and hungry art student, I was a model for other artists. They used to paint me for Jesus, see? That's *me*, yes. But I was posing as Jesus . . . Understand?

— Massa test Babu. Picture got red beard. Massa got red beard. Picture got blue eyes. Massa got blue eyes. Babu *know* you!

— Know . . . know what?

— Babu tear up picture now! Babu find real God!

— Oh, no! This is a nightmare, boy! You're *sick* . . .

— Babu stand face to face with God! God hide, but Babu find 'Im!

— No, no, no! You make me dizzy . . . Listen, boy—

— No, Massa! Massa now listen to Babu! *Massa you God!*

— Oh, Christ!

— You call Christ, but you no fool Babu, Massa! Massa brought Babu to Paris to test Babu! Like that time you test the Jew in Jerusalem . . . You test Jew to see if Jew follow you. But Jew fool; he no follow you . . . At first, Jew no believe God, like Babu didn't . . . But white man he believe in God and white man kill God and God came back from the grave and he say: *O.K. White man, you find me out. I bless you. You make me bleed and my blood make you pure . . . I give white man fine buildings . . . I make white man powerful . . .* Day and night Babu walk white-man streets and look at white man. All white man look alike. But Babu know God hides in white man's land. Then Babu find God's picture and Babu knows why God took Babu to Paris. Babu know God tests Babu like he tested white man long ago—

— You mixed-up fool!

— *Massa, you God!*

— Babu, you're insane! You've thought about this too much!

— Now God say to Babu: *If Babu pass test like white man pass test, then I make Babu and his people strong and power-ful like white man . . . Then Africa get buildings like white man.*

— Hunh? Ha ha! Yes, yes . . . Now, Babu, you just relax. I got to get to my show . . . People are waiting for me . . . We'll talk about this when I get back—

— *No! Babu no let God go!*

— Get out of my way, you fool! Don't you touch me!

— Massa, keep still! You test Babu and make it hard for Babu . . . But Babu stand test! Babu prove you!

— If you touch me, I'll kill you, you black bastard!

— Oh, Massa . . . You cry and shout . . . You make Babu so sorry for you . . . But Babu got hard, deep *faith!*

— What're you doing? Why are you opening that suitcase? You can't scare me with those bones . . . NO! PUT DOWN THAT KNIFE! Go 'way, you wild fool!

— Please, Massa . . . Be good like lamb in Bible . . .

Lamb he no say nothing when crown of thorns is put on his head . . .

— *You wild black savage!*

— Please, Massa. Don't scream! I know . . . You scream to make Babu scared . . . But Babu got faith! Babu love Massa. Babu want to wash in the blood of the lamb and be whiter than snow—

— Calm down, boy! Come to your senses . . . Think of what you are doing! I've helped you! I've been good to you! Listen, I'll give you money!

— Massa no lead Babu into temptation! Babu no live by bread alone!

— Oh . . . What can I do? Boy, you're in a dream . . .

— You test Babu like you test Jew that time. Jew, he no believe. White man kill you and prove you God. Then you rose from dead in three days and you make white man powerful. Now it's *black man's* turn!

— You maniac! Take your hand . . . off my . . . beard . . . You're hurting my neck!—

— *Babu prove God!*

— You're mad!

— Babu cry . . . But Babu got faith . . . BABU STRONG!

— NAW! TURN ME LOOSE! DOOOOOON'T . . .

— *Bon.* Jacques, let's examine the next dossier.

— *Oui, monsieur l'Inspecteur.* The case of John Franklin is one of the most baffling of all the unsolved murder cases in our files. John Franklin, American artist, was beheaded in a shockingly brutal manner five years ago by parties unknown—

— Ah, yes . . . I recall the case. Made quite a stir at the time. An African figured in the case, didn't he?

— That's right, sir.

— A psychologically interesting religious case, a fanatic who insisted upon confessing the crime . . . He had delusions, I believe . . . Hummnnn . . . He had no motive whatsoever for committing the crime and he tried ever so clumsily to invent one, but was too naive to know how . . . Hummnnn . . . The record says that he was shipped back to his African tribe, absolved completely of all complicity . . . It seems that he is now busy organizing a new religious cult. Ha ha! Believe it or not, he is preaching that his erstwhile master will rise like Jesus from the dead . . . Ha ha!

— Ha ha! *Drôle de type!*

— No new developments since then, Jacques?

— Nothing at all, sir.

— And John Franklin's wife . . . where is she?

— She is still living in Paris, sir.

— Any suggestions for further investigation into this case, Jacques?

— It has been my idea all along, sir, that Mrs. Franklin lied to us about her husband's death. It was clear that she herself had nothing to do with the murder; she was at John Franklin's exhibit at the time, in full view of more than a thousand people . . . But no one was ever able to understand her hysterical insistence that that demented African killed her husband. And, what was most astonishing, was that that crazy African boy said that Mrs. Franklin was *right!* That black boy went wild trying to incriminate himself . . . *But I'm convinced that the testimony of both Mrs. Franklin and that black boy was false.* Mrs. Franklin's testimony was motivated by pure hysteria, and that black boy had no motive for confessing the crime except his wild notion that his master was God—

— Jacques, have you any suspicions that would justify our reopening the case?

— Well, sir, my theory is this: Mrs. Franklin was a proud and vain woman and she did not wish to admit that she had been superseded in her husband's affections by *another woman*—

— *Tiens!* I'd not thought of that angle, Jacques. Let me have your reconstruction of the crime.

— Well, sir, my conviction is that while John Franklin was talking to that foolish boy, giving him his passport and ticket, this other woman, *Odile Dufour*, knocked on the door. Odile Dufour knew that her lover was destined to become famous and that this was her only chance to make him promise to leave his wife and live with her. I surmise that John Franklin dismissed the boy . . . I deduce this from the fact that the boy swore that, just as he left the room, he saw a vision of the Virgin . . . He saw Odile Dufour, of course . . .

— Of couse!

— Alone with her lover, Odile Dufour demanded a final decision. John Franklin brutally told her that what she wanted was impossible; he was impatient; crowds were waiting for him at the opening of his show . . . His cast-off mistress then went wild; she snatched up the knife that was lying upon the African's suitcase and attacked John Franklin, wounding him . . . Then, in her jealous rage, she beheaded him. She fled, fearing apprehension at any moment—

— Jacques, your theory's false. If the murder transpired as you've described it—and I admit that only an insanely jealous woman could behead a man like that—how do you account for the fact that the boy, *whom you say had left*, knew his master was dead when he was apprehended? . . .

— I was coming to that, sir. The police found the boy on the street; he was carrying his suitcase . . . He made no attempt to flee or evade arrest. When questioned, he said that,

just before the police had caught him, *he had gone back to
the Franklin apartment for his suitcase* . . . I maintain that
it was then that he found his murdered master. To his primitive
mind that dead, bloody body was like a supernatural sign. He
went to pieces, spouting a lot of gibberish about having killed
his master and about his master's rising from the dead, etc.

— Hold on, Jacques. Maybe that boy *was* telling the truth.
Perhaps he went back for that suitcase because it contained
the bones of his dead father? . . . Maybe he mixed Chistianity
with his paganism?

— No, sir. That boy swore in court that he went back to
retrieve that suitcase because it contained his *beautiful robes*
. . . He said that he did not care one whit about those bones,
that he was a staunch Christian.

— Bravo! I believe you've got it, Jacques! A crime of passion.

— Yes, sir. It ties all the loose ends together.

— Exactly.

— Therefore, sir, I say let us look for that *other woman* . . .
What fouled up this investigation were the wild ideas of that
crazy African . . .

— *Bon.* The case is reopened. Send out a tracer for Odile
Dufour. By God, it's never too late to bring a guilty person to
justice. *Chercher la femme! Bon. C'est midi . . . temps pour
manger! Prenons un apéritif . . .*

THE MAN WHO KILLED

A SHADOW

It ALL BEGAN long ago when he was a tiny boy who was already used, in a fearful sort of way, to living with shadows. But what were the shadows that made him afraid? Surely they were not those beautiful silhouettes of objects cast upon the earth by the sun. Shadows of that kind are innocent and he loved trying to catch them as he ran along sunlit paths in summer. But there were subtler shadows which he saw and which others could not see: the shadows of his fears. And this boy had such shadows and he lived to kill one of them.

Saul Saunders was born black in a little Southern town, not many miles from Washington, the nation's capital, which means that he came into a world that was split in two, a white world and a black one, the white one being separated from the black by a million psychological miles. So, from the very beginning, Saul looking timidly out from his black world, saw the shadowy outlines of a white world that was unreal to him and not his own.

It so happened that even Saul's mother was but a vague, shadowy thing to him, for she died long before his memory could form an image of her. And the same thing happened to Saul's father, who died before the boy could retain a clear picture of him in his mind.

People really never became personalities to Saul, for hardly had he ever got to know them before they vanished. So people became for Saul symbols of uneasiness, of a deprivation that evoked in him a sense of the transitory quality of life, which always made him feel that some invisible, unexplainable event was about to descend upon him.

He had five brothers and two sisters who remained strangers to him. There was, of course, no adult in his family with enough money to support them all, and the children were rationed out to various cousins, uncles, aunts, and grandparents.

It fell to Saul to live with his grandmother who moved constantly from one small Southern town to another, and even physical landscapes grew to have but little emotional meaning for the boy. Towns were places you lived in for a while, and then you moved on. When he had reached the age of twelve, all reality seemed to him to be akin to his mother and father, like the white world that surrounded the black island of his life, like the parade of dirty little towns that passed forever before his eyes, things that had names but not substance, things that happened and then retreated into an incomprehensible nothingness.

Saul was not dumb or lazy, but it took him seven years to reach the third grade in school. None of the people who came and went in Saul's life had ever prized learning and

Saul did likewise. It was quite normal in his environment to reach the age of fourteen and still be in the third grade, and Saul liked being normal, liked being like other people.

Then the one person—his grandmother—who Saul had thought would endure forever, passed suddenly from his life, and from that moment on Saul did not ever quite know what to do. He went to work for the white people of the South and the shadowlike quality of his world became terribly manifest. continuously present. He understood nothing of this white world into which he had been thrown; it was just there, a faint and fearful shadow cast by some object that stood between him and a hidden and powerful sun.

He quickly learned that the strange white people for whom he worked considered him inferior; he did not feel inferior and he did not think that he was. But when he looked about him he saw other black people accepting this definition of themselves, and who was he to challenge it? Outwardly he grew to accept it as part of that vast shadow-world that came and went, pulled by forces which he nor nobody he knew understood.

Soon all of Saul's anxieties, fears, and irritations became focused upon this white shadow-world which gave him his daily bread in exchange for his labor. Feeling unhappy and not knowing why, he projected his misery out from himself and upon the one thing that made him most constantly anxious. If this had not happened, if Saul had not found a way of putting his burden upon others, he would have early thought of suicide. He finally did, in the end, think of killing himself, but then it was too late . . .

At the age of fifteen Saul knew that the life he was then living was to be his lot, that there was no way to rid himself of his plaguing sense of unreality, no way to relax and forget.

He was most self-forgetful when he was with black people, and that made things a little easier for him. But as he grew older, he became more afraid, yet none of his friends noticed it. Indeed, many of Saul's friends liked him very much. Saul was always kind, attentive; but no one suspected that his kindness, his quiet, waiting loyalty came from his being afraid.

Then Saul changed. Maybe it was luck or misfortune; it is hard to tell. When he took a drink of whisky, he found that it helped to banish the shadows, lessened his tensions, made the world more reasonably three-dimensional, and he grew to like drinking. When he was paid off on a Saturday night, he would drink with his friends and he would feel better. He felt that whisky made life complete, that it stimulated him. But, of course, it did not. Whisky really depressed him, numbed him somewhat, reduced the force and number of the shadows that made him tight inside.

When Saul was sober, he almost never laughed in the presence of the white shadow-world, but when he had a drink or two he found that he could. Even when he was told about the hard lives that all Negroes lived, it did not worry him, for he would take a drink and not feel too badly. It did not even bother him when he heard that if you were alone with a white woman and she screamed, it was as good as hearing your death sentence, for, though you had done nothing, you would be killed. Saul got used to hearing the siren of the police car screaming in the Black Belt, got used to seeing white cops dragging Negroes off to jail. Once he grew wildly angry about it, felt that the shadows would some day claim him as he had seen them claim others, but his friends warned him that it was dangerous to feel that way, that always the black man lost, and the best thing to do was to take a drink. He did, and in a little while they were all laughing.

One night when he was mildly drunk—he was thirty years old and living in Washington at the time—he got married. The girl was good for Saul, for she too liked to drink and she was pretty and they got along together. Saul now felt that things were not so bad; as long as he could stifle the feeling of being hemmed in, as long as he could conquer the anxiety about the unexpected happening, life was bearable.

Saul's jobs had been many and simple. First he had worked on a farm. When he was fourteen he had gone to Washington, after his grandmother had died, where he did all kinds of odd jobs. Finally he was hired by an old white army colonel as chauffeur and butler and he averaged about twenty dollars every two weeks. He lived in and got his meals and uniform and he remained with the colonel for five years. The colonel too liked to drink, and sometimes they would both get drunk. But Saul never forgot that the colonel, though drunk and feeling fine, was still a shadow, unreal, and might suddenly change toward him.

One day, when whisky was making him feel good, Saul asked the colonel for a raise in salary, told him that he did not have enough to live on, and that prices were rising. But the colonel was sober and hard that day and said no. Saul was so stunned that he quit the job that instant. While under the spell of whisky he had for a quick moment felt that the world of shadows was over, but when he had asked for more money and had been refused, he knew that he had been wrong. He should not have asked for money; he should have known that the colonel was a no-good guy, a shadow.

Saul was next hired as an exterminator by a big chemical company and he found that there was something in his nature that made him like going from house to house and putting down poison for rats and mice and roaches. He liked seeing concrete evidence of his work and the dead bodies of rats were no shadows. They were real. He never felt better in his life than when he was killing with the sanction of society. And his boss even increased his salary when he asked for it. And he drank as much as he liked and no one cared.

But one morning, after a hard night of drinking which had made him irritable and high-strung, his boss said something that he did not like and he spoke up, defending himself against what he thought was a slighting remark. There was an argument and Saul left.

Two weeks of job hunting got him the position of janitor in the National Cathedral, a church and religious institution. It was the solitary kind of work he liked; he reported for duty each morning at seven o'clock and at eleven he was through. He first cleaned the Christmas card shop, next he cleaned the library; and his final chore was to clean the choir room.

But cleaning the library, with its rows and rows of books, was what caught Saul's attention, for there was a strange little shadow woman there who stared at him all the time in a most peculiar way. The library was housed in a separate building and, whenever he came to clean it, he and the white woman would be there alone. She was tiny, blonde, blue-eyed, weighing about 110 pounds, and standing about five feet three inches. Saul's boss had warned him never to quarrel with the lady in charge of the library. "She's a crackpot," he had told Saul. And naturally Saul never wanted any trouble; in fact, he did not even know the woman's name. Many times, however, he would pause in his work, feeling that his eyes were being drawn to her and he would turn around and find her staring at him. Then she would look away quickly, as though ashamed. "What in hell does she want from me?" he wondered uneasily. The woman never spoke to him except to say good morning and she even said that as though she did not want to say it. Saul thought that maybe she was afraid of him; but how could that be? He could not recall when anybody had ever been afraid of him, and he had never been in any trouble in his life.

One morning while sweeping the floor he felt his eyes being drawn toward her and he paused and turned and saw her staring at him. He did not move, neither did she. They stared at each other for about ten seconds, then she went out of the room, walking with quick steps, as though angry or afraid. He was frightened, but forgot it quickly. "What the hell's wrong with that woman?" he asked himself.

Next morning Saul's boss called him and told him, in a nice, quiet tone—but it made him scared and mad just the same— that the woman in the library had complained about him, had said that he never cleaned under her desk.

"Under her desk?" Saul asked, amazed.

"Yes," his boss said, amused at Saul's astonishment.

"But I clean under her desk every morning," Saul said.

"Well, Saul, remember, I told you she was a crackpot," his boss said soothingly. "Don't argue with her. Just do your work."

"Yes, sir," Saul said.

He wanted to tell his boss how the woman always stared at him, but he could not find courage enough to do so. If he had been talking with his black friends, he would have done so quite naturally. But why talk to one shadow about another queer shadow?

That day being payday, he got his weekly wages and that night he had a hell of a good time. He drank until he was drunk, until he blotted out almost everything from his consciousness. He was getting regularly drunk now whenever he had the money. He liked it and he bothered nobody and he was happy while doing it. But dawn found him broke, exhausted, and terribly depressed, full of shadows and uneasiness, a way he never liked it. The thought of going to his job made him angry. He longed for deep, heavy sleep. But, no, he had a good job and he had to keep it. Yes, he would go.

After cleaning the Christmas card shop—he was weak and he sweated a lot—he went to the library. No one was there. He swept the floor and was about to dust the books when he heard the footsteps of the woman coming into the room. He was tired, nervous, half asleep; his hands trembled and his reflexes were overquick. "So you're the bitch who snitched on me, hunh?" he said irritably to himself. He continued dusting and all at once he had the queer feeling that she was staring at him. He fought against the impulse to look at her, but he could not resist it. He turned slowly and saw that she was sitting in her chair at her desk, staring at him with unblinking eyes. He had the impression that she was about to speak. He could not help staring back at her, waiting.

"Why don't you clean under my desk?" she asked him in a tense but controlled voice.

"Why, ma'am," he said slowly, "I just did."

"Come here and look," she said, pointing downward.

He replaced the book on the shelf. She had never spoken so many words to him before. He went and stood before her and his mind protested against what his eyes saw, and then his senses leaped in wonder. She was sitting with her knees sprawled apart and her dress was drawn halfway up her legs. He looked from her round blue eyes to her white legs whose thighs thickened as they went to a V clothed in tight, sheer, pink panties; then he looked quickly again into her eyes. Her face was a beet red, but she sat very still, rigid, as though she was being impelled into an act which she did not want to

perform but was being driven to perform. Saul was so startled
that he could not move.

"I just cleaned under your desk this morning," he mumbled,
sensing that he was not talking about what she meant.

"There's dust there now," she said sternly, her legs still so
wide apart that he felt that she was naked.

He did not know what to do; he was so baffled, humiliated,
and frightened that he grew angry. But he was afraid to express his anger openly.

"Look, ma'am," he said in a tone of suppressed rage and
hate, "you're making trouble for me!"

"Why don't you do your work?" she blazed at him. "That's
what you're being paid to do, you black nigger!" Her legs
were still spread wide and she was sitting as though about to
spring upon him and throw her naked thighs about his body.

For a moment he was still and silent. Never before in his
life had he been called a "black nigger." He had heard that
white people used that phrase as their supreme humiliation
of black people, but he had never been treated so. As the insult sank in, as he stared at her gaping thighs, he felt over-
whelmed by a sense of wild danger.

"I don't like that," he said and before he knew it he had
slapped her flat across her face.

She sucked in her breath, sprang up, and stepped away from
him. Then she screamed sharply, and her voice was like a
lash cutting into his chest. She screamed again and he backed
away from her. He felt helpless, strange; he knew what he
had done, knew its meaning for him; but he knew that he
could not have helped it. It seemed that some part of him was
there in that room watching him do things that he should not
do. He drew in his breath and for a moment he felt that he
could not stand upon his legs. His world was now full of all

the shadows he had ever feared. He was in the worse trouble
that a black man could imagine.

The woman was screaming continuously now and he was
running toward the stairs. Just as he put his foot on the bottom
step, he paused and looked over his shoulder. She was backing
away from him, toward an open window at the far end of the
room, still screaming. Oh God! In her scream he heard the
sirens of the police cars that hunted down black men in the
Black Belts and he heard the shrill whistles of white cops
running after black men and he felt again in one rush of emotion all the wild and bitter tales he had heard of how whites
always got the black who did a crime and this woman was
screaming as though he had raped her.

He ran on up the steps, but her screams were coming so
loud that when he neared the top of the steps he slowed.
Those screams would not let him run any more, they weak-
ened him, tugged and pulled him. His chest felt as though it
would burst. He reached the top landing and looked round
aimlessly. He saw a fireplace and before it was a neat pile of
wood and while he was looking at that pile of wood the
screams tore at him, unnerved him. With a shaking hand he
reached down and seized in his left hand—for he was left-
handed—a heavy piece of oaken firewood that had jagged,
sharp edges where it had been cut with an ax. He turned and
ran back down the steps to where the woman stood screaming. He lifted the stick of wood as he confronted her, then
paused. He wanted her to stop screaming. If she had stopped,
he would have fled, but while she screamed all he could feel
was a hotness bubbling in him and urging him to do something. She would fill her lungs quickly and deeply and her
breath would come out at full blast. He swung down his left
arm and hit her a swinging blow on the side of her head, not

to hurt her, not to kill her, but to stop that awful noise, to stop that shadow from screaming a scream that meant death . . . He felt her skull crack and give as she sank to the floor, but she still screamed. He trembled from head to feet. Goddamn that woman . . . Why didn't she stop that yelling? He lifted his arm and gave her another blow, feeling the oaken stick driving its way into her skull. But still she screamed. He was about to hit her again when he became aware that the stick he held was light. He looked at it and found that half of it had broken off, was lying on the floor. But she screamed on, with blood running down her dress, her legs sprawled nakedly out from under her. He dropped the remainder of the stick and grabbed her throat and choked her to stop her screams. That seemed to quiet her; she looked as though she had fainted. He choked her for a long time, not trying to kill her, but just to make sure that she would not scream again and make him wild and hot inside. He was not reacting to the woman, but to the feelings that her screams evoked in him.

The woman was limp and silent now and slowly he took his hands from her throat. She was quiet. He waited. He was not certain. Yes, take her downstairs into the bathroom and if she screamed again no one would hear her . . . He took her hands in his and started dragging her away from the window. His hands were wet with sweat and her hands were so tiny and soft that time and again her little fingers slipped out of his palms. He tried holding her hands tighter and only succeeded in scratching her. Her ring slid off into his hand while he was dragging her and he stood still for a moment, staring in a daze at the thin band of shimmering gold, then mechanically he put it into his pocket. Finally he dragged her down the steps to the bathroom door.

He was about to take her in when he saw that the floor was

spotted with drippings of blood. That was bad . . . He had
been trained to keep floors clean, just as he had been trained
to fear shadows. He propped her clumsily against a wall and
went into the bathroom and took wads of toilet paper and
mopped up the red splashes. He even went back upstairs
where he had first struck her and found blood spots and wiped
them up carefully. He stiffened; she was hollering again. He
ran downstairs and this time he recalled that he had a knife
in his pocket. He took it out, opened it, and plunged it deep
into her throat; he was frantic to stop her from hollering . . .
He pulled the knife from her throat and she was quiet.

He stood, his eyes roving. He noticed a door leading down
to a recess in a wall through which steam pipes ran. Yes, it
would be better to put her there; then if she started yelling no
one would hear her. He was not trying to hide her; he merely
wanted to make sure that she would not be heard. He dragged
her again and her dress came up over her knees to her chest
and again he saw her pink panties. It was too hard dragging
her and he lifted her in his arms and while carrying her down
the short flight of steps he thought that the pink panties, if he
would wet them, would make a good mop to clean up the
blood. Once more he sat her against the wall, stripped her
of her pink panties—and not once did he so much as glance
at her groin—wetted them and swabbed up the spots, then
pushed her into the recess under the pipes. She was in full
view, easily seen. He tossed the wet ball of panties in after her.

He sighed and looked around. The floor seemed clean. He
went back upstairs. That stick of broken wood . . . He picked
up the two shattered ends of wood and several splinters; he
carefully joined the ends together and then fitted the splinters
into place. He laid the mended stick back upon the pile before the fireplace. He stood listening, wondering if she would

yell again, but there was no sound. It never occurred to him that he could help her, that she might be in pain; he never wondered even if she were dead. He got his coat and hat and went home.

He was nervously tired. It seemed that he had just finished doing an old and familiar job of dodging the shadows that were forever around him, shadows that he could not understand. He undressed, but paid no attention to the blood on his trousers and shirt; he was alone in the room; his wife was at work. When he pulled out his billfold, he saw the ring. He put it in the drawer of his night table, more to keep his wife from seeing it than to hide it. He climbed wearily into bed and at once fell into a deep, sound sleep from which he did not awaken until late afternoon. He lay blinking blood-shot eyes and he could not remember what he had done. Then the vague, shadowlike picture of it came before his eyes. He was puzzled, and for a moment he wondered if it had happened or had someone told him a story of it. He could not be sure. There was no fear or regret in him.

When at last the conviction of what he had done was real in him, it came only in terms of flat memory, devoid of all emotion, as though he were looking when very tired and sleepy at a scene being flashed upon the screen of a movie house. Not knowing what to do, he remained in bed. He had drifted off to sleep again when his wife came home late that night from her cooking job.

Next morning he ate the breakfast his wife prepared, rose from the table and kissed her, and started off toward the Cathedral as though nothing had happened. It was not until he actually got to the Cathedral steps that he became shaky and nervous. He stood before the door for two or three minutes, and then he realized that he could not go back in there this morning. Yet it was not danger that made him feel this way, but a queer kind of repugnance. Whether the woman was alive or not did not enter his mind. He still did not know what to do. Then he remembered that his wife, before she had left for her job, had asked him to buy some groceries. Yes, he would do that. He wanted to do that because he did not know what else on earth to do.

He bought the groceries and took them home, then spent the rest of the day wandering from bar to bar. Not once did he think of fleeing. He would go home, sit, turn on the radio, then go out into the streets and walk. Finally he would end up at a bar, drinking. On one of his many trips into the house, he changed his clothes, rolled up his bloody shirt and trousers, put the blood-stained knife inside the bundle, and pushed it into a far corner of a closet. He got his gun and put it into his pocket, for he was nervously depressed.

But he still did not know what to do. Suddenly he recalled that some months ago he had bought a cheap car which was now in a garage for repairs. He went to the garage and persuaded the owner to take it back for twenty-five dollars; the thought that he could use the car for escape never came to his mind. During that afternoon and early evening he sat in bars and drank. What he felt now was no different from what he had felt all his life.

Toward eight o'clock that night he met two friends of his and invited them for a drink. He was quite drunk now. Before him on the table was a sandwich and a small glass of whisky. He leaned forward, listening sleepily to one of his friends tell a story about a girl, and then he heard:

"Aren't you Saul Saunders?"

He looked up into the faces of two white shadows.

"Yes," he admitted readily. "What do you want?"

"You'd better come along with us. We want to ask you some questions," one of the shadows said.

"What's this all about?" Saul asked.

They grabbed his shoulders and he stood up. Then he reached down and picked up the glass of whisky and drank it. He walked steadily out of the bar to a waiting auto, a policeman to each side of him, his mind a benign blank. It was not until they were about to put him into the car that something happened and whipped his numbed senses to an apprehension of danger. The policeman patted his waist for arms; they found nothing because his gun was strapped to his chest. Yes, he ought to kill himself . . . The thought leaped into his mind with such gladness that he shivered. It was the answer to everything. Why had he not thought of it before?

Slowly he took off his hat and held it over his chest to hide the movement of his left hand, then he reached inside of his shirt and pulled out the gun. One of the policemen pounced on him and snatched the gun.

"So, you're trying to kill us too, hunh?" one asked.

"Naw. I was trying to kill myself," he answered simply.

"Like hell you were!"

A fist came onto his jaw and he sank back limp.

Two hours later, at the police station, he told them everything, speaking in a low, listless voice without a trace of emotion, vividly describing every detail, yet feeling that it was utterly hopeless for him to try to make them understand how horrible it was for him to hear that woman screaming. His narrative sounded so brutal that the policemen's faces were chalky.

Weeks later a voice droned in a court room and he sat staring dully.

". . . The Grand Jurors of the United States of America, in and for the District of Columbia aforesaid, upon their oath, do present:

"That one Saul Saunders, on, to wit, the first day of March, 19——, and at and within the District of Columbia aforesaid, contriving and intending to kill one Maybelle Eva Houseman . . ."

"So *that's* her name," he said to himself in amazement.

". . . Feloniously, wilfully, purposely, and of his deliberate and premeditated malice did strike, beat, and wound the said Maybelle Eva Houseman, in and upon the front of the head and in and upon the right side of the head of her, the said Maybelle Eva Houseman, two certain mortal wounds and fractures; and did fix and fasten about the neck and throat of her, the said Maybelle Eva Houseman, his hand or hands—but whether it was one of his hands or both of his hands is to the Grand Jury aforesaid unknown—and that he, the said Saul Saunders, with his hand or hands as aforesaid fixed and fastened about the throat of her, did choke and strangle the said Maybelle Eva Houseman, of which said choking and strangling the said Maybelle Eva Houseman, on, to wit, the said first day of March, 19——, and at and within the said District of Columbia, did die."

He longed for a drink, but that was impossible now. Then he took a deep breath and surrendered to the world of shadows about him, the world he had feared so long; and at once the tension went from him and he felt better than he had felt in a long time. He was amazed at how relaxed and peaceful it was when he stopped fighting the world of shadows.

". . . By force and violence and against resistance and by

putting in fear, did steal, take, and carry away, from and off the person and from the immediate, actual possession of one Maybelle Eva Houseman, then and there being, a certain finger ring, of the value of, to wit, ten dollars."

He listened now with more attention but no anxiety:

"And in and while perpetrating robbery aforesaid did kill and murder the said Maybelle Eva Houseman; against the form of the statute in such case made and provided, and against the peace and government of the said United States of America."

P.S. Thereupon Dr. Herman Stein was called as a witness and being first duly sworn testified as follows:

". . . On examination of the genital organs there was no evidence of contusion, abrasion, or trauma, and the decedent's hymen ring was intact. This decedent had not been criminally assaulted or attempted to be entered. It has been ascertained that the decedent's age was 40."

THE MAN WHO WENT

TO CHICAGO

WHEN I ROSE in the morning the temperature had dropped below zero. The house was as cold to me as the Southern streets had been in winter. I dressed, doubling my clothing. I ate in a restaurant, caught a streetcar, and rode south, rode until I could see no more black faces on the sidewalks. I had now crossed the boundary line of the Black Belt and had entered the territory where jobs were perhaps to be had from white folks. I walked the streets and looked into shop windows until I saw a sign in a delicatessen: PORTER WANTED.

I went in and a stout white woman came to me.

"Vat do you vant?" she asked.

The voice jarred me. She's Jewish, I thought, remembering with shame the obscenities I used to shout at Jewish store-keepers in Arkansas.

"I thought maybe you needed a porter," I said.

"Meester 'Offman, he eesn't here yet," she said. "Vill you vait?"

"Yes, ma'am."

"Seet down."

"No, ma'am, I'll wait outside."

"But eet's cold out zhere," she said.

"That's all right," I said.

She shrugged. I went to the sidewalk. I waited for half an hour in the bitter cold, regretting that I had not remained in the warm store, but unable to go back inside. A bald, stoutish white man went into the store and pulled off his coat. Yes, he was the boss man . . .

"Zo you vant a job?" he asked.

"Yes, sir," I answered, guessing at the meaning of his words.

"Vhere you vork before?"

"In Memphis, Tennessee."

"My brudder-in-law vorked in Tennessee vonce," he said.

I was hired. The work was easy, but I found to my dismay that I could not understand a third of what was said to me. My slow Southern ears were baffled by their clouded, thick accents. One morning Mrs. Hoffman asked me to go to a neighboring store—it was owned by a cousin of hers—and get a can of chicken à la king. I had never heard the phrase before and I asked her to repeat it.

"Don't you know nosing?" she demanded of me.

"If you would write it down for me, I'd know what to get," I ventured timidly.

"I can't vite!" she shouted in a sudden fury. "Vat kinda boy iss you?"

I memorized the separate sounds that she had uttered and went to the neighboring store.

"Mrs. Hoffman wants a can Cheek Keeng Awr Lar Keeng," I

said slowly, hoping he would not think I was being offensive.

"All vite," he said, after staring at me a moment.

He put a can into a paper bag and gave it to me; outside in the street I opened the bag and read the label: Chicken à la King. I cursed, disgusted with myself. I knew those words. It had been her thick accent that had thrown me off. Yet I was not angry with her for speaking broken English; my English, too, was broken. But why could she not have taken more patience? Only one answer came to my mind. I was black and she did not care. Or so I thought . . . I was persisting in reading my present environment in the light of my old one. I reasoned thus: though English was my native tongue and America my native land, she, an alien, could operate a store and earn a living in a neighborhood where I could not even live. I reasoned further that she was aware of this and was trying to protect her position against me.

It was not until I had left the delicatessen job that I saw how grossly I had misread the motives and attitudes of Mr. Hoffman and his wife. I had not yet learned anything that would have helped me to thread my way through these perplexing racial relations. Accepting my environment at its face value, trapped by my own emotions, I kept asking myself what had black people done to bring this crazy world upon them?

The fact of the separation of white and black was clear to me; it was its effect upon the personalities of people that stumped and dismayed me. I did not feel that I was a threat to anybody; yet, as soon as I had grown old enough to think, I had learned that my entire personality, my aspirations, had long ago been discounted; that, in a measure, the very meaning of the words I spoke could not be fully understood.

And when I contemplated the area of No Man's Land into which the Negro mind in America had been shunted I won-

dered if there had ever been in all human history a more cor-
roding and devastating attack upon the personalities of men
than the idea of racial discrimination. In order to escape the
racial attack that went to the roots of my life, I would have
gladly accepted any way of life but the one in which I found
myself. I would have agreed to live under a system of feudal
oppression, not because I preferred feudalism but because I
felt that feudalism made use of a limited part of a man, defined man, his rank, his function in society. I would have consented to live under the most rigid type of dictatorship, for
I felt that dictatorships, too, defined the use of men, however
degrading that use might be.

While working as a porter in Memphis I had often stood
aghast as a friend of mine had offered himself to be kicked
by the white men; but now, while working in Chicago,
I was learning that perhaps even a kick was better than un-
certainty . . . I had elected, in my fevered search for honor-
able adjustment to the American scene, not to submit and in
doing so I had embraced the daily horror of anxiety, of tension,
of eternal disquiet. I could now sympathize with—though I
could never bring myself to approve—those tortured blacks
who had given up and had gone to their white tormentors and
had said: "Kick me, if that's all there is for me; kick me and
let me feel at home, let me have peace!"

Color-hate defined the place of black life as below that of
white life; and the black man, responding to the same dreams
as the white man, strove to bury within his heart his awareness
of this difference because it made him lonely and afraid.
Hated by whites and being an organic part of the culture that
hated him, the black man grew in turn to hate in himself that
which others hated in him. But pride would make him hate
his self-hate, for he would not want whites to know that he was

so thoroughly conquered by them that his total life was conditioned by their attitude; but in the act of hiding his self-hate,
he could not help but hate those who evoked his self-hate in
him. So each part of his day would be consumed in a war
with himself, a good part of his energy would be spent in
keeping control of his unruly emotions, emotions which he had
not wished to have, but could not help having. Held at bay
by the hate of others, preoccupied with his own feelings, he
was continuously at war with reality. He became inefficient,
less able to see and judge the objective world. And when he
reached that state, the white people looked at him and laughed
and said:

"Look, didn't I tell you niggers were that way?"

To solve this tangle of balked emotion, I loaded the empty
part of the ship of my personality with fantasies of ambition
to keep it from toppling over into the sea of senselessness. Like
any other American, I dreamed of going into business and
making money; I dreamed of working for a firm that would
allow me to advance until I reached an important position;
I even dreamed of organizing secret groups of blacks to fight
all whites . . . And if the blacks would not agree to organize,
then they would have to be fought. I would end up again with
self-hate, but it was now a self-hate that was projected outward upon other blacks. Yet I knew—with that part of my
mind that the whites had given me—that none of my dreams
were possible. Then I would hate myself for allowing my mind
to dwell upon the unattainable. Thus the circle would complete itself.

Slowly I began to forge in the depths of my mind a mechanism that repressed all the dreams and desires that the Chicago
streets, the newspapers, the movies were evoking in me. I was
going through a second childhood; a new sense of the limit of

the possible was being born in me. What could I dream of that had the barest possibility of coming true? I could think of nothing. And, slowly, it was upon exactly that nothingness that my mind began to dwell, that constant sense of wanting without having, of being hated without reason. A dim notion of what life meant to a Negro in America was coming to consciousness in me, not in terms of external events, lynchings, Jim Crowism, and the endless brutalities, but in terms of crossed-up feeling, of emotional tension. I sensed that Negro life was a sprawling land of unconscious suffering, and there were but few Negroes who knew the meaning of their lives, who could tell their story.

Word reached me that an examination for postal clerk was impending and at once I filed an application and waited. As the date for the examination drew near, I was faced with another problem. How could I get a free day without losing my job? In the South it would have been an unwise policy for a Negro to have gone to his white boss and asked for time to take an examination for another job. It would have implied that the Negro did not like to work for the white boss, that he felt he was not receiving just consideration and, inasmuch as most jobs that Negroes held in the South involved a personal, paternalistic relationship, he would have been risking an argument that might have led to violence.

I now began to speculate about what kind of man Mr. Hoffman was, and I found that I did not know him; that is, I did not know his basic attitude toward Negroes. If I asked him, would he be sympathetic enough to allow me time off with pay? I needed the money. Perhaps he would say: "Go home and stay home if you don't like this job!" I was not sure of him. I decided, therefore, that I had better not risk it. I would forfeit the money and stay away without telling him.

The examination was scheduled to take place on a Monday; I had been working steadily and I would be too tired to do my best if I took the examination without benefit of rest. I decided to stay away from the shop Saturday, Sunday, and Monday. But what could I tell Mr. Hoffman? Yes, I would tell him that I had been ill. No, that was too thin. I would tell him that my mother had died in Memphis and that I had gone down to bury her. That lie might work.

I took the examination and when I came to the store on Tuesday, Mr. Hoffman was astonished, of course.

"I didn't sink you vould ever come back," he said.

"I'm awfully sorry, Mr. Hoffman."

"Vat happened?"

"My mother died in Memphis and I had to go down and bury her," I lied.

He looked at me, then shook his head.

"Rich, you lie," he said.

"I'm not lying," I lied stoutly.

"You vanted to do somesink, zo you zayed ervay," he said, shrugging.

"No, sir. I'm telling you the truth," I piled another lie upon the first one.

"No. You lie. You disappoint me," he said.

"Well, all I can do is tell you the truth," I lied indignantly.

"Vy didn't you use the phone?"

"I didn't think of it," I told a fresh lie.

"Rich, if your mudder die, you vould tell me," he said.

"I didn't have time. Had to catch the train," I lied yet again.

"Vhere did you get the money?"

"My aunt gave it to me," I said, disgusted that I had to lie and lie again.

"I don't vant a boy vat tells lies," he said.

"I don't lie," I lied passionately to protect my lies.

Mrs. Hoffman joined in and both of them hammered at me.

"Ve know. You come from ze Zouth. You feel you can't tell us ze truth. But ve don't bother you. Ve don't feel like people in ze Zouth. Ve treat you nice, don't ve?" they asked.

"Yes, ma'am," I mumbled.

"Zen vy lie?"

"I'm not lying," I lied with all my strength.

I became angry because I knew that they knew that I was lying. I had lied to protect myself, and then I had to lie to protect my lie. I had met so many white faces that would have violently disapproved of my taking the examination that I could not have risked telling Mr. Hoffman the truth. But how could I tell him that I had lied because I was so unsure of myself? Lying was bad, but revealing my own sense of insecurity would have been worse. It would have been shameful, and I did not like to feel ashamed.

Their attitudes had proved utterly amazing. They were taking time out from their duties in the store to talk to me, and I had never encountered anything like that from whites before. A Southern white man would have said: "Get to hell out of here!" or "All right, nigger. Get to work." But no white people had ever stood their ground and probed at me, questioned me at such length. It dawned upon me that they were trying to treat me as an equal, which made it even more impossible for me ever to tell them that I had lied, why I had lied. I felt that if I confessed I would be giving them a moral advantage over me that would have been unbearable.

"All vight, zay and vork," Mr. Hoffman said. "I know you're lying, but I don't care, Rich."

I wanted to quit. He had insulted me. But I liked him in

spite of myself. Yes, I had done wrong; but how on earth could I have known the kind of people I was working for? Perhaps Mr. Hoffman would have gladly consented for me to take the examination; but my hopes had been far weaker than my powerful fears.

Working with them from day to day and knowing that they knew I had lied from fear crushed me. I knew that they pitied me and pitied the fear in me. I resolved to quit and risk hunger rather than stay with them. I left the job that following Saturday, not telling them that I would not be back, not possessing the heart to say good-by. I just wanted to go quickly and have them forget that I had ever worked for them.

After an idle week, I got a job as a dishwasher in a North Side cafe that had just opened. My boss, a white woman, directed me in unpacking barrels of dishes, setting up new tables, painting, and so on. I had charge of serving breakfast; in the late afternoon I carted trays of food to patrons in the hotel who did not want to come down to eat. My wages were fifteen dollars a week; the hours were long, but I ate my meals on the job.

The cook was an elderly Finnish woman with a sharp, bony face. There were several white waitresses. I was the only Negro in the café. The waitresses were a hard, brisk lot, and I was keenly aware of how their attitudes contrasted with those of Southern white girls. They had not been taught to keep a gulf between me and themselves; they were relatively free of the heritage of racial hate.

One morning as I was making coffee, Cora came forward with a tray loaded with food and squeezed against me to draw a cup of coffee.

"Pardon me, Richard," she said.

"Oh, that's all right," I said in an even tone.

But I was aware that she was a white girl and that her body was pressed closely against mine, an incident that had never happened to me before in my life, an incident charged with the memory of dread. But she was not conscious of my blackness or of what her actions would have meant in the South. And had I not been born in the South, her trivial act would have been as unnoticed by me as it was by her. As she stood close to me, I could not help thinking that if a Southern white girl had wanted to draw a cup of coffee, she would have commanded me to step aside so that she might not come in contact with me. The work of the hot and busy kitchen would have had to cease for the moment so that I could have taken my tainted body far enough away to allow the Southern white girl a chance to get a cup of coffee. There lay a deep, emotional safety in knowing that the white girl who was now leaning carelessly against me was not thinking of me, had no deep, vague, irrational fright that made her feel that I was a creature to be avoided at all costs.

One summer morning a white girl came late to work and rushed into the pantry where I was busy. She went into the women's room and changed her clothes; I heard the door open and a second later I was surprised to hear her voice:

"Richard, quick! Tie my apron!"

She was standing with her back to me and the strings of her apron dangled loose. There was a moment of indecision on my part, then I took the two loose strings and carried them around her body and brought them again to her back and tied them in a clumsy knot.

"Thanks a million," she said, grasping my hand for a split second, and was gone.

I continued my work, filled with all the possible meanings that that tiny, simple, human event could have meant to any Negro in the South where I had spent most of my hungry days.

I did not feel any admiration or any hate for the girls. My attitude was one of abiding and friendly wonder. For the most part I was silent with them, though I knew that I had a firmer grasp of life than most of them. As I worked I listened to their talk and perceived its puzzled, wandering, superficial fumbling with the problems and facts of life. There were many things they wondered about that I could have explained to them, but I never dared.

During my lunch hour, which I spent on a bench in a near-by park, the waitresses would come and sit beside me, talking at random, laughing, joking, smoking cigarettes. I learned about their tawdry dreams, their simple hopes, their home lives, their fear of feeling anything deeply, their sex problems, their husbands. They were an eager, restless, talkative, ignorant bunch, but casually kind and impersonal for all that. They knew nothing of hate and fear, and strove instinctively to avoid all passion.

I often wondered what they were trying to get out of life, but I never stumbled upon a clue, and I doubt if they themselves had any notion. They lived on the surface of their days; their smiles were surface smiles, and their tears were surface tears. Negroes lived a truer and deeper life than they, but I wished that Negroes, too, could live as thoughtlessly, serenely, as they. The girls never talked of their feelings; none of them possessed the insight or the emotional equipment to understand themselves or others. How far apart in culture we stood! All my life I had done nothing but feel and cultivate my feelings; all their lives they had done nothing but strive for petty goals, the trivial material prizes of American life. We shared a common tongue, but my language was a different language from theirs.

It was in the psychological distance that separated the races that the deepest meaning of the problem of the Negro lay for me. For these poor, ignorant white girls to have understood my life would have meant nothing short of a vast revolution in theirs. And I was convinced that what they needed to make them complete and grown-up in their living was the inclusion in their personalities of a knowledge of lives such as I lived and suffered containedly.

As I, in memory, think back now upon those girls and their lives I feel that for white America to understand the significance of the problem of the Negro will take a bigger and tougher America than any we have yet known. I feel that America's past is too shallow, her national character too superficially optimistic, her very morality too suffused with color hate for her to accomplish so vast and complex a task. Culturally the Negro represents a paradox: Though he is an organic part of the nation, he is excluded by the entire tide and direction of American culture. Frankly, it is felt to be right to exclude him, and it is felt to be wrong to admit him freely. Therefore if, within the confines of its present culture, the nation ever seeks to purge itself of its color hate, it will find itself at war with itself, convulsed by a spasm of emotional and moral confusion. If the nation ever finds itself examining its real relation to the Negro, it will find itself doing infinitely more than that; for the anti-Negro attitude of whites represents but a tiny part—though a symbolically significant one— of the moral attitude of the nation. Our too-young and too-new America, lusty because it is lonely, aggressive because it is afraid, insists upon seeing the world in terms of good and bad, the holy and the evil, the high and the low, the white and the black; our America is frightened by fact, by history, by processes, by necessity. It hugs the easy way of damning those whom it cannot understand, of excluding those who look different; and it salves its conscience with a self-draped cloak of righteousness. Am I damning my native land? No; for I, too, share these faults of character! And I really do not think that America, adolescent and cocksure, a stranger to suffering and travail, an enemy of passion and sacrifice, is ready to probe into its most fundamental beliefs.

I knew that not race alone, not color alone, but the daily values that gave meaning to life stood between me and those white girls with whom I worked. Their constant outward-looking, their mania for radios, cars, and a thousand other trinkets, made them dream and fix their eyes upon the trash of life, made it impossible for them to learn a language that could have taught them to speak of what was in theirs or others' hearts. The words of their souls were the syllables of popular songs.

The essence of the irony of the plight of the Negro in America, to me, is that he is doomed to live in isolation, while those who condemn him seek the basest goals of any people on the face of the earth. Perhaps it would be possible for the Negro to become reconciled to his plight if he could be made to believe that his sufferings were for some remote, high, sacrificial end; but sharing the culture that condemns him, and seeing that a lust for trash is what blinds the nation to his claims, is what sets storms to rolling in his soul.

Though I had fled the pressure of the South, my outward conduct had not changed. I had been schooled to present an unalteringly smiling face and I continued to do so despite the fact that my environment allowed more open expression. I hid my feelings and avoided all relationships with whites that might cause me to reveal them.

Tillie, the Finnish cook, was a tall, ageless, red-faced, raw-boned woman with long snow-white hair, which she balled in a knot at the nape of her neck. She cooked expertly and was superbly efficient. One morning as I passed the sizzling stove, I thought I heard Tillie cough and spit, but I saw nothing; her face, obscured by steam, was bent over a big pot. My senses told me that Tillie had coughed and spat into that pot, but my heart told me that no human being could possibly be so filthy. I decided to watch her. An hour or so later I heard Tillie clear her throat with a grunt, saw her cough and spit into the boiling soup. I held my breath; I did not want to believe what I had seen.

Should I tell the boss lady? Would she believe me? I watched Tillie for another day to make sure that she was spitting into the food. She was; there was no doubt of it. But who would believe me if I told them what was happening? I was the only black person in the café. Perhaps they would think that I hated the cook. I stopped eating my meals there and bided my time.

The business of the café was growing rapidly and a Negro girl was hired to make salads. I went to her at once.

"Look, can I trust you?" I asked.

"What are you talking about?" she asked.

"I want you to say nothing, but watch that cook."

"For what?"

"Now, don't get scared. Just watch the cook."

She looked at me as though she thought I was crazy; and, frankly, I felt that perhaps I ought not to say anything to anybody.

"What do you mean?" she demanded.

"All right," I said. "I'll tell you. That cook spits in the food."

"What are you saying?" she asked aloud.

"Keep quiet," I said.

"Spitting?" she asked me in a whisper. "Why would she do that?"

"I don't know. But watch her."

She walked away from me with a funny look in her eyes. But half an hour later she came rushing to me, looking ill, sinking into a chair.

"Oh, God, I feel awful!"

"Did you see it?"

"She *is* spitting in the food!"

"What ought we do?" I asked.

"Tell the lady," she said.

"She wouldn't believe me," I said.

She widened her eyes as she understood. We were black and the cook was white.

"But I can't work here if she's going to do that," she said.

"Then you tell her," I said.

"She wouldn't believe me either," she said.

She rose and ran to the women's room. When she returned she stared at me. We were two Negroes and we were silently asking ourselves if the white boss lady would believe us if we told her that her expert white cook was spitting in the food all day long as it cooked on the stove.

"I don't know," she wailed, in a whisper, and walked away.

I thought of telling the waitresses about the cook, but I could not get up enough nerve. Many of the girls were friendly with Tillie. Yet I could not let the cook spit in the food all day. That was wrong by any human standard of conduct. I washed dishes, thinking, wondering; I served breakfast, thinking, wondering; I served meals in the apartments of patrons upstairs, thinking, wondering. Each time I picked up a tray of food I felt like retching. Finally the Negro salad girl came to me and handed me her purse and hat.

"I'm going to tell her and quit, goddamn," she said.

"I'll quit too, if she doesn't fire her," I said.

"Oh, she won't believe me," she wailed, in agony.

"You tell her. You're a woman. She might believe you."

Her eyes welled with tears and she sat for a long time; then she rose and went abruptly into the dining room. I went to the door and peered. Yes, she was at the desk, talking to the boss lady. She returned to the kitchen and went into the pantry; I followed her.

"Did you tell her?" I asked.

"Yes."

"What did she say?"

"She said I was crazy."

"Oh, God!" I said.

"She just looked at me with those gray eyes of hers," the girl said. "Why would Tillie do that?"

"I don't know," I said.

The boss lady came to the door and called the girl; both of them went into the dining room. Tillie came over to me; a hard cold look was in her eyes.

"What's happening here?" she asked.

"I don't know," I said, wanting to slap her across the mouth.

She muttered something and went back to the stove, coughed, and spat into a bubbling pot. I left the kitchen and went into the back areaway to breathe. The boss lady came out.

"Richard," she said.

Her face was pale. I was smoking a cigarette and I did not look at her.

"Is this true?"

"Yes, ma'am."

"It couldn't be. Do you know what you're saying?"

"Just watch her," I said.

"I don't know," she moaned.

She looked crushed. She went back into the dining room, but I saw her watching the cook through the doors. I watched both of them, the boss lady and the cook, praying that the cook would spit again. She did. The boss lady came into the kitchen and stared at Tillie, but she did not utter a word. She burst into tears and ran back into the dining room.

"What's happening here?" Tillie demanded.

No one answered. The boss lady came out and tossed Tillie her hat, coat, and money.

"Now, get out of here, you dirty dog!" she said.

Tillie stared, then slowly picked up her hat, coat, and the money; she stood a moment, wiped sweat from her forehead with her hand, then spat—this time on the floor. She left.

Nobody was ever able to fathom why Tillie liked to spit into the food.

Brooding over Tillie, I recalled the time when the boss man in Mississippi had come to me and had tossed my wages to me and said:

"Get out, nigger! I don't like your looks."

And I wondered if a Negro who did not smile and grin was as morally loathsome to whites as a cook who spat into the food.

The following summer I was called for temporary duty in the post office, and the work lasted into the winter. Aunt Cleo succumbed to a severe cardiac condition and, hard on the heels of her illness, my brother developed stomach ulcers. To rush my worries to a climax, my mother also became ill. I felt that I was maintaining a private hospital. Finally, the post-office work ceased altogether and I haunted the city for jobs. But when I went into the streets in the morning I saw sights that killed my hope for the rest of the day. Unemployed men loitered in doorways with blank looks in their eyes, sat dejectedly on front steps in shabby clothing, congregated in sullen groups on street corners, and filled all the empty benches in the parks of Chicago's South Side.

Luck of a sort came when a distant cousin of mine, who was a superintendent for a Negro burial society, offered me a position on his staff as an agent. The thought of selling insurance policies to ignorant Negroes disgusted me.

"Well, if you don't sell them, somebody else will," my cousin told me. "You've got to eat, haven't you?"

During that year I worked for several burial and insurance societies that operated among Negroes, and I received a new kind of education. I found that the burial societies, with some exceptions, were mostly "rackets." Some of them conducted their business legitimately, but there were many that exploited the ignorance of their black customers.

I was paid under a system that netted me fifteen dollars for every dollar's worth of new premiums that I placed upon the company's books, and for every dollar's worth of old premiums that lapsed I was penalized fifteen dollars. In addition, I was paid a commission of ten per cent on total premiums collected, but during the Depression it was extremely difficult to persuade a black family to buy a policy carrying even a dime premium. I considered myself lucky if, after subtracting lapses from new business, there remained fifteen dollars that I could call my own.

This "gambling" method of remuneration was practiced by some of the burial companies because of the tremendous "turnover" in policyholders, and the companies had to have a constant stream of new business to keep afloat. Whenever a black family moved or suffered a slight reverse in fortune, it usually let its policy lapse and later bought another policy from some other company.

Each day now I saw how the Negro in Chicago lived, for I visited hundreds of dingy flats filled with rickety furniture and ill-clad children. Most of the policyholders were illiterate and did not know that their policies carried clauses severely restricting their benefit payments, and, as an insurance agent, it was not my duty to tell them.

After tramping the streets and pounding on doors to collect premiums, I was dry, strained, too tired to read or write. I hungered for relief and, as a salesman of insurance to many young black girls, I found it. There were many comely black housewives who, trying desperately to keep up their insurance payments, were willing to make bargains to escape paying a ten-cent premium. I had a long, tortured affair with one girl by paying her ten-cent premium each week. She was an illiterate black child with a baby whose father she did not know. During the entire period of my relationship with her, she had but one demand to make of me: she wanted me to take her to a circus. Just what significance circuses had for her, I was never able to learn.

After I had been with her one morning—in exchange for the dime premium—I sat on the sofa in the front room and began to read a book I had with me. She came over shyly.

"Lemme see that," she said.

"What?" I asked.

"That book," she said.

I gave her the book; she looked at it intently. I saw that she was holding it upside down.

"What's in here you keep reading?" she asked.

"Can't you really read?" I asked.

"Naw," she giggled. "You know I can't read."

"You can read *some*," I said.

"Naw," she said.

I stared at her and wondered just what a life like hers meant in the scheme of things, and I came to the conclusion that it meant absolutely nothing. And neither did my life mean anything.

"How come you looking at me that way for?"

"Nothing."

"You don't talk much."

"There isn't much to say."

"I wished Jim was here," she sighed.

"Who's Jim?" I asked, jealous. I knew that she had other men, but I resented her mentioning them in my presence.

"Just a friend," she said.

I hated her then, then hated myself for coming to her.

"Do you like Jim better than you like me?" I asked.

"Naw. Jim just likes to talk."

"Then why do you be with me, if you like Jim better?" I asked, trying to make an issue and feeling a wave of disgust because I wanted to.

"You all right," she said, giggling. "I like you."

"I could kill you," I said.

"What?" she exclaimed.

"Nothing," I said, ashamed.

"Kill me, you said? You crazy, man," she said.

"Maybe I am," I muttered, angry that I was sitting beside a human being to whom I could not talk, angry with myself for coming to her, hating my wild and restless loneliness.

"You oughta go home and sleep," she said. "You tired."

"What do you ever think about?" I demanded harshly.

"Lotta things."

"What, for example?"

"You," she said, smiling.

"You know I mean just one dime to you each week," I said.

"Naw, I thinka lotta you."

"Then what do you think?"

" 'Bout how you talk when you talk. I wished I could talk like you," she said seriously.

"Why?" I taunted her.

"When you gonna take me to a circus?" she demanded suddenly.

"You ought to be in a circus," I said.

"I'd like it," she said, her eyes shining.

I wanted to laugh, but her words sounded so sincere that I could not.

"There's no circus in town," I said.

"I bet there is and you won't tell me 'cause you don't wanna take me," she said, pouting.

"But there's no circus in town, I tell you!"

"When will one come?"

"I don't know."

"Can't you read it in the papers?" she asked.

"There's nothing in the papers about a circus."

"There is," she said. "If I could read, I'd find it."

I laughed, and she was hurt.

"There *is* a circus in town," she said stoutly.

"There's no circus in town," I said. "But if you want to learn to read, then I'll teach you."

She nestled at my side, giggling.

"See that word?" I said, pointing.

"Yeah."

"That's an 'and,'" I said.

She doubled, giggling.

"What's the matter?" I asked.

She rolled on the floor, giggling.

"What's so funny?" I demanded.

"You," she giggled. "You so funny."

I rose.

"The hell with you," I said.

"Don't you go and cuss me now," she said. "I don't cuss you."

"I'm sorry," I said.

I got my hat and went to the door.

"I'll see you next week?" she asked.

"Maybe," I said.

When I was on the sidewalk, she called to me from a window.

"You promised to take me to a circus, remember?"

"Yes." I walked close to the window. "What is it you like about a circus?"

"The animals," she said simply.

I felt that there was a hidden meaning, perhaps, in what she had said, but I could not find it. She laughed and slammed the window shut.

Each time I left her I resolved not to visit her again. I could not talk to her; I merely listened to her passionate desire to see a circus. She was not calculating; if she liked a man, she just liked him. Sex relations were the only relations she had ever had; no others were possible with her, so limited was her intelligence.

Most of the other agents also had their bought girls and they were extremely anxious to keep other agents from tampering with them. One day a new section of the South Side was given to me as a part of my collection area, and the agent from whom the territory had been taken suddenly became very friendly with me.

"Say, Wright," he asked, "did you collect from Ewing on Champlain Avenue yet?"

"Yes," I answered, after consulting my book.

"How did you like her?" he asked, staring at me.

"She's a good-looking number," I said.

"You had anything to do with her yet?" he asked.

"No, but I'd like to," I said laughing.

"Look," he said. "I'm a friend of yours."

"Since when?" I countered.

"No, I'm really a friend," he said.

"What's on your mind?"

"Listen, that gal's sick," he said seriously.

"What do you mean?"

"She's got the clap," he said. "Keep away from her. She'll lay with anybody."

"Gee, I'm glad you told me," I said.

"You had your eye on her, didn't you?" he asked.

"Yes, I did," I said.

"Leave her alone," he said. "She'll get you down."

That night I told my cousin what the agent had said about Miss Ewing. My cousin laughed.

"That gal's all right," he said. "That agent's been fooling around with her. He told you she had a disease so that you'd be scared to bother her. He was protecting her from you."

That was the way the black women were regarded by the black agents. Some of the agents were vicious; if they had claims to pay to a sick black woman and if the woman was able to have sex relations with them, they would insist upon it, using the claims money as a bribe. If the woman refused, they would report to the office that the woman was a malingerer.

The average black woman would submit because she needed the money badly.

As an insurance agent, it was necessary for me to take part in one swindle. It appears that the burial society had originally issued a policy that was—from their point of view—too liberal in its provisions, and the officials decided to exchange the policies then in the hands of their clients for other policies carrying stricter clauses. Of course, this had to be done in a manner that would not allow the policyholder to know that his policy was being switched—that he was being swindled. I did not like it, but there was only one thing I could do to keep from being a party to it: I could quit and starve. But I did not feel that being honest was worth the price of starvation.

The swindle worked in this way. In my visits to the homes of the policyholders to collect premiums, I was accompanied by the superintendent who claimed to the policyholder that he was making a routine inspection. The policyholder, usually an illiterate black woman, would dig up her policy from the bottom of a trunk or chest and hand it to the superintendent. Meanwhile I would be marking the woman's premium book, an act which would distract her from what the superintendent was doing. The superintendent would exchange the old policy for a new one which was identical in color, serial number, and beneficiary, but which carried smaller payments. It was dirty work and I wondered how I could stop it. And when I could think of no safe way I would curse myself and the victims and forget about it. (The black owners of the burial societies were leaders in the Negro communities and were respected by whites.)

When I reached the relief station, I felt that I was making a public confession of my hunger. I sat waiting for hours, resentful of the mass of hungry people about me. My turn finally came and I was questioned by a middle-class Negro woman who asked me for a short history of my life. As I waited, I became aware of something happening in the room. The black men and women were mumbling quietly among themselves; they had not known one another before they had come here, but now their timidity and shame were wearing off and they were exchanging experiences. Before this they had lived as individuals, each somewhat afraid of the other, each seeking his own pleasure, each stanch in that degree of Americanism that had been allowed him. But now life had tossed them together, and they were learning to know the sentiments of their neighbors for the first time; their talking was enabling them to sense the collectivity of their lives, and some of their fear was passing.

Did the relief officials realize what was happening? No. If they had, they would have stopped it. But they saw their "clients" through the eyes of their profession, saw only what their "science" allowed them to see. As I listened to the talk, I could see black minds shedding many illusions. These people now knew that the past had betrayed them, had cast them out; but they did not know what the future would be like, did not know what they wanted. Yes, some of the things that the Communists said were true; they maintained that there came times in history when a ruling class could no longer rule. And now I sat looking at the beginnings of anarchy. To permit the birth of this new consciousness in these people was proof that those who ruled did not quite know what they were doing, assuming that they were trying to save themselves and their class. Had they understood what was happening, they would never have allowed millions of perplexed and defeated people to sit together for long hours and talk, for out of their talk was rising a new realization of life. And once this new conception of themselves had formed, no power on earth could alter it.

I left the relief station with the promise that food would be sent to me, but I also left with a knowledge that the relief officials had not wanted to give to me. I had felt the possibility of creating a new understanding of life in the minds of people rejected by the society in which they lived, people to whom the Chicago *Tribune* referred contemptuously as the "idle" ones, as though these people had deliberately sought their present state of helplessness.

Who would give these people a meaningful way of life? Communist theory defined these people as the molders of the future of mankind, but the Communist speeches I had heard in the park had mocked that definition. These people, of course, were not ready for a revolution; they had not abandoned their past lives by choice, but because they simply could not live the old way any longer. Now, what new faith would they embrace? The day I begged bread from the city officials was the day that showed me I was not alone in my loneliness; society had cast millions of others with me. But how could I be with them? How many understood what was happening? My mind swam with questions that I could not answer.

I was slowly beginning to comprehend the meaning of my environment; a sense of direction was beginning to emerge from the conditions of my life. I began to feel something more powerful than I could express. My speech and manner changed. My cynicism slid from me. I grew open and questioning. I wanted to know.

If I were a member of the class that rules, I would post men in all the neighborhoods of the nation, not to spy upon or club rebellious workers, not to break strikes or disrupt unions, but to ferret out those who no longer respond to the system under which they live. I would make it known that the real danger does not stem from those who seek to grab their share of wealth through force, or from those who try to defend their property through violence, for both of these groups, by their affirmative acts, support the values of the system under which they live. The millions that I would fear are those who do not dream of the prizes that the nation holds forth, for it is in them, though they may not know it, that a revolution has taken place and is biding its time to translate itself into a new and strange way of life.

I feel that the Negroes' relation to America is symbolically peculiar, and from the Negroes' ultimate reactions to their trapped state a lesson can be learned about America's future. Negroes are told in a language they cannot possibly misunderstand that their native land is not their own; and when, acting upon impulses which they share with whites, they try to assert a claim to their birthright, whites retaliate with terror, never pausing to consider the consequences should the Negroes give up completely. The whites never dream that they would face a situation far more terrifying if they were confronted by Negroes who made no claims at all than by those who are buoyed up by social aggressiveness. My knowledge of how Negroes react to their plight makes me declare that no man can possibly be individually guilty of treason, that an insurgent act is but a man's desperate answer to those who twist his environment so that he cannot fully share the spirit of his native land. Treason is a crime of the State.

Christmas came and I was once more called to the post office for temporary work. This time I met many young white men and we discussed world happenings, the vast armies of unemployed, the rising tide of radical action. I now detected a change in the attitudes of the whites I met; their privations were making them regard Negroes with new eyes, and, for the first time, I was invited to their homes.

When the work in the post office ended, I was assigned by the relief system as an orderly to a medical research institute in one of the largest and wealthiest hospitals in Chicago. I cleaned operating rooms, dog, rat, mice, cat, and rabbit pans, and fed guinea pigs. Four of us Negroes worked there and we occupied an underworld position, remembering that we must restrict ourselves—when not engaged upon some task—to the basement corridors, so that we would not mingle with white nurses, doctors, or visitors.

The sharp line of racial division drawn by the hospital authorities came to me the first morning when I walked along an underground corridor and saw two long lines of women coming toward me. A line of white girls marched past, clad in starched uniforms that gleamed white; their faces were alert, their step quick, their bodies lean and shapely, their shoulders erect, their faces lit with the light of purpose. And after them came a line of black girls, old, fat, dressed in ragged gingham, walking loosely, carrying tin cans of soap powder, rags, mops, brooms . . . I wondered what law of the universe kept them from being mixed? The sun would not have stopped shining had there been a few black girls in the first line, and the earth would not have stopped whirling on its axis had there been a few white girls in the second line. But the two lines I saw graded social status in purely racial terms.

Of the three Negroes who worked with me, one was a boy about my own age, Bill, who was either sleepy or drunk most of the time. Bill straightened his hair and I suspected that he kept a bottle hidden somewhere in the piles of hay which we fed to the guinea pigs. He did not like me and I did not like

him, though I tried harder than he to conceal my dislike. We
had nothing in common except that we were both black and
lost. While I contained my frustration, he drank to drown his.
Often I tried to talk to him, tried in simple words to convey
to him some of my ideas, and he would listen in sullen silence.
Then one day he came to me with an angry look on his
face.

"I got it," he said.

"You've got what?" I asked.

"This old race problem you keep talking about," he said.
"What about it?"

"Well, it's this way," he explained seriously. "Let the government give every man a gun and five bullets, then let us all
start over again. Make it just like it was in the beginning. The
ones who come out on top, white or black, let them rule."

His simplicity terrified me. I had never met a Negro who was
so irredeemably brutalized. I stopped pumping my ideas into
Bill's brain for fear that the fumes of alcohol might send him
reeling toward some fantastic fate.

The two other Negroes were elderly and had been employed
in the institute for fifteen years or more. One was Brand, a
short, black, morose bachelor; the other was Cooke, a tall, yellow, spectacled fellow who spent his spare time keeping
track of world events through the Chicago *Tribune*. Brand
and Cooke hated each other for a reason that I was never
able to determine, and they spent a good part of each day
quarreling.

When I began working at the institute, I recalled my adolescent dream of wanting to be a medical research worker. Daily
I saw young Jewish boys and girls receiving instruction in
chemistry and medicine that the average black boy or girl
could never receive. When I was alone, I wandered and poked

my fingers into strange chemicals, watched intricate machines trace red and black lines on ruled paper. At times I paused and stared at the walls of the rooms, at the floors, at the wide desks at which the white doctors sat; and I realized— with a feeling that I could never quite get used to—that I was looking at the world of another race.

My interest in what was happening in the institute amused the three other Negroes with whom I worked. They had no curiosity about "white folks' things," while I wanted to know if the dogs being treated for diabetes were getting well; if the rats and mice in which cancer had been induced showed any signs of responding to treatment. I wanted to know the princi- ple that lay behind the Aschheim-Zondek tests that were made with rabbits, the Wassermann tests that were made with guinea pigs. But when I asked a timid question I found that even Jewish doctors had learned to imitate the sadistic method of humbling a Negro that the others had cultivated.

"If you know too much, boy, your brains might explode," a doctor said one day.

Each Saturday morning I assisted a young Jewish doctor in slitting the vocal cords of a fresh batch of dogs from the city pound. The object was to devocalize the dogs so that their howls would not disturb the patients in the other parts of the hospital. I held each dog as the doctor injected Nembutal into its veins to make it unconscious; then I held the dog's jaws open as the doctor inserted the scalpel and severed the vocal cords. Later, when the dogs came to, they would lift their heads to the ceiling and gape in a soundless wail. The sight became lodged in my imagination as a symbol of silent suffer- ing.

To me Nembutal was a powerful and mysterious liquid, but when I asked questions about its properties I could not obtain

a single intelligent answer. The doctor simply ignored me
with:

"Come on. Bring me the next dog. I haven't got all day."

One Saturday morning, after I had held the dogs for their
vocal cords to be slit, the doctor left the Nembutal on a bench.
I picked it up, uncorked it, and smelled it. It was odorless. Suddenly Brand ran to me with a stricken face.

"What're you doing?" he asked.

"I was smelling this stuff to see if it had any odor," I said.

"Did you really smell it?" he asked me.

"Yes."

"Oh, God!" he exclaimed.

"What's the matter?" I asked.

"You shouldn't've done that!" he shouted.

"Why?"

He grabbed my arm and jerked me across the room.

"Come on!" he yelled, snatching open the door.

"What's the matter?" I asked.

"I gotta get you to a doctor 'fore it's too late," he gasped.

Had my foolish curiosity made me inhale something danger-
out?

"But—Is it poisonous?"

"Run, boy!" he said, pulling me. "You'll fall dead."

Filled with fear, with Brand pulling my arm, I rushed out of
the room, raced across a rear areaway, into another room, then
down a long corridor. I wanted to ask Brand what symptoms I
must expect, but we were running too fast. Brand finally
stopped, gasping for breath. My heart beat wildly and my
blood pounded in my head. Brand then dropped to the concrete floor, stretched out on his back, and yelled with laughter,
shaking all over. He beat his fists against the concrete; he
moaned, giggled, he kicked.

I tried to master my outrage, wondering if some of the white doctors had told him to play the joke. He rose and wiped tears from his eyes, still laughing. I walked away from him. He knew that I was angry and he followed me.

"Don't get mad," he gasped through his laughter.

"Go to hell," I said.

"I couldn't help it," he giggled. "You looked at me like you'd believe anything I said. Man, you was scared."

He leaned against the wall, laughing again, stomping his feet. I was angry, for I felt that he would spread the story. I knew that Bill and Cooke never ventured beyond the safe bounds of Negro living, and they would never blunder into anything like this. And if they heard about this, they would laugh for months.

"Brand, if you mention this, I'll kill you," I swore.

"You ain't mad?" he asked, laughing, staring at me through tears.

Sniffing, Brand walked ahead of me. I followed him back into the room that housed the dogs. All day, while at some task, he would pause and giggle, then smother the giggling with his hand, looking at me out of the corner of his eyes, shaking his head. He laughed at me for a week. I kept my temper and let him amuse himself. I finally found out the properties of Nembutal by consulting medical books; but I never told Brand.

One summer morning, just as I began work, a young Jewish boy came to me with a stop watch in his hand.

"Dr.——wants me to time you when you clean a room," he said. "We're trying to make the institute more efficient."

"I'm doing my work, and getting through on time," I said.

"This is the boss's order," he said.

"Why don't you work for a change?" I blurted, angry.

"Now, look," he said. "*This* is my work. Now *you* work."

I got a mop and pail, sprayed a room with disinfectant, and scrubbed at coagulated blood and hardened dog, rat, and rabbit feces. The normal temperature of a room was ninety, but, as the sun beat down upon the skylights, the temperature rose above a hundred. Stripped to my waist, I slung the mop, moving steadily like a machine, hearing the boy press the button on the stop watch as I finished cleaning a room.

"Well, how is it?" I asked.

"It took you seventeen minutes to clean that last room," he said. "That ought to be the time for each room."

"But that room was not very dirty," I said.

"You have seventeen rooms to clean," he went on as though I had not spoken. "Seventeen times seventeen make four hours and forty-nine minutes." He wrote upon a little pad. "After lunch, clean the five flights of stone stairs. I timed a boy who scrubbed one step and multiplied that time by the number of steps. You ought to be through by six."

"Suppose I want relief?" I asked.

"You'll manage," he said and left.

Never had I felt so much the slave as when I scoured those stone steps each afternoon. Working against time, I would wet five steps, sprinkle soap powder, and then a white doctor or a nurse would come along and, instead of avoiding the soapy steps, would walk on them and track the dirty water onto the steps that I had already cleaned. To obviate this, I cleaned but two steps at a time, a distance over which a ten-year-old child could step. But it did no good. The white people still plopped their feet down into the dirty water and muddied the other clean steps. If I ever really hotly hated unthinking whites, it was then. Not once during my entire stay at the institute did a single white person show enough courtesy to avoid a wet step. I would be on my knees, scrubbing, sweating, pouring out what limited energy my body could wring from my meager diet, and I would hear feet approaching. I would pause and curse with tense lips:

"These sonofabitches are going to dirty these steps again, goddamn their souls to hell!"

Sometimes a sadistically observant white man would notice that he had tracked dirty water up the steps, and he would look back down at me and smile and say:

"Boy, we sure keep you busy, don't we?"

And I would not be able to answer.

The feud that went on between Brand and Cooke continued. Although they were working daily in a building where scientific history was being made, the light of curiosity was never in their eyes. They were conditioned to their racial "place," had learned to see only a part of the whites and the white world; and the whites, too, had learned to see only a part of the lives of the blacks and their world.

Perhaps Brand and Cooke, lacking interests that could absorb them, fuming like children over trifles, simply invented their hate of each other in order to have something to feel deeply about. Or perhaps there was in them a vague tension stemming from their chronically frustrating way of life, a pain whose cause they did not know; and, like those devocalized dogs, they would whirl and snap at the air when their old pain struck them. Anyway, they argued about the weather, sports, sex, war, race, politics, and religion; neither of them knew much about the subjects they debated, but it seemed that the less they knew the better they could argue.

The tug of war between the two elderly men reached a climax one winter day at noon. It was incredibly cold and an icy gale swept up and down the Chicago streets with blizzard force. The door of the animal-filled room was locked, for we always insisted that we be allowed one hour in which to eat and rest. Bill and I were sitting on wooden boxes, eating our lunches out of paper bags. Brand was washing his hands at the sink. Cooke was sitting on a rickety stool, munching an apple and reading the Chicago *Tribune*.

Now and then a devocalized dog lifted his nose to the ceiling and howled soundlessly. The room was filled with many rows of high steel tiers. Perched upon each of these tiers were layers of steel cages containing the dogs, rats, mice, rabbits, and guinea pigs. Each cage was labeled in some indecipherable scientific jargon. Along the walls of the room were long charts with zigzagging red and black lines that traced the success or failure of some experiment. The lonely piping of guinea pigs floated unheeded about us. Hay rustled as a rabbit leaped restlessly about in its pen. A rat scampered around in its steel prison. Cooke tapped the newspaper for attention.

"It says here," Cooke mumbled through a mouthful of apple, "that this is the coldest day since 1888."

Bill and I sat unconcerned. Brand chuckled softly.

"What in hell you laughing about?" Cooke demanded of Brand.

"You can't believe what that damn *Tribune* says," Brand said.

"How come I can't?" Cooke demanded. "It's the world's greatest newspaper."

Brand did not reply; he shook his head pityingly and chuckled again.

"Stop that damn laughing at me!" Cooke said angrily.

"I laugh as much as I wanna," Brand said. "You don't know what you talking about. The *Herald-Examiner* says it's the coldest day since 1873."

"But the *Trib* oughta know," Cooke countered. "It's older'n that *Examiner*."

"That damn *Trib* don't know nothing!" Brand drowned out Cooke's voice.

"How in hell you know?" Cooke asked with rising anger.

The argument waxed until Cooke shouted that if Brand did not shut up he was going to "cut his black throat." ◀

Brand whirled from the sink, his hands dripping soapy water, his eyes blazing.

"Take that back," Brand said.

"I take nothing back! What you wanna do about it?" Cooke taunted.

The two elderly Negroes glared at each other. I wondered if the quarrel was really serious, or if it would turn out harmlessly as so many others had done.

Suddenly Cooke dropped the Chicago *Tribune* and pulled a long knife from his pocket; his thumb pressed a button and a gleaming steel blade leaped out. Brand stepped back quickly and seized an ice pick that was stuck in a wooden board above the sink.

"Put that knife down," Brand said.

"Stay 'way from me, or I'll cut your throat," Cooke warned.

Brand lunged with the ice pick. Cooke dodged out of range. They circled each other like fighters in a prize ring. The cancerous and tubercular rats and mice leaped about in their cages. The guinea pigs whistled in fright. The diabetic dogs bared their teeth and barked soundlessly in our direction. The Aschheim-Zondek rabbits flopped their ears and tried to hide in the corners of their pens. Cooke now crouched and sprang forward with the knife. Bill and I jumped to our feet, speechless with surprise. Brand retreated. The eyes of both men were hard and unblinking; they were breathing deeply.

"Say, cut it out!" I called in alarm.

"Them damn fools is really fighting," Bill said in amazement.

Slashing at each other, Brand and Cooke surged up and down the aisles of steel tiers. Suddenly Brand uttered a bellow and charged into Cooke and swept him violently backward. Cooke grasped Brand's hand to keep the ice pick from sinking into his chest. Brand broke free and charged Cooke again, sweeping him into an animal-filled steel tier. The tier balanced itself on its edge for an indecisive moment, then toppled.

Like kingpins, one steel tier lammed into another, then they all crashed to the floor with a sound as of the roof falling. The whole aspect of the room altered quicker than the eye could follow. Brand and Cooke stood stock-still, their eyes fastened upon each other, their pointed weapons raised; but they were dimly aware of the havoc that churned about them.

The steel tiers lay jumbled; the doors of the cages swung open. Rats and mice and dogs and rabbits moved over the floor in wild panic. The Wassermann guinea pigs were squealing as though judgment day had come. Here and there an animal had been crushed beneath a cage.

All four of us looked at one another. We knew what this meant. We might lose our jobs. We were already regarded as black dunces; and if the doctors saw this mess they would take it as final proof. Bill rushed to the door to make sure that it was locked. I glanced at the clock and saw that it was 12:30. We had one half-hour of grace.

"Come on," Bill said uneasily. "We got to get this place cleaned."

Brand and Cooke stared at each other, both doubting.

"Give me your knife, Cooke," I said.

"Naw! Take Brand's ice pick *first*," Cooke said.

"The hell you say!" Brand said. "Take his knife *first!*"

A knock sounded at the door.

"Sssssh," Bill said.

We waited. We heard footsteps going away. We'll all lose our jobs, I thought.

Persuading the fighters to surrender their weapons was a difficult task, but at last it was done and we could begin to set things right. Slowly Brand stooped and tugged at one end of a steel tier. Cooke stooped to help him. Both men seemed to be acting in a dream. Soon, however, all four of us were working frantically, watching the clock.

As we labored we conspired to keep the fight a secret; we agreed to tell the doctors—if any should ask—that we had not been in the room during our lunch hour; we felt that that lie would explain why no one had unlocked the door when the knock had come.

We righted the tiers and replaced the cages; then we were faced with the impossible task of sorting the cancerous rats and mice, the diabetic dogs, the Aschheim-Zondek rabbits, and the Wassermann guinea pigs. Whether we kept our jobs or not depended upon how shrewdly we could cover up all evidence of the fight. It was pure guesswork, but we had to try to put the animals back into the correct cages. We knew that certain rats or mice went into certain cages, but we did not know *what* rat or mouse went into *what* cage. We did not know a tubercular mouse from a cancerous mouse—the white doctors had made sure that we would not know. They had never taken time to answer a single question; though we worked in the institute, we were as remote from the meaning of the experiments as if we lived in the moon. The doctors had laughed at what they felt was our childlike interest in the fate of the animals.

First we sorted the dogs; that was fairly easy, for we could remember the size and color of most of them. But the rats and mice and guinea pigs baffled us completely.

We put our heads together and pondered, down in the underworld of the great scientific institute. It was a strange scientific conference; the fate of the entire medical research institute rested in our ignorant, black hands.

We remembered the number of rats, mice, or guinea pigs—we had to handle them several times a day—that went into a given cage, and we supplied the number helter-skelter from those animals that we could catch running loose on the floor. We discovered that many rats, mice, and guinea pigs were missing—they had been killed in the scuffle. We solved that problem by taking healthy stock from other cages and putting them into cages with sick animals. We repeated this process until we were certain that, numerically at least, all the animals with which the doctors were experimenting were accounted for.

The rabbits came last. We broke the rabbits down into two general groups; those that had fur on their bellies and those that did not. We knew that all those rabbits that had shaven bellies—our scientific knowledge adequately covered this point because it was our job to shave the rabbits—were undergoing the Aschheim-Zondek tests. But in what pen did a given rabbit belong? We did not know. I solved the problem very simply. I counted the shaven rabbits; they numbered seventeen. I counted the pens labeled "Aschheim-Zondek," then proceeded to drop a shaven rabbit into each pen at random. And again we were numerically successful. At least white America had taught us how to count . . .

Lastly we carefully wrapped all the dead animals in newspapers and hid their bodies in a garbage can.

At a few minutes to one the room was in order; that is, the

kind of order that we four Negroes could figure out. I unlocked the door and we sat waiting, whispering, vowing secrecy, wondering what the reaction of the doctors would be.

Finally a doctor came, gray-haired, white-coated, spectacled, efficient, serious, taciturn, bearing a tray upon which sat a bottle of mysterious fluid and a hypodermic needle.

"My rats, please."

Cooke shuffled forward to serve him. We held our breath. Cooke got the cage which he knew the doctor always called for at that hour and brought it forward. One by one, Cooke took out the rats and held them as the doctor solemnly injected the mysterious fluid under their skins.

"Thank you, Cooke," the doctor murmured.

"Not at all, sir," Cooke mumbled with a suppressed gasp.

When the doctor had gone we looked at one another, hardly daring to believe that our secret would be kept. We were so anxious that we did not know whether to curse or laugh. Another doctor came.

"Give me A-Z rabbit number 14."

"Yes, sir," I said.

I brought him the rabbit and he took it upstairs to the operating room. We waited for repercussions. None came.

All that afternoon the doctors came and went. I would run into the room—stealing a few seconds from my step-scrubbing —and ask what progress was being made and would learn that the doctors had detected nothing. At quitting time we felt triumphant.

"They won't ever know," Cooke boasted in a whisper.

I saw Brand stiffen. I knew that he was aching to dispute Cooke's optimism, but the memory of the fight he had just had was so fresh in his mind that he could not speak.

Another day went by and nothing happened. Then another day. The doctors examined the animals and wrote in their little black books, in their big black books, and continued to trace red and black lines upon the charts.

A week passed and we felt out of danger. Not one question had been asked.

Of course, we four black men were much too modest to make our contribution known, but we often wondered what went on in the laboratories after that secret disaster. Was some scientific hypothesis, well on its way to validation and ultimate public use, discarded because of unexpected findings on that cold winter day? Was some tested principle given a new and strange refinement because of fresh, remarkable evidence? Did some brooding research worker—those who held stop watches and slopped their feet carelessly in the water of the steps I tried so hard to keep clean—get a wild, if brief, glimpse of a new scientific truth? Well, we never heard . . .

I brooded upon whether I should have gone to the director's office and told him what had happened, but each time I thought of it I remembered that the director had been the man who had ordered the boy to stand over me while I was working and time my movements with a stop watch. He did not regard me as a human being. I did not share his world. I earned thirteen dollars a week and I had to support four people with it, and should I risk that thirteen dollars by acting idealistically? Brand and Cooke would have hated me and would have eventually driven me from the job had I "told" on them. The hospital kept us four Negroes as though we were close kin to the animals we tended, huddled together down in the underworld corridors of the hospital, separated by a vast psychological distance from the significant processes of the rest of the hospital—just as America had kept us locked in the dark underworld of American life for three hundred years—and we had made our own code of ethics, values, loyalty.

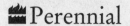 **Perennial**

BOOKS BY RICHARD WRIGHT:

"[An] American author as distinctive as any of those writing today."
—*New York Times*

NATIVE SON
WITH AN INTRODUCTION BY THE AUTHOR AND AN AFTERWORD BY JOHN REILLY
ISBN 0-06-053348-X (abridged paperback) • ISBN 0-89845-916-8 (audio)
ISBN 0-06-092980-4 (Perennial Classics paperback)

Wright reflects on the poverty and feelings of hopelessness experienced by people in Chicago's inner city and what it meant to be black in the 1930s. The abridged edition represents the original publication in which several passages were omitted.

BLACK BOY
WITH AN INTRODUCTION BY JERRY W. WARD, JR.
ISBN 0-06-092978-2 (Perennial Classics paperback)

An eloquent autobiography about growing up in the Jim Crow South that gives unique voice to being Southern, black, and male in early 20th-century America.

EIGHT MEN: *Short Stories*
WITH AN INTRODUCTION BY PAUL GILROY
ISBN 0-06-097681-0 (paperback)

Eight men tell eight stories about what it means to be a black male in America.

THE OUTSIDER
WITH AN INTRODUCTION BY MARYEMMA GRAHAM
NOTES BY ARNOLD RAMPERSAD
ISBN 0-06-053925-9 (paperback)

A compelling story of a black man's attempt to escape his past and start anew in Harlem. Damon is a man at odds with society and with himself, who hungers for peace but who brings terror and destruction wherever he goes.

UNCLE TOM'S CHILDREN
ISBN 0-06-081251-6 (paperback)

A fascinating collection of five short stories that bring to life post-slavery characters in their full emotional depth.

Want to receive notice of new books by Richard Wright?
Sign up for Richard Wright's AuthorTracker at www.AuthorTracker.com

Available wherever books are sold, or call 1-800-331-3761 to order.